THE *haunted* RECTORY

IMAGE BOOKS / DOUBLEDAY

New York   London   Toronto

Sydney   Auckland

The St. Francis Xavier Church Hookers

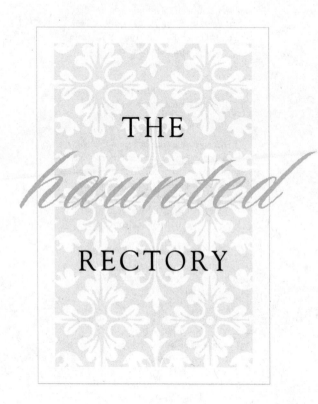

THE

haunted

RECTORY

KATHERINE VALENTINE

AN IMAGE BOOK
PUBLISHED BY DOUBLEDAY

Published in the United States by Doubleday,
an imprint of The Doubleday Broadway
Publishing Group, a division of Random
House, Inc., New York.
www.doubleday.com

IMAGE, DOUBLEDAY, and the portrayal of a deer
drinking from a stream are registered
trademarks of Random House, Inc.

Book design by Jennifer Ann Daddio

Library of Congress
Cataloging-in-Publication Data
Valentine, Katherine.
The haunted rectory / Katherine Valentine.
—1st Image Books ed.
p.   cm.—(The St. Francis Xavier Church
hookers)
1. Parsonages—Fiction. 2. Catholics—Fiction.
3. Connecticut—Fiction. I. Title.
PS3622.A44H38 2006
813'.54—dc22
2005042433

ISBN 10: 0-385-51202-3
ISBN 13: 978-0-385-51202-2

PRINTED IN THE UNITED STATES OF AMERICA

1   3   5   7   9   10   8   6   4   2

First Edition

To my beloved son Matthew

and my dear daughter-in-law, Tricia—

parents extraordinaire.

You make my heart fill with pride.

For we wrestle not against flesh and blood

but against the rulers, against the

authorities, against the powers of this

dark world and against the spiritual forces

of evil in the heavenly realms.

— EPHESIANS 6:12

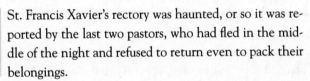 St. Francis Xavier's rectory was haunted, or so it was reported by the last two pastors, who had fled in the middle of the night and refused to return even to pack their belongings.

The first was Father Jack Naves, a pale, shy man who seldom smiled, more from his fear of dentists than from a lack of mirth. He was known in the diocese as a plodder without ambition who could be counted on to do what was required of him but nothing more. In some respects, Archbishop Gerard Kerry welcomed his lack of ardor. He had enough prelates who constantly sought his favor in hopes of gleaning a coveted place on one of his special councils, which were widely considered rungs on the ladder to Rome.

But Father Naves never expressed an interest in church politics or any other diocesan function outside his role as pastor of St. Bridget's, a parish in the northwest quadrant of the state that pretty much ran itself. It was blessed (or cursed, depending on what side of the clerical collar you happened to be speaking from) with a roster of "active" parishioners.

In fact, the bishop was barely aware of Father Naves's presence until a parishioner paid him a visit, complaining about the priest's lackluster homilies and his refusal to entertain any new parish programs or to take part in the community's ecumenical events. This particular parish served an affluent, quintessential New England town along with Congregational and Baptist churches and a bustling synagogue. All were nestled along a town green and took enormous pride in a religious esprit de corps. The synagogue shared Passover with Christians, and the Christians lit a menorah each December—functions that previous St. Bridget pastors had openly embraced. Father Naves, however, had no such leanings, and his continued absence from these affairs was proving to be an embarrassment to the parish.

Normally, the bishop would have ignored the complaints. Lord knows, he received dozens each month. Ever since Vatican II, and the inclusion of parishioners in areas that had once been dictated solely by priests, the complaints had been coming in a steady flow. As far as the bishop was concerned, many practicing Catholics overstepped their boundaries. They felt that their opinions mattered far more than they should.

Much to his chagrin, however, they sometimes did.

Take this case, for instance. The man from Father Naves's parish who had paid the bishop a visit was a heavy contributor to the Bishop's Annual Appeal, a fund whose coffers had drastically declined with the recent sex scandals in the Church. Without those funds, the many programs provided throughout the archdiocese would be severely restricted. More important, the cutbacks would be seen as an act of failure by Rome. There was only one thing to do. As a matter of survival, the bishop decided that it would be prudent to move Naves to another, less visible parish. Arrangements were hastily made for Father Naves to pastor St. Francis Xavier, whose predecessor, Father Stephens, had recently died from heart failure. Father Stephens had been seventy-five at the time.

The bishop considered the matter settled and completely forgot about the appointment until he received a strange phone call from Father Naves complaining about an infestation of rodents in the rectory. He couldn't imagine why the priest was troubling him about such mundane matters.

"Call an exterminator," he snapped.

"I did."

"And?"

"It's kind of curious . . ."

"Can we move this along?"

Naves's voice took on a nervous edge. "The exterminator found nothing, but I had an electrician come in to check out things because the lights keep going on and off. I figured whatever had been gnawing inside the walls had shorted some wires. This morning the electrician took down a portion of wall."

"Is there a point to this? I have a meeting in a few minutes."

"Behind the wall were hundreds of black snakes."

"Did you say snakes?"

"I called the exterminator back in, and he says we have to rip apart all the Sheetrock throughout the rectory and make certain they didn't breed, which is the reason for my call. As you can imagine, this is something of an emergency which our church finances cannot handle. We'll need your assistance."

The bishop approved the funds (although he would later concede that this was the beginning of an even stranger course of events), and he dismissed the matter until one night, at three in the morning, he was awakened by his bleary-eyed assistant.

"Father Naves is downstairs," he said. "I think you'd better go down and take a look at him."

The bishop tightened his robe as he clamored down the stairs, not at all pleased to have been awakened in the middle of the night. At the sight of Father Naves, he came to a dead halt.

"Good heavens, Naves . . ." the bishop exclaimed, not believing his eyes.

Father Naves stood in the middle of the Italian marble entryway, clad in a tattered pair of pajamas. His face was covered with deep gouges that resembled claw marks, and his eyes were filled with a sense of madness.

"What's that he's mumbling?"

The assistant leaned closer.

"Well . . . what is it?"

"He's saying, 'Please, don't make me go back there.' "

The next appointee was Father David St. Martin. This was to be his first assignment as pastor. He had arrived at St. Francis at 3 PM and spent the afternoon unpacking his clothes and books before sitting down in front of the television set in the library to eat his dinner, which had been brought over earlier by one of the church ladies.

The noises began at around 9 PM. Just as Father St. Martin was headed upstairs to bed, he heard the sound of something moving behind the walls. Having been brought up in an old farmhouse in upstate New York, he was accustomed to the creaks and groans associated with aging buildings, and he figured it was probably the sound of the water coursing through the heating system. Without giving it a second thought, he ignored the rumblings, took a shower, then dressed for bed before settling in with a book. Father St. Martin was partial to mysteries, and the one he was reading kept him guessing right to the end.

It was nearing midnight, and he had finally arrived at the point in the story where the killer was about to be revealed when the temperature in the room plummeted. Within seconds, the room grew as cold as a crypt. Teeth chattering, he threw back the covers and reached for his robe, figuring that the furnace must have conked out—not an unusual problem with old homes. He got as far as the downstairs hall when he noticed a black mist rising near the foot of the basement stairs. He rubbed his eyes, thinking he must be experiencing a combination of overtiredness and eye strain. Perhaps the light fixture needed a brighter bulb. The mist began to take shape.

He felt something quicken inside his chest. His heartrate increased as fear surged through his system, sending him warning signals to run. This was not a product of reading too late in bed. Whatever this thing was, it had shape and form and substance. He paused for just a moment, his feet refusing to obey, his eyes fixated on the shape that was morphing into a creature that would haunt his dreams for years.

Father St. Martin spent the rest of the night huddled in the backseat of his car and left the next morning after eliciting the help of Marvin Woodruff, the groundskeeper, who accompanied him back inside so that he could pack.

The Church is a small community, and as in any small town, gossip travels quickly. Within weeks, rumors that St. Francis Xavier's rectory was haunted reached the Hartford archdiocese.

Being a practical man, Archbishop Kerry knew these allegations must be quashed before the situation got out of hand and found its way to Rome. After giving it considerable thought, he decided to call on the one priest who he was certain could make this all go away—his old friend Father William Braxton.

Braxton had recently retired to Florida, but the bishop knew that it wouldn't take much to persuade him to return to active priesthood. Father Braxton was a man of action, and from the tone of his past few letters it was obvious that retirement fit his friend like a poorly made suit.

Braxton began his career as an army chaplain during the Korean War and quickly became a legend. His exploits eventually earned him a Purple Heart. Their camp had come under attack. A skilled marksman, he had picked up a rifle and fired blindly into advancing enemy forces as he dashed to rescue a wounded comrade. Although he managed to save the boy, he took a piece of mortar in the calf— a wound that continued to give him trouble throughout his life whenever the weather was damp or cold.

After the war, he returned to the States and passed on what was considered by others to be the most favored parish in the archdiocese. It was nestled in an affluent community, filled with wealthy parishioners who were eager to share their lavish lifestyle with the parish priest. The rectory came complete with a retinue of servants, a generous expense account, a new BMW each year, and a six-week vacation often spent at one of the parishioners' luxurious vacation homes. It also provided a 401(k) that was supplemented each Christmas and birthday with blue-chip stocks.

But none of this interested Father Braxton. Instead, he elected to take on one of New Haven's most crime-infested parishes. Before his arrival, gang members that proliferated along the streets outside the church had gathered before Mass every day to terrorize parish members. Women repeatedly had their purses snatched. Old men were robbed of their wallets and their Timex watches. Parents refused to allow their children to attend any of the church functions unless security guards were present, and by the time Father Braxton arrived there were fewer than a handful of parishioners either brave or foolish enough to attend morning Mass.

Father Braxton stood six feet four, had arms like ham shanks, and was afraid of no one. His nose had been broken so many times over the years that it gave him repeated sinus trouble, yet he refused to have it repaired. He felt that it added to his rough-and-tumble image.

He had never been afraid of confrontation, and as soon as he arrived he dressed in sweatpants and a shirt that said, "If you don't like the way I swagger, get off my sidewalk," marched right up to the gang leaders, and made it clear that he wouldn't tolerate anyone harassing his people, adding that if he found out otherwise he would personally see to it that it never happened again.

One evening, a couple of the gang members took him up on the threat. No one knew exactly what happened that night, but three of the youths spent several months in the hospital. Father Braxton required twenty-one stitches to sew up the knife wound on his arm, but that didn't stop him from saying Mass the next morning.

So when Archbishop Kerry called, Father Braxton eagerly accepted the challenge. In fact, he saw it as an answer to his prayer. For a man accustomed to action, a Florida retirement community offered few challenges. He packed a suitcase, made arrangements to have his belongings stored and his condo rented out, then hopped on a plane—all within twenty-four hours. A few days later, he was snugly ensconced within the walls of St. Francis Xavier's rectory and enjoying a late-night glass of brandy.

The fire blazing in the living-room fireplace snapped and hissed in concert with Andrea Bocelli's *Arie Sacre*, which wafted from the double speakers that he had carefully positioned for maximum listening pleasure. Eyes closed, he allowed the music to underline his thoughts, which centered on the recent talk of hauntings here at the rectory.

He found it impossible to fathom that anyone in this day and age, let alone a priest, still believed in ghosts and goblins and who knows what else that went bump in the night. Why, it was laughable! These were the ravings of religious fanatics, priests who saw evil hiding behind every vice of man. Bah! Humbug! As far as he was concerned, these clerics should be cloistered, locked away with their archaic superstitions, instead of being allowed to infect parishes with their lunacy.

A sudden chill snaked through the room, curling around his slippered feet. "Darn drafty place," he swore, casting about for an open window, a loosened floorboard, anything that might account for the cold air funneling in.

He didn't try to temper his annoyance, which showed in his stiffened shoulders, and the way his lips had unfurled into a straight, pencil-thin line. Feeling every bit the martyr at having his evening disturbed, he threw himself off the chair and marched heavily across the room in search of the thermostat. He found it hidden behind a potted palm in the hallway. The thermometer read seventy-two degrees but was clearly incorrect. The house had grown as cold as a tomb.

He found the basement door, switched on the light, and headed downstairs to investigate. As he descended, the air grew heavy with mold, instantly triggering an allergy attack. His eyes began to water, blurring his vision. What this place needed was a decent dehumidifier, he thought. He certainly hoped that nothing of importance was stored down here. It would be ruined for sure.

This was just one more thing he planned to add to his growing list of improvements. He'd present these to the bishop at next week's lunch. They included a whirlpool for the upstairs bathroom (New England winters played havoc with his arthritis), a satellite dish, thus ensuring access to all future sporting events, and a new groundskeeper. He had just fired the old one. The fellow's name was Marvin Woodruff, and for some reason the locals called him Marvin-in-the-Corner. He refused to speak. Instead, whenever Father Braxton asked him a question he whistled and made hand motions. A real nutcase.

Something dashed across the foot of the stairs.

"Who's there?" Father Braxton called out.

Faint voices whispered in the shadows.

"I said . . . who's down there?" he shouted again.

The wooden door to the left of the furnace slowly creaked open.

"Show yourself!"

Something slithered across the floor and began to take shape at the foot of the stairs. He leaned forward, straining to make it out.

He screamed like a man whose heart has been ripped from his chest, frantically retracing his steps. The top of the stairs meant safety.

He crashed through the basement door, falling face-first onto the marble floor. He heard the familiar sound of cartilage breaking inside his nose. Blood dripped from both nostrils, but he didn't feel any physical pain, only terror. He resisted the urge to look back, scrambling to right himself for fear that at any moment a hand would reach out through the open door and drag him back into darkness.

For the next several weeks, Archbishop Kerry repeatedly called Father Braxton's Florida residence, but no one answered. In fact, the priest seldom spoke to anyone after that night, preferring to spend his days alone, seated on a metal chair at the end of the abandoned pier outside his condo, staring into the brackish waters . . . trying to forget what it was he had seen.

two

The sign in the front window of the Sit and Sip Café said "Closed for the Day," but no one in the sleepy New England town of Bend Oaks paid any heed. Folks ambled in and out as if it were any other Saturday morning. Some had kids in tow, although most were men, blue-collar workers, looking as though they had tumbled out of the shower only minutes ago—hair plastered to their scalps with ridges where the comb's teeth had made a path, like furrows in a field of newly plowed earth. Working Saturdays meant overtime.

Dressed in an assortment of worn, faded blue jeans, plaid flannel shirts with fraying cuffs and collars, and thick-soled work boots stained to match their occupations—paint, cement, grease, mud, and clay—the men made their way to the line of parked pickup trucks. They nodded their greetings as they sipped from Styrofoam cups filled with coffee whose steam angled off under a brisk autumn wind.

Coffee this morning was being made by patrons. Instructions were tacked above the coffeemaker, next to which sat a basket filled with blueberry, cranberry-nut, and pumpkin muffins baked the night before by Jane Edwell, the owner. The customers were regulars, so they knew that coffee and a muffin cost $1.25 plus six cents tax. Jane had left the cash register open so folks could make their own change.

The men, especially, tried not to let their disappointment show. Jane's muffins were good, but nothing could take the place of her homemade corn beef hash topped with a couple of fried eggs and filled with so much artery-clogging cholesterol that Doc Fedder said it should come with a health warning. But it was this very staple that had put Jane in the café business—that and the backing from her husband and his two best friends, Ted Hopkins and Barry Newfield, who decided that Bend Oaks needed a sit-down place for breakfast and lunch. Until then, folks got their morning coffee and their newspapers at the pharmacy.

Jane had always loved to cook and had fantasized for years about owning a small luncheon place. Nothing fancy—just plain food folks around town were used to, like her famous corn beef hash. A café would also ensure a steady income. Vance's excavation business was often brought to its knees during bad weather, and with the kids reaching college age they sure could use a few extra dollars.

Jane wistfully mentioned all of this to Vance every time they passed the old Tyler's Hardware Store. Greg Tyler had closed it down a few years ago when a Wal-Mart showed up over in the next county.

On their anniversary two years ago, Vance handed her a small gold box tied with a ribbon. Inside was the key to Tyler's old place. He and his friends, Ted and Barry, had pooled their money and bought the place, then called in every favor that was owed them. During the next few weeks, the space was completely gutted and refashioned. A bank of booths now flanked the north wall where racks of plumbing supplies had once hung; the display window made a perfect setting for a round table and six chairs, donated by the Lion's Club, whose members were doing some renovations of their own. They also included four square wooden tables, perfect for the center of the space, and several more spindly-type chairs. Vance regraded the club's driveway in exchange.

The base of the original front counter remained and was refitted with Formica in a soft dove gray. Facing the back side of the counter, a wall was erected to separate the kitchen from the restaurant. Along the side of the restaurant, a large gas grill and double fryer was installed for short orders like hamburgers, fries, eggs, and breakfast meats.

On the other side of the wall was the kitchen, formerly a storeroom. The shelves were removed, making room for two industrial-size dishwashers and a stainless-steel, eight-jet stove with two baking ovens. In the center of the room was a long wooden table over which hung an array of pots and pans. Underneath, baking utensils were stored.

The Sit and Sip Café had been a hit since the day Jane opened the doors. She took care of all the cooking but employed a full-time dishwasher and two part-time waitresses, both of whom had today off. Jane and her rug-hooking group, the St. Francis Xavier Church Hookers, were meeting for the first time after their summer hiatus to dye yards of wool on the cafés huge stove in preparation for this year's hooked rug.

Every year since 1952, a handful of St. Francis Xavier churchwomen had gathered once a week from September to May to create some of the finest hooked rugs in all New England. Folks would come from as far away as New Jersey to try their luck at winning these highly prized rugs. They were raffled off at the Bend Oaks Strawberry Festival, which took place on the second Saturday each May and brought in enough money to fix whatever portion of the church had fallen apart or worn away during the previous year.

Rug hooking is as indigenous to the New England culture as maple sugaring. Ask any man or woman from the mountains of Maine down through the Connecticut shoreline and chances are they can tell you about watching their mothers or grandmothers turn old woolen clothing into hooked rugs.

The term *hooking* was derived from the instrument used, which was crafted from metal and shaped like a hook. A rug maker plunged the hook through loosely woven spaces in a burlap pattern, snagged a woolen strip that was held below, and drew it up through the cloth to make a loop. Although the process was relatively simple, it took a skilled hooker to maintain the same height throughout the design when creating the row upon row of woolen loops that make up a rug.

Myla Whitcomb (the group's oldest member) and Judith Kochan (Father Stephens's sister and housekeeper) had started the St. Francis Xavier Church Hookers group back in the 1950s. The church vestibule needed painting, so the women thought they'd hook a rug and raffle it off, then use the proceeds toward the repairs. They had such a good time together that they decided to continue, and thus the St. Francis Xavier Church Hookers was formed and the yearly raffle became a tradition. Each year the ticket sales increased, due in part to the rugs' vibrant colors, which seemed to grow more brilliant with each passing year. Myla was responsible for that.

She had learned the dyeing process from her mother, who had learned it from her mother, and by experimenting with these family formulas Myla created some of the most eye-catching colors in rug-hooking design anywhere. Women said they could always spy one of Myla's rugs—the colors seemed to "pop." Her golds looked as though they had been burnished; the greens sparkled like lush foliage; and the blacks (created by bleeding red and green pieces of wool in boiling water) had a soft, faded quality that was perfect for rendering the borders a rich, old-fashioned charm.

The theme of this year's rug was "Nautical Whimsies." It was a design filled with mermaids, tall-masted ships, and sea urchins. Kay Sprage, the club's newest member, who hailed from New York City, had suggested it. Kay owned a high-profile public-relations firm and hobnobbed with the rich and famous. She insisted that she could sell hundreds of raffle tickets to her swanky East Hampton friends.

The kitchen door swung open. Vance peeked in, wearing his favorite sweatshirt. Jane grimaced. It was stained under the arms and unraveling along the hem. On the front, the faded image of his dog, Rufus, was now barely discernible. Rufus had been dead for ten years.

"Hi, hon. Just thought I'd check in and see if you need anything before I take Alex to his soccer practice."

Jane had been standing at the sink, filling a large white enamel dye pot with water. She smiled into her husband's crystal-blue eyes, thinking that he was a man who would never age. He still had the same boyish grin he had worn in high school.

"Thanks, but I think I've got everything under control. Everything except the way my husband dresses himself," she teased. "I thought I threw that old thing away."

"You did, but I pulled it out of the trash."

"How did you know it was in the trash . . . again?"

"I told him," Alex said. Their ten-year-old son burst into the room dressed in full soccer regalia, including his new pair of cleats.

"Alex!"

"Sorry, Mom, but Dad promised to take me camping if I kept him informed."

"Vance!"

"We men have to look out for each other," Vance said, grabbing his son and tousling his hair. The boy struggled to get free. "Besides, someday it could be his."

Alex made a face. "Don't take this the wrong way, Dad, but I'd go naked before I wore that thing."

Vance feigned offense, while Jane laughed. She loved to hear their easy banter.

"Why don't you go back out front," Vance told his son. "I have some serious making-out to do with your mother." Vance walked over, his six-foot-four frame taking the length of the kitchen in three easy strides. "I didn't get my morning kiss. You left before I got out of the shower."

"I'm sorry, I was running late."

He pulled her close and gave her a kiss full on the lips. She felt her body fold into his like the missing piece of a puzzle.

"Oh, yuck!" Alex said, turning his back on his parents. "Come on, Dad. We're going to be late for practice."

"In a minute. I'm not finished here." He ran his hand along the nape of her neck and down the V of her blouse.

"Ugh! Why can't you two act like other parents," Alex complained. "Mom, can I take some muffins for my friends?"

"Sure, just leave a few for the customers, okay?" The door swung closed behind him.

"I'll be back around noon and fire up the grill," Vance told her, kissing her softly on the nose.

"You'll find a bowl of sliced onions in the deep fridge, along with your staples of hamburgers and hot dogs."

Once a year, Jane handed the café over to Vance and his football buddies. While the ladies worked in the kitchen, the men would station themselves out front, eat hamburgers smothered in mountains of fried onions with beer chasers, and watch football on the thirty-six-inch Sony kept in the storage closet just for this occasion. For the rest of the afternoon, the women's conversation would be punctuated by shouts and foot-stomping and an occasional colorful phrase spit out like chewing tobacco. By suppertime, the men would be laid out in the booths, snoring.

"You're a woman who knows how to please her man," Vance said, pinching her on the behind.

She gave him a swat. "Get out of here. I have work to do."

"I'm going," he said, clipping a piece of cold toast off Jane's plate. "Oh, I forgot. Marilee wants me to drop her and her friends off at the mall when I'm finished with Alex. Something about shopping for an outfit for the Apple Harvest Dance. Midsy's mom is going to pick them up. That okay with you?"

Marilee was their fourteen-year-old daughter, and Midsy Harriman was her best friend. Jane preferred that Marilee not hang around the mall unsupervised, but she knew that she had to compromise occasionally. There was a dance next weekend, and she had told her daughter she could buy a new outfit.

"It's all right with me as long as they don't spend the entire day there," she said.

"I'll pass that along."

As soon as Vance was gone, Jane felt the space around her thicken. Because she had lost her parents and her brothers in a car accident when she was a teenager, Vance and the children were her universe. When they weren't around, she felt as if she were adrift in a black void. This was why the café was closed on Sundays. That was family time—hikes in the woods, camping across the river, bike rides through the surrounding countryside.

It saddened her that lately the kids had protested against family time, especially Marilee. They had once been so close, but that bond had begun to unravel. Jane tried not to think of what it would be like when both of her children no longer needed her. Marilee had already transferred the mother-daughter intimacies they once shared to her friends. Alex was at the age where boys worked to distance themselves from any feminine influence. The boy who had to be pried from her arms on the first day of kindergarten now seldom took notice when she wasn't around. His dad, however, he couldn't get enough of.

She knew that within a few short years they would both be on their own, living separate lives, no longer needing her advice or her company. The thought made her throat grow tight. She couldn't imagine their home without the sound of her children's voices.

As the pots of water heated on the back of the stove, Jane began to sort through the six twenty-one-gallon storage containers of wool that had been collected during the past year. Each was filled to overflowing with old skirts, pants, and jackets—all freshly laundered then cut into large squares of fabric, which was easily handled during the dyeing.

Some of the wool had been collected from folks in town. Most everyone had a bag of woolen castoffs labeled "For the Hookers" somewhere in their closets. Other items came from the yearly clearance sale over at the Salvation Army across the river.

The dyeing process called for the wool to be soaked in water first, then rung dry. This assured that the dye was evenly distributed. Several yards of wool were now soaking in the sink while Jane scurried around the kitchen, getting things ready for the others. She glanced nervously at the clock. Myla would be here shortly. She liked to arrive early, and to make certain everything was in place.

Myla had soft gray hair the color and texture of lamb's wool, a sweet disposition, and the look of old money. Everyone in town knew her car, a rusted-out 1974 Volvo that she drove as proudly as if it were a new Mercedes. For the past ten years, there had been a betting pool at Sam's Bar and Grill over whether it would survive another winter.

Myla was widowed now. Her husband, Justin Whitcomb, had died of a stroke several years back, leaving her with a few shares of GE stock and the ancestral home—a huge, tumbledown clapboard structure that consumed fuel at an alarming rate. Recently, Myla had closed the upstairs and had taken to sleeping in the kitchen next to the stove. Although there were programs that might have helped subsidize the rising costs of fuel and food, she was too proud to accept help.

Townsfolk, however, made a point of finding ways to help without letting it seem like charity. Vance delivered loads of wood to Myla, convincing her that he had gotten it free from one of his jobs. Jane dropped over with containers of soup or bags of muffins from the café with the pretext that she'd just have to throw it all away. And someone always made certain that her driveway was shoveled in winter and her lawn was mowed in summer.

A small bank of windows along the east wall highlighted Jane's profile in the soft morning light. Her body, lean and fit, moved as easily as an athlete's (Jane had once been Bend Oaks High School's track star), her arms sculpted from lifting racks of heavy dishes and coffee cups, twenty-five-pound bags of potatoes, barrels of garlic pickles, and cartons of milk. Her silhouette was more like her fourteen-year-old daughter's than that of a middle-aged woman. Only the small traces of gray that threaded her rich auburn hair like the basting stitches on a quilt might have hinted at her age. Her hair was thick and heavy, and she drew it back tight against her head into a ponytail, accenting the high cheekbones and amber eyes framed by thick dark lashes.

Loose strands of hair curled around her face as the humidity in the room rose, but she didn't notice the change in the temperature. She pushed them impatiently out of her way. She had never been one to fuss over her looks. Her hair-style was the same standard-issue ponytail she had worn since high school. Not a trace of makeup lined her face.

People said that if she paid a little more attention to her looks she'd be such a pretty woman. But pretty was reserved for girls who were more fluff than substance—girls who would be knocked down by the slightest wind of adversity, like gladiolus under a driving rain.

Jane, by contrast, was solid and dependable, which was fortunate, because those were the qualities she had needed during the harrowing days that followed the accident. It still haunted her dreams, often jolting her out of a sound sleep. Her pillow would be soaked with sweat, her heart beating like a kettledrum against her chest. Each time it came, it sent her hurtling back through time to that exact moment when she heard the impact.

The family was returning from one of her track meets. Their team had taken second place, and she remembered feeling slightly let-down, even though her father told her repeatedly that she'd done a wonderful job. She had been seated on the passenger side beside the window. Her brothers had been sandwiched to her left and were fighting over whose foot got to rest on the floor hump. She let them argue as she tried to find a comfortable position for a short nap.

None of them saw the tractor-trailer coming. It was hauling fourteen thousand pounds of Maytag washing machines and dryers. The trucker lost control coming around a curve and swerved onto their side. There was no time for her father to react. It all happened so fast. All she remembered of that moment was the eerie silence seconds before the sickening sound of metal exploding, and the feeling of being hurled into the air. The rescue team later found her lying in a gulley, twenty-five feet from the scene. The doctors said the fact that she was thrown from the wreckage was the only thing that saved her. In this instance, it was a good thing that she wasn't wearing a seat belt. The rest of her family and the trucker had died instantly.

But she had been wearing one. She was certain of it, so why was she thrown free and the others weren't? It was a mystery that still plagued her. Her leg had nearly been severed, but surgeons were able to reattach it in an eighteen-hour operation. She would never run track again, and she would always walk with a slight limp, which grew more pronounced on rainy days.

The injury to her leg was not the only one she suffered. Something inside her had changed as well. A psychic gift had been triggered by the accident, a barrier removed that separated the seen and unseen worlds, revealing ancient forms of evil that lay in wait for mankind's soul.

Outside the swinging kitchen doors, Jane heard a chorus of greetings followed by Rose Rinkleman's signature laugh—a raucous, low-pitched bellow that always made strangers turn and stare. Voices began to escalate, climbing higher with every verbal exchange. Jane smiled—no need to open the kitchen door to know what was going on out front.

Rose was a terrible flirt who had a way of reducing men to a pubescent awkwardness. The loudest, most obnoxious, opinionated, boisterous man became tongue-tied when she walked into a room. Some of it had to do with her ability to outcuss, outsmart-talk, and deliver jokes that made even the men blush. But mostly it was because Rose Rinkleman was the sexiest woman who had ever sauntered into Bend Oaks. She was partial to spandex and tight-fitting knits in bright shades of orange, pink, and turquoise, which made her easy to pick out of a crowd. Her favorite eye shadow was Revlon's metallic green, which she accented with liquid black eyeliner; she wore five-inch stiletto heels during even the most savage winter storms. But her biggest asset was her size 38D bust, which she set off with plunging necklines, and formfitting sweaters and T-shirts. Most men in town, regardless of age, had a hard time keeping their eyes level with her face while they were engaged in conversation.

Rose had arrived ten years ago to apply for the post of assistant high-school principal. For the interview, she wore a conservative black suit and a pair of flat patent-leather pumps. She knew that if there's anything that gives a school superintendent confidence it's seeing a candidate dressed in sober-minded black.

Rose was hired, but she couldn't hide her true personality for long. It was like trying to fit a size 14 behind into a pair of size 6 jeans. Sooner or later, things were bound to break loose. In Rose's case, it happened right after her probationary period ended and she had been officially signed on as vice principal of Bend Oaks High, but once folks got over the initial shock of seeing their vice principal dressed like a streetwalker, they discovered that Rose was a hard-nosed educator who loved her students as though they were her own children.

The door swung open and Rose walked through with Myla, who was dressed in a blue wool jacket and pants that had been purchased with an eye to someday fashioning them into a rug. She dropped her canvas bag on a chair and surveyed the stacks of wool Jane had piled neatly on the table.

"I had no idea that we'd collected so much this year," she said, her Bermuda-blue eyes twinkling merrily.

"Abby's been collecting along her postal route again," Jane explained.

Rose threw herself into the nearest chair. "I guess this means we're doing the eight by ten this year. I hope the church appreciates the crimp this puts in my social calendar."

The ladies joked that there wasn't a man within a hundred-mile radius whom she hadn't dated. Rose went through men the way most people went through a bag of potato chips.

The group hooked either a seven by five or an eight by ten, depending on the amount of wool the women collected. The larger one meant they might have to meet twice a week, but it was bound to take in more ticket sales.

"By the way, we passed the rectory on the way over," Rose told Jane. "It's still empty. That makes three priests who have taken off in the middle of the night."

"The whole thing is pretty peculiar, if you ask me," Myla said. "Father Stephens lived there—how many years? He never had a problem."

"What's peculiar?" Kay Sprage asked, breezing in the back door. She was impeccably dressed as always, looking as though she had just stepped out of a designer show room, which, of course, she probably had. Kay owned a New York City PR firm. Among her clients was a stable of major fashion designers.

"Rumor about the rectory," Rose told her. "What happened to Gail? I thought she was coming with you."

Gail Honeychurch was a real-estate broker who had sold Kay a lakeside home and introduced her to the group.

"She's waiting for Ralph," Kay explained, placing her Valentino Garavani calfskin handbag on a nearby chair. "She wanted to tell him about RJ's recent incident at school."

"How many days' detention did he get this time?" Jane asked.

"Four," Rose replied, shaking her head. "I'm beginning to think Gail has bitten off more than she can chew. I can't understand why she allowed Ralph's ex-wife to just drop those kids at her front door and then take off."

"Where did she go again?" Jane asked.

"Memphis. She wants to be a country singing star."

"And I want to be the Queen of Sheba," Myla quipped. "Someone hand me that measuring spoon. Well, if you ask me, Gail's just too kindhearted. Always was. She has to learn to put her foot down. Tell that no-good husband of hers to stay home. What kind of business is he in, anyway? I never heard of anyone taking so many business trips."

Although Kay felt that Myla was right on target, she had a steadfast rule against talking about anyone unless he or she was present. She changed the subject. "So what do you think made him leave?"

"Who?" Myla asked.

"The priest."

"Oh, that. Well . . ." Rose began, twirling a piece of hair. "There's a rumor that the rectory is haunted."

"Like in 'ghosts'?" Kay asked with a chuckle. "You can't be serious."

"Maybe we should meet somewhere else," Jane suggested, trying not to let her apprehension show.

"What? And break tradition? We've been meeting here since this group began," Myla said indignantly. "Besides, my husband's grandfather built that house. I'll be darned if I'm going to let some silly rumors about ghosts keep me away."

three

The midafternoon sky was gunmetal gray, which matched Father Rich Melo's mood as he turned out of the archdiocese parking lot and onto Farmington Avenue. A light drizzle lent a soft sheen to the asphalt.

Traffic moved freely. Hartford, the insurance capital, had not yet discharged its fleet of workers. Within minutes, the brick building that housed the diocesan offices quickly faded from his rearview mirror, along with what he perceived might easily be his carefully crafted career.

A Toyota 4Runner swerved out in front of him. He slammed on the brakes, turned the wheel sharply to the right, and leaned his head out the window and swore in Italian—a bad habit he had picked up in Rome. If he had any sense at all, he would make some carefully placed calls to have himself summoned back.

What lunacy had made Archbishop Kerry think he was inclined to pastor a church? He was here on sabbatical. Besides, he didn't have those kinds of skills or the patience to deal with people on that level, not even on an interim basis. So why was he headed up north to take over a parish? Catholic guilt, pure and simple. The bishop had been in a bind, and he had allowed himself to be talked into this. He just hoped neither of them would live to regret it.

Rich was an academic. Research, facts, dates, and a strong analytical mind—that was where he excelled. And he had proved it by heading the Department of Ancient Semitic Languages at the University of Rome for the past fifteen years. A few weeks ago, he had been granted a sabbatical to further those studies. Yale University had recently acquired a two-thousand-year-old parchment that had been bequeathed by an alumnus. Although the artifact was reportedly not intact, college officials felt that it would still make a noteworthy addition to their collection.

No one was saying how this alumnus had gotten hold of the text, or how it had been smuggled out of the Middle East, but Rich was anxious to try to decipher its contents before some Department of Antiquities yelled foul. All the arrangements between the two universities had been finalized. The dean expected to meet with him the day after tomorrow to work out the details.

Rich had tried to explain all of that to the bishop, and had reminded him that, even if he wanted to shelve his research, he had no experience in overseeing a parish.

"I realize that," the bishop said. "But you have other, more important skills."

"May I ask what you think those are?"

"You come highly recommended by Father Malachi."

Rich got a sinking feeling.

"You see, there is a situation in a parish up north from here. Small town. Simple people. A few months back they lost their pastor. He was elderly. Died of a heart attack in his sleep. And since then I've sent several replacements, all of whom have fled in the middle of the night and refused to go back. They said the rectory was haunted. Frankly, I didn't know what to do. The parish needs a priest. What was I going to tell them? So I made some calls to the Vatican. I have friends there whom I can trust to be discreet, and they led me to Father Malachi, who, in turn, led me to you."

"Did those other priests say what they saw or heard?"

"Noises from behind the walls. Objects disappearing, then reappearing. Furniture levitating. Things straight out of *The Exorcist*."

"Have you investigated any of these claims? I mean, there could be a hundred explanations for any of this."

"Yes, yes, of course. In fact, I sent a good friend. A priest I've known since my days at the seminary. He served in the Korean War, even received the Purple Heart. Not the kind of man who would allow himself to be chased away by something that went bump in the night."

"And?"

"He fled, too. He wouldn't tell me what he saw, just refused to go back."

"I see."

The bishop took a seat opposite Rich. "The whole thing has me puzzled."

"And you think I can somehow right this problem?" Rich asked. "Excuse me, Bishop, but I'm a professor, not a Ghostbuster."

The bishop laughed. "Father Malachi said you have a rare gift, and that if anyone could sort this out you could."

"He's wrong," Rich said emphatically. He had traveled this road before. He was not going down that path again.

"He told me about the incident with the young girl in Rome," the bishop said quietly.

Rich had spent the past eight months trying to forget what he had seen, and now with one sentence the horror he had experienced came flooding back. "One exorcism does not an exorcist make," he said philosophically. "Listen, I empathize with your problem, but you've got the wrong guy. I prefer the world of books and classrooms. I'm sure there's someone else on your staff who could take care of this. I just want to do my research and then hightail it back to Rome."

"There isn't anyone else. Certainly not anyone I can trust, or anyone who has any expertise in these matters." The bishop leaned forward and spoke with an earnestness that compelled Rich to listen.

"The American church here has suffered one scandal after another these last few months. If rumors of this supposed haunting get out, it will only fuel the public relations nightmare that we bishops have been trying to contain.

"All I'm asking is that you go up there and let the parishioners assume that you've simply been assigned as an interim pastor. You can delegate most of the parish duties while you do your research. Father Stephens was ill for years. The folks there are used to practically running the place. All you'll be required to do is say Mass.

"While you're there, just keep your eyes and ears open, then report back to me. I won't force this on you, Rich. You have to be willing. If you turn me down, I won't hold it against you. God knows, I wouldn't want to take it on myself. I'm not normally one who believes in all this mumbo jumbo, but my gut tells me this time something supernatural is happening there."

Rich thought of a hundred reasons that he should say no. "I never wanted to get involved with this sort of thing again," he told the bishop.

"No, I don't suppose you would. Father Malachi gave me the details of the case you worked on together. It scared the hell out of me."

What had he gotten himself into? he wondered, traversing the familiar country roads that he had once traveled as a young man.

A simple "Sorry, Bishop, but I think I'll pass on this one" would have sufficed. But no, he had let himself get suckered into this. This was all Malachi's fault. Damn the man! What part of *I refuse to get involved in exorcisms* didn't he understand? Let Malachi and his secret order inhabit the world of the paranormal. He wanted no part of it.

Rich was perfectly happy living the sane and highly respected lifestyle of an academic in a field that he had worked hard to master. He held advanced degrees in both Petroglyphy and Assyriology. His study of Hittite myths and legends had won him a prestigious OAT

Award, presented by *Choice* magazine, which was published by the American Library Association. The association reviewed more than seven thousand academic titles annually and was heavily referenced by undergraduate librarians when making acquisitions. Rich was the envy of all his colleagues.

Unfortunately, the very book that had won him such acclaim had also attracted Father Malachi's attention. Eight months ago, Rich had just finished grading the last test of the spring semester when he was summoned by the Pope's assistant with a request from the pontiff himself. Would Rich go to a small enclave in a northern section of the city where a sect of cloistered priests had procured a manuscript they wished to have deciphered? It seemed an innocuous request, hardly one that should elicit the Pope's attention, but Rich didn't question it. He had decoded hundreds of similar texts for the Vatican down through the years. He figured this was just one more. So he filled a backpack with reference materials and headed out. What that parchment entailed, however, was anything but ordinary, and neither was what followed.

Rich turned onto Route 10, passing by Avon, then on to Farmington. Good Lord, things had changed while he was away. The road that had been flanked by cow paths in the late eighties now looked like one long strip mall—T.J. Maxx, Marshall's, Ethan Allen, Target, supersize grocery stores, designer outlets. It went on and on. He wondered why Americans felt they needed so much "stuff." He kept the accumulation of "things" to a minimum. He liked the freedom of being able to pick up and leave at a moment's notice. Upon reflection, of course, he knew that freedom was illusory. He was, after all, tied to the Church.

Rich maneuvered the rented sedan into the right-hand lane, angling toward Route 44, a back road that ambled through the quiet countryside, eventually taking him to the upper northwest portion of the state. He knew it well. He had grown up around here. A few towns over was the Catholic orphanage where his father had dropped him off like a piece of excess baggage when he was six years old. He had lived there until he was seventeen, when he entered St. Joseph's seminary.

Outside, the rain had tapered off. At the next traffic light he hit the button for the electric windows and let a fine, fresh mist blow in, lifting his wavy blond hair and revealing a high, intelligent forehead. A stylish young woman driving a BMW convertible glanced his way and smiled an open invitation. He smiled slightly, nodded, then refocused his attention on the traffic light.

He had driven directly to the archdiocese from the airport and was still dressed in a hand-tailored Italian merino-wool sports jacket and a custom-made shirt. But even if he had been garbed in clerical black there was a strong probability that the woman would still have flirted. Women seemed drawn to his clean, Nordic profile, his piercing blue eyes, and his broad shoulders. Of course, a six-foot-two rock-hard body and the looks of a professional sportsman didn't hurt, either. Rich was fastidious about keeping fit. He ran five miles every morning before Mass and combined this with a weight-training regimen. The only thing that marred his otherwise good looks was the crescent-shaped birthmark on the side of his neck, which he was always careful to hide. Much to his chagrin, however, it seemed to grow more pronounced with age.

The power of appearing fit and attractive had been Rich's first life lesson. His parents couldn't afford to keep two children. Rich was a plain, scrawny child. His baby brother, however, with his dimpled cheeks and perfectly shaped head, was declared a beauty. They had kept him.

He came to a turn in the road. If he went east, it would take him along the river that ran through Riverton. He could stop at the Riverton Inn and have an early supper (he had only dreamed of going there as a young boy; only the well-to-do dined there), or he could travel the back roads that wound through the Litchfield hills. It was a much longer route, but infinitely more scenic. He threw on the directional and headed toward the hills. Heck, he wasn't in a hurry, and it had been years since he'd wandered these back roads.

An overwhelming sense of nostalgia made him opt for the latter course. The sun had broken through the clouds, backlighting what was left of autumn's plumage. That was one thing he had sorely missed. There was nothing as spectacular as a New England fall.

The road wound through state conservation lands thick with pines. With nothing to draw his attention, his thoughts ambled back to Malachi and the days he'd spent in the villa perched on a hill with a commanding view of the city of Rome. The ancient drama that had played out within its walls was an anachronism against the modern metropolis below.

Rich had felt an inner door opening that night. A power had been unleashed, a sense of destiny forged. He had fought against it even though Malachi had sensed it, too.

"You have been given a rare gift," Malachi had told him. "A priest with your powers appears in Church history only once every five hundred years or so."

Rich visualized what he had witnessed in the locked room at the head of the stairs and shuddered. "Then I give it back," he said.

Malachi poured two glasses of wine. He handed one to Rich. "You may not have a choice in this matter," he said.

"I have my free will."

"You have your priestly vows," he reminded him. "Evil has suddenly been given unprecedented access to our world. I believe that you, my friend, have been sent at this time to help overcome it."

"Me?" he had laughed. "I'm afraid that you've got me confused with someone else."

"He uses the foolish things of the world to confound the wise."

"Gee, thanks," Rich said with a weak smile.

"There are some who believe that the prophesies that were foretold in the Book of Revelation are being played out in our time."

"Every generation since the Resurrection has believed that," Rich reminded him.

Malachi searched his face. "But what do you believe?"

"Me?" He studied his wine. "I don't know. I guess, like most, that something is off balance. Anyone who watches the news has to believe that."

"Do you believe in the reality of Satan at work in our world?"

Before he arrived, Rich would have answered that question by saying only in concept. But now, having just witnessed the unfathomable in the locked room upstairs, he had to believe.

"Yes." He finished off what was left in his glass and took the liberty of pouring himself another while Malachi continued.

"It seems as though Satan has suddenly loosed an all-out war against all that God stands for. He's doing everything he can to win souls before the final conflict, including attacking an innocent child."

"How can God allow this?" Rich asked. He sank back into his chair, feeling a heavy weight attach itself to his heart.

"It is not our place to question God," Malachi reminded him. "Just to obey."

"But how can one blindly obey a God who would allow that upstairs"—he motioned toward the room above their heads—"to take place."

"We walk by faith, not by sight, my son. Our finite minds could never understand the myriad complexities of God's plan. We can only place ourselves at his disposal and pray that he will find us worthy enough to use us in his service to combat the Devil's schemes."

"As exorcists?" Rich rebelled. He shuddered at the thought of having to accept that path, yet something long dormant had been awakened in him. Could it be?

Malachi studied the remaining wine in his glass. "It may not be what we would have chosen, but it is our destiny."

Rich turned onto Route 202, working his way farther north with a sense of predestination, as though what he was about to undertake had been foretold since ancient times. Some other hand was now directing his life. Some say that when we arrive at the place where we were destined to be, we will look back over our lives and see that everything—the heartaches, tragedies, victories, valleys, and hilltops—has been in preparation for this moment.

Rich had felt it that day, seated in the villa with the sienna-colored walls and the terra-cotta tiled floor and the French doors thrown open to the jasmine-scented air. He knew it with absolute certainty, coupled with dread.

His abandonment as a child had made him rely alone on a heavenly Father and had forged a deep and abiding bond of trust in God. Since the beginning of his study for the priesthood, fellow clerics had sensed his unwavering faith and often came to him to help bolster their secret doubts and fears. Being brought up in a Catholic orphanage had shaped his love of the Church, which later led to his becoming a priest. Even his leaning toward the study of ancient times—an era when demons and evil were spoken of in the same commonplace manner in which people spoke of the stock market today—provided him with insights into a world that the modern-day man had jettisoned from his vernacular. It was labeled archaic, superstitious. But it was a world that Rich was finding increasingly real.

Was it a call within his calling to the priesthood? The thought deeply troubled him. He was just a priest, a professor, a sinner like everyone else. How could a sinner help save the damned?

And so he had run from the call, back to the safety of academia's hallowed halls, safe from the stigma attached to those who spoke of the unseen. But it had followed him, and there was no place else to hide.

four

Somewhere during the past five years, Gail Honey-church had finally accepted the fact that she was never going to be a size 10 again, that is, not without exerting an anormous amount of effort, which she clearly was not doing. She studied her reflection in the full-length mirror behind the bathroom door, the one that gave a clear view of anyone seated on the john. What had her husband, Ralph, been thinking?

She sucked in her stomach and turned sideways, showcasing her Talbots size 12 figure in a more slenderizing silhouette. If she shopped at Wal-Mart or the Dress Barn she was a size 14, which is why her Talbots balance was pushing $2,500 this month. She studied the reflection critically. Not bad for a forty-two-year-old woman, she concluded. At twenty she wore a size 6, but a few extra pounds were to be expected with each decade, right?

She exhaled and watched the rolls of flesh settle like an inner tube around her waist. Damn that Jane Fonda for propounding that "women should look great at any age" myth! And damn Oprah for perpetuating it! Why couldn't they just leave middle-aged women alone—let them morph into the soft, pliable, matronly shape of their forebears guilt-free? Her mother and grandmother never worried about their figure, yet back then men treated women with more respect than they did today's figure-conscious, emaciated youth worshippers. When was the last time a man took off his hat in an elevator or offered her a seat on a bus? Not that she traveled much by bus.

Still, the guilt lingered. Maybe she should really make a commitment to exercising more frequently. All she needed was an extra five or six hours pinned on to every day. It seemed that her business alone took up most of her time. When was the last time she enjoyed a weekend off without the phone ringing?

"My father-in-law promised to lend us the down payment on the house. But he won't give us the money unless he inspects the house first, and he's only available on Sundays."

She sighed. She couldn't remember when.

Gail was helping to raise two stepsons—Jerry, fourteen, and Ralph Junior, whom everyone called RJ, seventeen. At times they seemed hell-bent on turning her into the proverbial wicked stepmother.

"No, Jerry, you can't have a pet python. No, RJ, you can't borrow my car. Why? Remember the last time? You were clocked at eighty in a thirty-five zone, and when the officer told you to get out of the car you gave him the finger."

Although the boys could be exhausting, Gail loved them as though they were her own. RJ was especially dear to her heart. He had a sweet vulnerability that he tried to mask behind an insolent facade. There were even those special moments when he watched her make supper and confided his dreams.

"Do you think I could be a pediatrician? A brother of one of my friends is really sick. I'd like to be able to help kids like that someday."

She and Ralph decided not to have children when they got married. Ralph had his two sons, and Gail was in her late thirties and struggling with a new business. It wasn't that she didn't want to have children. The timing just hadn't seemed right.

Then fate threw her a curve. One Monday morning as she was rushing around the house, trying to make an 8 AM appointment with a builder, the doorbell rang. Ralph's first wife, Chirley (with a "C," she informed Gail), stood on the front porch, flanked by two mammoth duffel bags and dozens of plastic shopping bags stuffed with clothes and toys. Ralph, as usual, had been away on a business trip.

"Here," she said, pushing the boys through the front door, as though she were returning an item that didn't fit. "I've got a chance to cut a record down in Memphis on a new label, but I have to be there by midweek. I can't travel that distance with two kids in the backseat of my car," she said.

Chirley fancied herself the next Faith Hill. The problem was she couldn't carry a tune, which was why her career had gone no further than a string of sleazy back-alley bars. Gail later discovered that the new label she mentioned was being launched in someone's garage.

"I can see how your . . . er . . . career goals are very important to you and how the boys might interfere with that," Gail began tentatively. Since the boys were listening, she wanted to make certain that her words were chosen carefully. "But I really can't take them. You see, I have an appointment and I'm late. You'll have to wait and talk to Ralph when he gets back in town. RJ . . . Jerry . . . I'm sorry, but you'll have to go back with your mother."

"Honey, I'm done with waiting on that man," Chirley said. Then, without as much as a goodbye to her sons, she sauntered down the front walk and into her car while Gail stood watching in hopeless disbelief.

That was five years ago. They hadn't seen her since, although she did send a Christmas card every year, with a photo of some new redneck band that she felt certain was her ticket to stardom, along with two ten-dollar bills. "Give one to each of the boys," she scrawled on the back of the card. Gail noticed that she never referred to them as her sons.

Eventually, Gail adjusted—as she did to everything in life—with an "if life gives you lemons, make lemonade" attitude. Like other working women, she learned to balance her schedule between work and children, although lately she was spending an inordinate amount of time at the boys' high school. Fortunately, Rose—from the hooking group—was the vice principal and could pinch-hit for her when she just couldn't break away. She had tried to get Ralph more involved, urging him to reduce his monthly business trips.

"Excuse me for trying to make a living," Ralph quipped. "The less I travel, the less money there'll be for the boys' college fund. Education doesn't come cheap."

Of course, he was right. But somehow that didn't lessen the feeling she got that he didn't enjoy spending time with his sons. If he did, he would make time. Even when he wasn't traveling, he found ways to keep busy away from the house—golf, beers with his buddies. More distressing were the times when the boys stepped over the boundaries. Ralph just shrugged it off with a "Boys will be boys." Or he would make a flippant remark, such as "They're just letting off some steam." Unfortunately, he never saw their antics for what they were—a bid for his attention. Nor did he see it as his responsibility to step in and intervene.

Last week that "steam" had caused the entire school to be evacuated. Jerry put a stink bomb in one of the air vents. If Rose hadn't intervened, he would have been suspended. But Gail could tell when she called that Rose's tolerance for these repeated incidents had been exhausted.

"I'm sorry, Gail," Rose said. "You're one of my best friends, but I'm afraid that if either of these boys pulls another stunt I'm going to have to expel him."

Gail couldn't blame her. She had a school to run, and its main purpose was educating minds, not reforming delinquents. Maybe if she and Ralph had a little extra money they could send the boys to one of those private schools, the ones that specialize in redirecting defiant behavior. There seemed to be a plethora of them in New England.

Extra money? That was a rare commodity in their house these

days. Every month it grew harder to make ends meet. The food bills alone were staggering, and clothing expenses for the boys sent shock waves through her budget for months. (Who would have imagined, a few years back, that sneakers would someday cost more than a hundred dollars a pair!)

Meanwhile, their paychecks kept dwindling. Ralph's paycheck was a third of what he brought home last year. He sold hospital pharmaceutical supplies.

"Sales are off," he said simply, handing her the grocery money—a pittance of what it had been a few months ago. "You'll have to make do with this."

Adding to their economic woes was a decline in real-estate sales, Gail's bread and butter. Sales were down 35 percent this quarter from the same period last year. She didn't understand it. The rest of the country was enjoying record housing sales, so why was Bend Oaks's housing market in the dumps?

Last month she had to let one of her salespeople go, which had helped some, but she still had to maintain an office with phones and heat as well as pay taxes. She worried constantly. Where was the money going to come from? And what if Jerry needed braces to correct his overbite? She'd probably have to refinance their home. God help them if they were ever hit with a financial emergency. They'd be out on the streets.

She kept all of this to herself, even from her mother-in-law, Vera, who had just returned from one of her extended travels. Unlike other in-law relationships, she and Vera were extremely close—probably because Vera thought so little of her son and so highly of a woman who could put up with his nonsense.

"You see, that's why I sold my home and now travel," Vera announced right after the boys had come to live with Gail and Ralph. "I was done raising kids or doctoring relatives. If you don't put down roots, there's no place for them to dump them off."

Gail leaned back from the sink and studied her face in the mirror. Kay had given her a makeup kit for her birthday.

"You're stuck in a time warp," Kay had told her. "Blue eye shadow went out in the sixties." She wasn't sure how she felt about this brown. It seemed to make her eyes look muddy. At least the blue had given her face a splash of color. She bit her lower lip. She didn't want to offend Kay, but . . . She rummaged through her makeup case and found the blue eye shadow. So she was stuck in the sixties.

She looked at her watch. Shoot! She was supposed to have picked up Kay fifteen minutes ago. "Boys, I'm leaving," she yelled into the family room, heading toward the back door. Jerry was sitting in front of the television set, eyes locked on a gyrating J. Lo. RJ was on the phone. "Turn that thing off," she told Jerry, scooping her keys off a side table. "And, RJ, get off the phone. You both have homework to do."

RJ sighed heavily into the phone. "I gotta go."

Jerry had completely zoned out. She raced over to the sofa, grabbed the remote, and turned off the TV.

"Hey! I was watching that."

"No TV until homework's done, remember? And no phone either, RJ. Understood?"

"Yeah."

"If you need me, I'm at the rectory. Jerry, leave your homework on the kitchen counter. I'll check it when I get home. Got it?"

"Yeah, we got it."

Gail had barely gotten out the back door when she heard the TV snap back on.

The entrance to St. Francis Xavier's rectory was tucked away off a seldom used road three-quarters of a mile from the church. It was an imposing property, completely inappropriate for a rectory but very much in keeping with its original intent. It had been a wedding gift to the wealthy Whitcombs' only child, Charles II, in 1929.

Charles, however, died before ever taking possession of the house. His death was shrouded in mystery, which was further fueled by the Whitcombs' insistence that the facts concerning the case remain sealed. The Whitcombs had both the money and the influence to make certain their request was carried out.

The sheriff, an elected official, made certain that his main campaign contributors' wishes were followed to the letter. Nothing was ever leaked to the press. Apart from a small obituary that listed Charles's academic history and the charities he had chaired, it was as if nothing unusual had happened that night at the estate.

After their son's death, the Whitcombs boarded up the house, and it remained that way for nearly a quarter of a century. In the early 1950s, upon the death of Viola Whitcomb, who had survived her husband, Charles I, by nearly two decades, the property was deeded to St. Francis Xavier—a happenstance that its parishioners viewed as an act of divine and timely intervention. The baby boomers were having babies, and the church had grown by leaps and bounds. Sunday Masses had taken on the appearance of so many sardines stuffed into a tin can. The church was in desperate need of expansion.

The pastor at that time was Father O'Donnell. He petitioned the archdiocese to have the former rectory incorporated into the church's expansion program and the Whitcomb property designated as the new rectory–parish center. The bishop approved. Unfortunately, Father O'Donnell never got to enjoy the fruits of his labor. Both he and his assistant, a young man just six months away from being ordained, were found dead in their respective beds a few days after they had moved in. The coroner's report listed the cause of death as heart failure, noting that neither of the men had any indication of heart disease. He also found it rather strange that both of them had died between the hours of midnight and 3 AM.

Once again the house was boarded up, and it remained that way until Father Jonathan Stephens arrived, two years later. A man of deep spirituality, he immediately sensed that something inside the house wasn't right. Until the day he died, he tried to discourage his parishioners from visiting the rectory. It wasn't much of a problem, really, since the parishioners were so happy to have a full-time, resident priest again. Hardly a word of protest was uttered.

Then his sister and housekeeper Judith decided to start a rug-hooking group, and she insisted that its meetings be held at the rectory. "The rug is too big to be transported from one member's home to the next," she told him. "Besides, I hate driving at night."

What about the church basement? he suggested. He'd drive her.

"Do you know how many groups use that space?" she countered, with an "I can't believe you would even suggest this" tone to her voice. "I can just imagine one of the preschoolers spilling a cup of juice all over our rug."

Since Father Stephens had never been able to dissuade his sister of anything once she had set her mind on it, he acquiesced. He did, however, insist on opening each meeting with a prayer, through which he solicited the protection of St. Michael.

Tonight's meeting would be the first time in all those years that the hookers had met without Father Stephens. Jane had tried to persuade the women to meet elsewhere, but to no avail.

"You're not afraid of all those silly rumors now, are you?" Rose had teased.

What could she say? That she saw things gathering around the rectory that would rival any Hollywood horror flick? No wonder the other priests had fled. No one knew of her gift—not the hookers, not even Vance—and she preferred to keep it that way, so she kept her silence.

Dusk was settling as Jane pulled the Pathfinder in front of the massive wrought-iron gates that flanked the entrance to the rectory's driveway. The gates had always struck her as formidable—as if they were sending a clear message to all visitors to stay out unless they had been invited. This was hardly the kind of welcome Catholics expected from their parish rectory. But then this was hardly your ordinary rectory. She put the car in park and studied the iron structure and the grounds they sealed off, remembering the day that Father Stephens had first brought her here to live. There had been no gates then.

"This is your home for as long as you like," he said, his face reflecting her own deep sorrow. He and her parents had been good friends.

She was eternally grateful for this kindness. She had no living relatives. All of her grandparents had died before she was born, and with two more years before she would be considered an adult she would most certainly have been placed in a foster home had he not intervened.

But her sense of security was quickly shaken the moment she stepped through the front door of the rectory and sensed the evil that resided there. She had kept silent, afraid that if she voiced what she saw Father Stephens would send her away. What if he thought she was suffering from trauma and needed psychiatric help? What if he felt that it was necessary to commit her to one of those institutions? Ridgecrest was just a few towns away. She had heard stories about what went on there. Horrifying stories. The thought of being sent there evoked a deeper terror than her fear of confronting the entities she saw wandering the halls at night. They were menacing, demonic creatures who, she sensed, felt threatened by her ability to see into their world.

Each night they grew bolder, taunting her. Suddenly things in her room began to levitate. Sounds emanated from behind the walls, as though something were trying to claw its way through. Sleep was no longer an option. She felt that she must be on guard both for herself and for Father Stephens and his sister.

Finally, the emotional strain proved too much. She began to lose weight. Always a good student, her grades now began to plummet. Then one day she fainted in class from sheer exhaustion. The school nurse summoned Father Stephens.

"I realize that the child has been through a great ordeal, but she seems incredibly high-strung and nervous," the nurse told the priest. "Is she getting the proper rest at night?"

Father Stephens took her back to the rectory in his aging Rambler station wagon. The doors creaked like the hinges on a coffin, and the engine spewed black smoke thick enough to completely obliterate the cars behind. He was silent until they reached the rectory's front entrance. He put the car in park and asked her to stay seated for a moment. He wanted to know if anything was wrong.

She considered making excuses—it was a new environment, she missed her family—but Father Stephens had a way of seeing through half-truths, so she decided to tell him about her gift and what she sensed in the house.

When she finished, there was a silence that seemed to stretch out for an eternity. Finally, he looked at her with eyes filled with compassion coupled with deep concern.

"I believe you," he said. "I feel it, too."

She experienced an immediate rush of relief, and asked, "Then you don't think I'm crazy?"

"No," he said, patting her hand reassuringly. "The Bible says that Satan goes among us like a roaring lion, trying to devour those he can. For whatever reason, God has given you the ability to see his activity and perhaps warn people."

"But who would listen?" she wanted to know.

The priest had smiled knowingly. "Yes, that's always been the problem, hasn't it?"

But Father Stephens *did* listen, and within a few hours Jane was seated on a Trailway bus with her best friend, Gail, and they were headed to Gail's grandparents' place at the Cape for a short holiday. When she returned a week later, exterior changes had been made. A wrought-iron gate adorned with a circular wreath had been installed along the front driveway, and Marvin had laid a new walkway that encircled the house.

Marvin . . .

Thoughts of this simpleminded man trained her thoughts back on the present. She hadn't seen him for several days, and that worried her. He was a fixture at the Sit and Sip, arriving at 8:03 every morning, dressed in the same outfit regardless of the weather—a threadbare dirty brown cable sweater and faded green corduroy pants. He always took the same seat, wedged in the corner between the front window and the coat rack, and if anyone was sitting there he would begin to whistle "When the Saints Go Marching In" until they moved. Patrons had christened him Marvin-in-the-Corner. The name stuck, but he took it in stride. He had been labeled "different" since he was a child.

But what he lacked in social graces and intellect, he made up for in mechanical savvy. There wasn't a thing that Marvin couldn't fix, from toasters to John Deere tractors. That was one of the reasons Father Stephens had hired him as a groundskeeper; something at the rectory always needed fixing.

Then one day Marvin asked if he might clean out some of the old garden beds, which had originally been designed by the famous English gardener Gertrude Jekyll. Within weeks, the garden was transformed from a patch of overgrown briars and weeds to a lush cottage garden filled with Shasta daisies, Scottish broom, decorative grasses, native phlox, chicory, and bee balm. Father Stephens called it a "feast for the eyes."

Marvin had been lost since Father Stephens's death. The townsfolk hired him to do odd jobs, but it wasn't the same. He had grown accustomed to a routine. Part of his day had been spent working at the church, the other at the rectory. Since being fired by Father Braxton, Marvin had wandered aimlessly around town. Occasionally, someone would spy him peering through the rectory gates at his unattended gardens.

Jane wished he were here now. The gates were locked at night. It had been Marvin's job to open them. While he was employed at the rectory, he had lived in the stone cottage just beyond the gates. The cottage windows were dark now. No light flicked on at the sound of gravel crunching beneath her car. She stared out into the darkness. It felt strange and empty not having him there.

She still carried the key that Father Stephens had given her so many years ago. She slipped out of the car, ignoring the bell that chimed as a reminder that she had left the key in the ignition. The iron gate felt cold and clammy as she grasped it. The key slid into place. She gave it a turn and heard the familiar click. Then, leaning all her weight against the heavy iron gates, she pushed hard. The gates moved slowly; the hinges squealed, frightening a flock of sparrows that had bedded down in a nearby tree. They took flight, the flutter of their wings mimicking the flutter of her heart.

A twig snapped. She swung around, searching for any movement in the foliage. Thickening shadows gave form and motion to ordinary shapes. A cluster of lilac bushes flanked the stone pillars. In spring, their color and fragrance filled her with delight. But tonight they swayed in the breeze, a gesture of mock welcome; their leaves trailed behind like the fringes on an ancient magician's robe.

She pushed hard on the gates, eager to be back in the safety of the car and away from the thickening shadows that seemed to be closing in on her. Finally, the gates were open. She raced back, her feet sending gravel flying into the air, and hopped into the car. She hit the lock button and was about to put the car in drive when she had a paralyzing thought. What if someone had slipped inside while her back was turned?

She worked to squelch a rising flood of panic, but it was useless. She felt for the door lock, flipped it open, and jumped out of the car as though the seat were on fire. Her heart was racing like a thorough-bred's at the Kentucky Derby. She knew she was being ridiculous, but she couldn't help herself. Slowly, she peered into the car windows and studied the inside. No one was there. Her level of anxiety went down a notch.

But what if someone was hunched down on the floor?

Adrenaline began to pump again. She stood on her tiptoes and peered into the back windows. If something or someone peered back at her, she'd have a heart attack for certain. Except for the two bags of groceries she had brought along for tonight's snacks, the backseat was empty. She breathed easier.

You've got to get hold of yourself, girl.

She slipped back inside the car and hit the lock button. All four locks snapped into place, and for a brief moment this gave her a sense of protection. But in her heart she knew that no physical barrier could keep what she feared from breaking through.

She started down the long, winding driveway canopied by ancient oaks, some of which were said to have given shelter to Benedict Arnold's troops when they camped here. A quarter mile into the estate, the rectory came into view.

The moonlight draped itself across the stone facade, which had been quarried in a neighboring state. The corners of the building were capped with quoins that set off the large rectilinear blocks in mottled shades of gray and fused with specks of mica that sparkled like glitter. Although the building was much too grand for a rectory, it was extremely handsome. The Whitcombs had spared no expense in its design. The decorative details alone had cost upwards of $25,000, an enormous amount back in the 1920s.

Four pilasters supported the arcaded porch at the front of the house (fashioned after the ones Mrs. Whitcomb had seen guarding a temple in Rome). They lent protection to the massive paneled oak doors, which were adorned with intricate hand carvings. Tall, slender windows with two-over-two paned glass were paired symmetrically. Bracketed cornices with paneled frieze set off the gable roof and the small tower to the left of the house.

As Jane neared the house, she could feel it—something dark and sinister staring out at her through the windows. It was waiting. She wanted to flee, but what would she tell her friends? More important, who would warn them if the shadows began to thicken? Disregarding her fears, she stepped on the gas and pulled up next to the back kitchen door. The motion light came on, and for a moment the darkness receded.

five

The hookers always said that it felt like a lifetime between meetings. There was always so much to tell, so many subjects that needed to be discussed. Even though it had been only five days since the women last met at the café, there were new things to share as they gathered around the coarse brown piece of burlap that would slowly be transformed into a magical seascape.

Tonight's first topic of discussion was what were they going to do about Marvin. The sheriff had found him sleeping in his car.

"Winter is coming," Myla said, as though the group of staunch New Englanders needed reminding. "If someone doesn't find him a place to stay soon, he's going to freeze to death in that car."

"If he needs a temporary home, I can set up a cot in the café's kitchen," Jane offered, trying to focus on her section of the rug instead of on the deathlike chill she felt gathering in the corner. "I'd let him stay permanently, but the Board of Health might disapprove. Rose, would you pass me the turquoise blue?"

"So, Rose, how's Harold?" Kay asked, looking smart as always in a cashmere sweater, an Hermes scarf, and gold earrings. Her wardrobe was an anomaly in a sea of sweatshirts, polyester pants, and Rose's pink satin bustier.

"It's over," Rose said, shading in a seahorse.

"I thought you said he was 'the one,' " Gail said, slipping out of her red polyester jacket, which was monogrammed with a "Bend Oaks Realty" logo above the breast pocket and smelled so heavily of cigarette smoke that it made her gag. Her last client today had been a chain-smoker. She tossed it on a chair on the other side of the room, then took a seat with the others.

"I thought so, too. At first it seemed that we had so much in common. He liked old movies, historic houses, and cheap wine." Rose made it a point never to pay more than ten dollars a bottle. "He even liked to line-dance. Now, I ask you, how many men do you know who like to line-dance?"

"I tried line-dancing once at the senior center," Myla offered. "Couldn't get the hang of it. I kept crashing into people."

"So what happened?" Gail asked.

"I caught him with another woman."

"Where?" Kay asked, as though it mattered.

"At the Fireside Grill. I went for a drink after work and found him dancing cheek to cheek with his ex-wife."

"Not another ex-wife," Myla moaned, making a perfect line of small loops along what was to become a lighthouse. Rose's last two boyfriends had all had issues with former wives.

"Did you confront him?" Gail wanted to know.

"You bet."

"And what did he say?"

"That his ex was on some new kind of exercise program and he was helping her to lose weight."

"Come again . . ."

"He said it was a new diet regimen that used dancing as a form of exercise. The theory was that if you danced three hours a week you would lose twenty pounds a month."

"So let me calculate this. If she kept dancing three hours a week every month for, say, ten months, she would eventually disappear?" Kay asked, laughing.

"I lost five pounds one summer when I took up belly-dancing at the Y," Gail offered, tightening the large wooden hoop over a nest of seashells, then pulling the burlap taut. It was not in Gail's nature to think poorly of anyone.

"Ditch him and keep looking" was Myla's suggestion.

"Already done. I've just signed on with Dateline Harmony."

"The Internet dating service? Do you think that's safe?" Gail asked, grateful that she was happily married and never had to go through the dating scene again. "I mean, you hear all kinds of stories about the strange people who sign up for those sorts of things."

"I'm not worried. I still remember some of my wrestling moves from my college days. Besides, I make a point of carrying my stun gun on every new date."

"Were did you get that?" Gail asked.

"A cop I once dated." Rose paused and looked out into space. A smile moved slowly across her lips. "His name was Fred. What a hunk. I had almost forgotten about him."

"What happened to Fred?" Kay asked, finishing off a strand of wool and reaching for another.

"Found out he was gay."

"Rose, your life plays out like a soap opera," Kay said, smiling.

"Is that coffee I smell brewing?" Rose asked.

"I'll bring in the pot," Jane said, getting up.

"Look at your pants," Myla said.

Jane looked down. She was covered with lint from the wool.

"Hookers' rule number one . . ." Myla began.

"Never wear dark colors when hooking," the others intoned.

Jane brushed self-consciously at the lint. "I must have forgotten that over the summer. Oh, well, these needed to be dry-cleaned. Anyone else want a cup of coffee?"

All hands went up.

Rose waited until Jane had disappeared down the hall. "Does Jane seem unusually quiet tonight, or is it me?"

"No, you're right," Gail said, looking at Jane's empty chair. "This is the first time she's been here since Father Stephens died. I'm sure it can't be easy for her."

A branch scraped against the outside window above the kitchen sink. Jane pushed the curtain aside to glance out into the inky darkness. She hated nightfall. It was impossible to see what was out there lurking in the shadows. Tonight, however, she was more fearful of what might be lurking within these walls.

She reached inside the cabinet for the sugar and creamer while an inner dialogue played on: *What are you so afraid of? Whatever evil resided in this house before was vanquished by Father Stephens. There's absolutely nothing here that can harm you or the others. You're letting your emotions get the better of you. The house seems strange because Father Stephens is gone, that's all.*

She straightened her shoulders, feeling slightly better after the lecture, closed the cabinet door, and gasped. There was a woman's reflection staring back at her in the glass. The creamer clattered to the floor.

"I'm so sorry," Kay apologized, reaching out to help steady her. "I didn't mean to scare you. I thought you heard me coming down the hall."

"I was lost in thought. You startled me, that's all." She bent down to pick up the creamer, which, surprisingly, was still in one piece.

Kay paused to watch Jane rinse out the creamer. "I realized that I've never formally expressed my condolences," she said. "I know how much Father Stephens meant to you. I wish I could have been here this summer to lend my support, but I was tied up in London."

"I know," Jane assured her. "Your assistant told me. The flowers you sent were beautiful." She placed the creamer on the counter and turned away as a heavy tightness spread across her chest. She was on the verge of tears and quickly changed the subject. "Excuse me, I need to get to the refrigerator," she said.

Kay moved to one side.

"I brought some cream from the café." Jane wished she would go away and leave her alone. The loss was still so new.

"It must be hard for you tonight, being here for the first time since . . ."

Tears began to gather. A single tear slipped down her cheek. She tasted its saltiness. Darn Kay. Even if she wanted to, she couldn't stop them now. "Yes, he was like a parent. I miss him a great deal. He was always there when the gift became—"

"Gift?"

Had she really said that? She threw up her hands like a traffic cop. She couldn't go on. Kay got the message.

"Since I'm here, want me to help you set up the coffee?" Kay asked, swiftly changing the subject.

"Sure. Would you take down that carafe and—"

Jane's instructions were suddenly interrupted by a blood-curdling scream. It had come from the front hall.

"What in the name of . . .?" Kay asked

Jane flew past her and into the front hall, Kay close on her heels. They found the others gathered around the front door.

"What happened?" Jane asked.

"Gail saw a man peering through the library window," Rose said. She stood wielding a poker from the fireplace.

"I'll call the police," Kay said.

"Wait," Jane said. "What if it's Vance or someone we know just fooling around?"

"What if it's not?" Kay asked, punching in 911. New Yorkers didn't believe in taking chances.

Two loud knocks sounded against the front door.

"Don't open it!" Myla cautioned.

"Who's there?" Rose demanded.

The others packed closely behind her.

"Father Rich Melo," a man said. "I've been sent by Archbishop Kerry."

It took Rich several minutes to get things sorted out. Apparently the bishop's secretary had forgotten to call, so no one had expected him, and the key he had been given was for an earlier lock system. Once the women were convinced that he was neither ghoul nor masher, introductions were made and they welcomed him warmly, urging him to come in out of the damp night air.

"This is quite a place," he said, handing one of the women his coat while pausing to admire the front entrance hall. "This kind of architecture isn't something I expected to find in a small New England town."

Rich studied the domed ceiling, which soared three flights, encapsulating the balustrade staircase like a bell jar. A stained-glass window capped the dome, and on sunny days sent shards of colored prisms dancing along the imported silk-screened wallpaper. Thick Persian carpet lined the stairway, each riser held in place by a brass bar that over the years had been buffed to a soft patina. At the end of the balustrade, two graceful nymphs held aloft lanterns that Rich's trained eye told him were most certainly made by Tiffany.

The main entrance hall, a large rectangular space with some twenty by forty feet of inlaid marble, was paneled in rich mahogany that had been aged to the color of fine Merlot. The hallway was flanked by two sets of massive pocket doors. One led to the library and revealed the hookers' work-in-progress; the other, to a formal living room. Directly opposite the entryway was the dining room, which ran across the entire back of the house. From where Rich was standing, he had a clear view of a marble fireplace, above which hung a gold-leaf mirror that soared toward the ceiling. Later, on closer inspection, he would discover that it had been designed by a master craftsman, adorned with a smiling Bacchus and a cascade of grapes, the vines and leaves intricately woven together.

Myla watched him taking it all in and beamed with pride. "My husband's grandparents built this house," she said.

"They must have really liked the pastor," he joked, his handsome face softening into a smile.

She laughed. "No, this was designed as a wedding gift for their son."

"Lucky man."

"I'm afraid not. He died before he and his bride could move in."

"That's a pity."

"You know something about architecture, Father?" Myla asked.

"It's a hobby of mine. Italianate, correct?"

"Yes, it was quite the rage when it was commissioned."

"If memory serves me, it was drawn from the country villas in the Old World. A redesign of the Italian Renaissance derived from classical Rome." He ran a hand along the paneling. "My guess is that it was built around the early twentieth century. Andrew Jackson Downing, I believe, popularized it here in the Northeast."

"Yes, in fact he designed this home. It was built in 1925 after the Whitcombs returned from the grand tour. While in Italy, they had fallen in love with a Tuscan villa."

"They chose wisely."

"We were just going to have some cake and coffee. Would you like to join us before you settle in?" Jane asked.

"Are you sure I'm not taking you from your work?" he asked. He had spied the rug through the open library doors as he encircled the hallway. He walked over now and studied its outlined design more closely. "This is going to be quite beautiful. Reminds me of the tapestries that are so prolific in Rome."

"Did you spend a lot of time there?" Kay asked.

"Come in and sit down," Myla said, indicating a leather chair.

"Thank you. I teach at the university." He sank into the soft leather and crossed his legs.

"So, how did you land here?" Rose asked.

"I'm on sabbatical, doing some research at Yale. The bishop asked if I would cover as interim pastor until he finds someone full-time."

"And who won't leave screaming in the middle of the night," Myla whispered under her breath.

Rich pretended not to hear.

"Let me fix you that cup of coffee, Father," Rose said, giving him a sassy smile.

The others looked at her strangely. Handsome men were her undoing. They sincerely hoped she wouldn't make any moves on a priest, though.

"And, if you like, I'll show you to your room when you're through," she added, handing him a mug.

"Why not let Jane show him?" Gail suggested. "After all, she lived here and knows where everything is."

The others sighed with relief.

Rose made no attempt to hide her disappointment.

"Jane?" Gail said.

Jane hesitated for just a moment. "I'd be glad to help you settle in, Father."

Rose leaned over to whisper in Myla's ear. "God, he's drop-dead gorgeous. What a waste."

"This was Father Stephens's room," Jane explained.

St. Francis Xavier's new interim pastor had been plied with cake and several cups of coffee, along with a multitude of questions, before Kay had sagely suggested that he be shown to his room, reminding the others that he must be tired from traveling.

Jane switched on the lights and felt her heart flood with a deep sadness.

"Are you all right?" Rich asked.

"Yes, it's just that I've not been up in this part of the house since . . ." She quickly changed the subject. "This is the only room with an adjoining bathroom, but if you'd rather have another room there are six more on this floor. I suggest, however, you that you stay here. It's saf—"

He watched her pause.

"It's nicer than the others."

"It will do nicely." He placed his carry-on bag on the bed. His other belongings would arrive from Rome tomorrow. He watched her draw the curtains and got the distinct impression that there was something she wanted to say but wasn't quite sure how to begin.

"It has a wonderful view of the back gardens during the spring and summer," she told him, bending down to adjust the folds in the drapes. "That is, if you like gardens. It was one of Father Stephens's passions. Of course, you can't see them at night. And there's a nice-size closet over there"—she pointed—"and lots of bookcases in case you like to read. Father Stephens was a prolific reader."

"So I see," Rich said. The shelves were tightly packed.

"You'll need some fresh sheets and towels. The linen closet is just down the hall. I'll only be a minute."

Rich studied the room. Two mismatched chairs flanked the large bay window, separated by a round pedestal table, the top covered in water stains. The table also held a lamp, the most hideous thing he had ever seen. He switched it on and was somewhat disappointed that it provided a good deal of light. He would have liked an excuse to get rid of it.

A pine four-poster bed, nicked and scarred, stood opposite the fireplace. Small painted bookcases crammed with more books had been turned into makeshift nightstands with swivel light fixtures mounted on the wall above. It looked like a room that was well used.

He hitched up the legs of his trousers and bent down to scan the titles: *Hostage to the Devil, Un Escorista Raconta: The Roman Ritual of*

Exorcism, The Handbook of Parapsychology. Not exactly light reading. He moved to the taller bookcases. Books of similar subjects also lined those shelves.

Jane returned just as he was inspecting a red leather-bound volume.

"Interesting choice of reading material," he commented, flipping through the pages as she passed en route to the bathroom with an armload of towels. "*Spiritual Warfare*. Nothing like a little light reading before you go to bed."

He slid the book back into the empty space and dusted off his hands. He wondered if the priests who had fled had used this room. These titles could easily have planted the seed that later grew into a state of paranoia.

"Jane?" he called, following her into the bathroom. "Do you know if the others used this room?"

"The other priests?" she asked, placing the last towel on the shower rack. "No, I don't think so. The room has remained locked until a few weeks ago. Father Stephens's sister had requested that we keep it closed until she had time to remove her brother's things."

He followed her back into the bedroom. "What about the books? Why were they left behind?"

Jane threw back the bedspread and shook out a fresh bottom sheet. "You want to give me a hand here, Father?"

He grabbed a corner.

Jane paused slightly. "He left instructions with his sister that they were to remain in case the next pastor needed to refer to them."

Why would Father Stephens feel that anyone would need reference material on the occult? he wondered. Unless, of course, the house truly was haunted.

Jane tucked a pillow under her chin and slipped on a pillowcase.

"Didn't she want to stay on? I mean, the new pastor would still need a housekeeper, or was it just too hard for her to stay since her brother was gone?"

"She didn't feel . . . comfortable here after his death."

"Where is she now?"

"She moved in with a nephew and his wife. They live about forty miles from here. Well, that should do it," Jane said, placing the last pillow on the bed and quickly checking to make sure everything was in place.

"If you need extra blankets, the linen closet is just down the hall on the right, and you're welcome to take your meals at the café until you find a new housekeeper. It's in the center of town. You can't miss it."

"Thank you, Jane, for all your help. I hope I haven't kept you away from your rug hooking too long."

She smiled. "No, I'm sure the others will take up the slack. Well, if there's nothing else."

He walked her to the door. "I'm sure I'll be fine."

"I'll leave my phone number on the kitchen counter. If you need anything, please don't hesitate to call."

She turned, then suddenly swung back. He caught a hint of fear on her face, another intimation that there was something else she wanted to say.

"I know this might sound strange, but please don't wander the halls at night. It isn't safe. Stay inside this room."

"If you're talking about those rumors—"

"No. I'm talking about what I know."

His curiosity was piqued. He started to question her further, but she cut him off.

"Good night, Father," she said, and disappeared down the hall.

He stepped out into the hallway and watched her shadow descend the staircase. What did Jane know about this house that might explain the paranormal disturbances that had been reported? She had certainly hinted that something wasn't quite right, going so far as to say that she "knew" that the rumors had substance. Was she implying a firsthand experience with these phenomena? She was certainly someone he would need to interview.

A cold chill began to snake around his feet. He turned, taking in the upstairs quarters. The bedroom doors were all closed, and an eerie stillness had settled over the space. How easy it would be to let oneself become influenced by another's fears, he thought, stepping back inside the room. Still, he paused only briefly before securely locking the bedroom door.

six

The skies held the promise of rain as Jane stepped out the front door dressed in jeans and a lightweight sweat jacket. The countryside lay like a slumbering child as she stood on the front porch, limbering up for the walk into town.

Like most New Englanders, Jane especially loved autumn with its bejeweled landscape. But by late October only a vestige of the countryside's former splendor remained. A heavy downpour was certain to strip away the remaining beauty. Already there were pockets of barren woodland, exposing sharp edges of gullies, fallen trees, and wild tangles of brush and limb that had been craftily hidden behind the summer's lush foliage and autumn's dazzling kaleidoscope of colors. Soon the hills and valleys would be naked, stripped, barren, and ready for the onslaught of winter that would seal it under a covering of icy snow.

A pale glow of light filtered behind the mountains as Jane headed out. The café was exactly one and seven-tenths miles from her circa-1950s Cape Cod, which she and Vance had purchased from his parents. While shopping for a Christmas tree, his mother had fallen on a patch of ice and broken her hip. Six weeks later, Jane's in-laws signed over the house and moved down South.

Having lost a sense of continuity when her family died, Jane reveled in the connections she found scattered throughout Vance's childhood home. Everywhere she looked there were reminders of the years he, his parents, and his two brothers had spent as a family within these walls. The bathroom door bore notches of height measurements. Vance had been six feet tall by his fourteenth birthday. Their son, Alex, practiced shooting baskets through the same hoop above the garage door that his father and uncles had used when they were his age, and he loved the fact that he slept in their old bedroom.

She set out along the familiar route, which had been mapped out with an eye to the changing tableau. Nature had always provided a balm for her soul. She drew strength from the cycle of seasons and the affirmation of renewal. Spring brought tulips, daffodils, wild roses, and the return of the blue heron to the river, along with flocks of wild geese, mallards, and bullfrogs. With summer came a profusion of wildflowers—bee balm, Queen Anne's lace, jack-in-the-pulpit, and chicory—that reflected a clear blue sky. There was also an abundance of wildlife—deer, coyotes, and beavers—most of which stayed hidden within the foliage, although she once spied a bobcat crossing the road by the state campgrounds.

Later, fall would bring with it the madcap race to prepare for winter. Squirrels thrashed about overhead in the trees; chipmunks, with their tails high, sailed across the road with mouths stuffed like cushions. Deer moved deeper into the woods to hide among spires of joe-pyre turned deep mauve and sandstone-colored cattails. Jane savored it all, even nature's finale: a winter landscape that stretched for miles like a new canvas, awaiting the first brushstroke of spring.

Up ahead, Doc Fedder's place came into view with its sagging porch. Several townsfolk, including Vance, had repeatedly offered to help fix it, but Doc said he liked it just the way it was. A noted tightwad, he was averse to the increase in property taxes that came with major home improvements.

She made a left turn onto Spruce Lane. Here the dirt road turned to asphalt as the lane filled with older homes, some of which had been built during the early 1800s. Side roads splintered off from this main course and ran down toward the river.

Over the past few years, New Yorkers, including Kay Sprage, had discovered this area with its bungalows perched atop small knolls, providing unobstructed views of the river. Many houses had been renovated into year-round residences, with additions and architectural designs reconfigured to meet the needs of today's buyers. A few homes, however, would remain as cottages—particularly the ones that rested on thick layers of shale, making excavation nearly impossible. Builders dynamited when they could, but with the homes along the river in such close proximity this wasn't always an option.

Jane hated the changes. Vance, however, was thrilled. His excavating business had never been so busy. As the scenery flitted by, her mind wandered over today's to-do list. She walked briskly, filling her lungs with the cool morning air that smelled richly of autumn. Payroll checks had to be made out. Ugh! She hated bookkeeping and longed for the business to grow large enough for her to hand that task over to an accountant. The walk-in freezer also needed a deep cleaning. Maybe she could get one of the waitresses to tackle that chore without complaining too heavily. She would have done it herself yesterday, but the dishwasher had sprung a leak in the middle of lunch, leaving them without a clean fork or spoon in the place. Thank God Gail had come in to pick up her turkey club. Jane had sent her dashing to the grocer's for a supply of plastic silverware and paper plates.

She tried to turn her attention back to the scenery, but, like a noisome tune, once she allowed the day's issues to invade her consciousness there was no shutting them out. Sometimes, reviewing all that had to be done, she almost lost heart. But what was she to do? Close the café? Fat chance. She was no quitter. The road inclined along this stretch. She increased her pace, arms pumping like pistons. Somehow, she would fit it all in. She always did.

But some days it did seem as though she had been shot out of a cannon. Up at five o'clock, out the door by five-twenty. Work at the café until four-fifteen, then home again to clear away the breakfast dishes that, invariably, were still scattered around the kitchen and the family room (she had given up trying to persuade her family to confine their meals to the kitchen table); throw in a load of wash, start supper, then head out for the first round of carpooling—Alex to karate lessons; Marilee to choir practice or the library. Later she would rack them up like billiard balls, trying to keep them stationary long enough to eat something that resembled a healthful meal, then back into the car, where they would once again be shot off in different directions.

Alex was heavily into sports, which she and Vance encouraged, believing that it helped kids stay out of trouble and taught them about commitment and teamwork. Basketball was his current favorite, followed by karate and ice hockey. Pick a night, and somewhere she or Vance—or both of them—would be sitting on a cold wooden bench yelling themselves hoarse.

Marilee preferred more tempered pursuits, like the choir and the drama club. Much to Jane's chagrin, her favorite activity of late was shopping, or, more specifically, wandering the mall aimlessly with her friends. Jane didn't approve of it, not one bit. It wasn't fair to the merchants and, as far as she was concerned, it was a recipe for trouble. Of course, whenever she voiced this opinion it brought a wail of protest. "It's just a place for kids to meet and talk," Marilee said repeatedly. "Why do you always have to think that something bad will happen? Why can't you trust me like the other mothers do? I'm old enough to handle myself."

Jane doubted that. This was just one more issue that had divided them lately. They used to be so close, and now they were like planets orbiting the same solar system but never touching, light-years apart. Jane felt that she was losing her daughter, this girl child inside a woman's body. The thought filled her with fear. What was she doing wrong? She wished her mother were alive. Theirs had been a good relationship. That's what Jane wanted with her daughter, but she had no idea how to get there. She knew only that no matter what else she might accomplish in life, if she failed as a mother she had failed in all things.

The sun was breaking through the cloud cover just as Jane climbed the last hill—a half-mile steep climb to the top of Main Street. Head down, she bent into the incline, her breath coming in short, hard pulses as she maintained her pace.

At the top of the rise, she paused, gazing out over the sleepy valley. Specks of house lights punctuated the dawn as a soft down of mist rolled in off the river in steamy waves. The café lay a few doors down. She resumed her walk, hands thrust into the pockets of her sweat jacket, occasionally turning to watch her reflection in the storefront windows. It showed a tall, lithe woman, well proportioned but with a slight limp. Hard exercise always made her damaged leg a little stiff, but she felt that it was a fair trade-off. The healthy glow in her checks testified to that.

The café was sandwiched in between the grocer's and the post office. As Jane reached above the doorsill for her key, the lights went on across the street at the *Bend Oaks Gazette*, meaning that its owner-editor, Henry Moffat, had come in early. The weekly paper hit the newsstands tomorrow.

Jane let herself in and went right to work. In small, fluid movements she exchanged her jacket for an apron and fired up the grill, started the coffee, then went into the back to gather up a ten-pound tub filled with parboiled sliced potatoes, several pounds of bacon, equal amounts of sausage links, and a five-pound slab of butter. The bread orders would arrive later.

With practiced skill, she quickly arranged things on top of the grill—meat to the left, potatoes on the right. Later, the front would be divided into quadrants. Two sections for eggs (scrambled and fried), one for pancakes, the other for French toast. Within minutes everything was gently sizzling. She poured herself a mug of coffee, then went to the front window and flashed the "Open" sign on and off to let Henry know that the coffee was ready. He responded by flashing his desk light on and off, which meant that he'd be right over.

She looked out over the sleepy town while sipping her coffee and watching a bank of dark gray clouds move steadily in this direction. Her two waitresses should be arriving shortly, just in time for the morning regulars. Before things got busy, she wondered if she should give Father Rich a call and see if he was all right. But what would she say if he asked why she was concerned? She could hardly say that she felt the evil that Father Stephens had once vanquished had returned and that it wasn't safe for him to be there.

The bell above the doorway jingled.

"Morning, Jane." Henry marched in, a line of regulars trailing behind him and shouting out orders.

Jane finished her coffee and headed toward the grill. Now where were those two waitresses?

Vera Honeychurch stubbed out her Phillies Slim cigar, feeling slightly winded and a little light-headed from the walk into town. Darn cigars. They'd be the death of her yet. But then they were her only vice. That and a shot of whiskey once or twice a week. She needn't have walked. Gail had offered to drive her into town, but she'd had to get off by herself before she marched into their bedroom and kicked her son's sorry butt from here to Tuesday. Vera loved Gail as a daughter and hated the way her son treated her like a serving wench. Thank God she lived with them only in between her trips. Since retiring, Vera had become quite the world traveler.

Take this morning, for instance. It started off with Ralph bellowing from the bedroom that the television was blaring and he couldn't sleep. Meanwhile, Gail was in the kitchen packing lunches for *his* sons before running off to work.

"Jerry, do as he says," she told her stepson. "You know how tired he is after a business trip."

Vera looked over at Gail and thought, My Lord, woman, you've aged five years since the last time I visited. If anyone needs more rest it's you.

"Gail, I said turn the television down!" Ralph screamed, slamming the bedroom door.

Gail jumped as if a firecracker had gone off. "Now, see what you've done?"

"There's no reason he can't get up and talk to the boy himself," Vera said, dumping her cup of tea into the kitchen sink. "I think I'll head down to the café and let folks know that I'm back." She figured that if she didn't get out of the house fast, she might do something she'd regret. She had restrained herself in deference to Gail, who asked her not to interfere.

"Jerry, turn it down. *Pleassse . . .*" Gail said. Her elbow hit a glass of milk that she'd poured for RJ. It gushed over the counter like a waterfall and puddled on the tiled floor. Tears sprang to her eyes.

Vera noted that something like compassion had registered in RJ's eyes. That was new. The last time she was here, the boy acted as though Gail were the proverbial wicked stepmother. She wondered what had happened while she was away?

"Hold on," RJ told the person he was talking to on his cell phone. Then he walked over to his brother, threw him off the couch, grabbed the remote hidden behind one of the cushions, and hit mute.

"Hey!" Jerry shrieked.

"Leave it," RJ snarled. His brother thought briefly about protesting, then, sensing an ominous threat, decided instead to go back to his Pop-Tart without further comment.

By the time Vera left the house, the air was so thick with tension that you could have cut it with a knife. For the life of her, she couldn't figure out why Gail put up with any of it. She had a husband who was never home, and two stepsons who had been dumped on her. She took care of the household, oversaw the kids' schoolwork, ran a business, and pretty much did everything that needed doing. And what did her son do? He took trips. He slept in hotels with room service, laundry pickups, and never so much as made up a bed. And *he* was tired?

But Gail loved Ralph and wouldn't hear a bad word spoken against him. Vera hoped that someday her son would wake up and discover what a gem he had married, but knowing Ralph, she wasn't counting on it.

The first selectman, Gerald Hacket, was seated by the front window next to Barrie Cheshire, the building inspector, and Tommy Hawkins, who was in charge of public works. The men waved when they saw her. Vera had been the town clerk for thirty-three years before retiring.

Since then her small pension, Social Security, and an occasional side job had allowed her to pursue her love of travel, which she had managed to do nonstop for the past seven years, and, God willing, might continue for another seven. But like all things Vera did, these travels were far from being ordinary. No senior tour buses for her.

She had traveled to Bavaria with a nonprofit church group and helped to build an orphanage. Through Elderhostel, she was sent to Mesa, Arizona, to teach English to Hopi second graders. And she had joined the Seafarers Antiquities Association, which had allowed her to help sail a replica of an eighteenth-century tall-masted ship across the Atlantic.

On this last trip, she had accompanied a Columbia University biologist, whom she had met on an earlier Elderhostel trip. If he had been just fifteen years older, she might have followed Rose's example and done some serious flirting. Instead, she contented herself with collecting water samples as they traveled down the Amazon River by barge. In the process, she had nearly lost a finger to piranhas and, while coursing down a stream that flowed through a cave, had come close to being bitten by a vampire bat.

"It sure beats playing pinochle," she told her friend Myla, who was convinced that Vera had lost her mind.

As soon as Vera stepped through the front door, folks began calling out greetings.

"So how's Bend Oaks's intrepid traveler?" someone shouted.

It was a full thirty minutes before she finally made her way to the front counter. Jane reached over and gave her a big hug.

"Coffee?"

"Sounds good."

"So how are you?"

"Still breathing," Vera said, squeezing in between Pete Carlson, who worked down at the lumberyard, and St. Francis Xavier's new interim pastor, who had slipped in while she was talking to the new town clerk.

"You must be Father Rich," she said without preamble. She studied him over the rim of her glasses. "Gail said you were a looker. I can see she didn't exaggerate."

"Vera!" Jane said, laughing. "Father Melo, this is Gail's mother-in-law, Vera Honeychurch."

"Nice to meet you," Rich said, liking Vera instantly.

"Vera is our world traveler," Jane explained. "How long are you with us this time?"

"Just long enough to save up a little money for my next adventure."

"Where's it going to be this time? The Arctic? Outer space, perhaps?" As far-fetched as that might sound, Jane knew that with Vera anything was possible.

"I'm headed off to the Australian outback."

"Have you ever been there?" Rich asked.

"No, which is why I'm going."

"Makes sense," Rich said, laughing.

"Jane, may I have an order of toast?" Vera watched Jane pop two slices of white bread into the toaster. "I'm looking for a job," she told her, stirring sugar into her coffee. "You got any waitress openings?"

"I wish I had known you were coming back. I just hired a new girl last week. Sorry."

"What kind of job are you looking for?" Rich asked.

"Anything that doesn't involve babies, pets, or old people," Vera said. "I hate working with old people."

Rich had an idea. "It just so happens that I'm in need of a temporary housekeeper over at the rectory. You interested?"

"Interested? You bet!"

Jane clutched the piece of toast she was buttering so tightly that it crumbled in her hands.

"You're hired," Rich told her. "When can you start?"

"How about today?"

"Sounds good to me. I can drop you off on my way over to the church."

"Make that toast to go," she told Jane, searching for her wallet.

"Let me get this," Rich said, pulling out his billfold.

"Why, thanks, Father. I just want to say hello to some folks before we leave," she said, heading over to the round table by the front window.

He laid a five-dollar bill on the counter. "Is that enough?"

"Enough for a whole breakfast," Jane said, handing him a bag with Vera's toast, then sliding over to the cash register. She rang up fifty cents and handed him back the change.

"Jane, would you drop by the rectory this evening?" he said. "There's something I want to talk to you about."

Her face grew tight with concern. "Is anything wrong?"

"I'm curious about the rectory's past, that's all."

"Then you should probably talk to Myla," Jane said. "I don't know much about the building."

"It's not the building that I'm interested in," he said, slipping his billfold inside his jacket. "It's what's happened inside the house that concerns me, and I think you might know more about that than anyone else."

Jane parked the SUV under the portico and hurried toward the porch. The floodlights were on, which helped to push back the shadows that crept and crawled along the perimeter. She reached for the handle on the front door and it opened from inside. Father Rich had been waiting for her.

"I've lit a fire in the parlor," he told her, ushering her through the hallway. "It seemed a bit chilly in here tonight. May I get you some sherry?"

"That would be nice," she said, slipping out of her coat and laying it over the arm of a chair.

While Rich poured drinks, Jane looked around the room. It had always been her least favorite. She found the dark paneling and the heavily carved mantel oppressive.

"How are you settling in?" she asked, watching him place the stopper back on the Waterford decanter, part of an extensive set of priceless cut glass that was original to the house.

"Let's just say that the house isn't as compatible as I might have liked," he said, motioning to the set of chairs flanking the fireplace. He waited until she was settled, then said, straight out, "Last night you said I shouldn't wander around the halls at night because it might not be safe. What did you mean by that?"

She paused, uncertain how to respond. "It's hard to explain. Not many people would understand."

"Try me."

There was something in the way he was poised on the edge of his chair, elbows resting on his knees, his brow furrowed in a look of deep interest, that made her go on.

"I have a gift."

He studied her quietly for a moment before asking, "What kind of gift?"

"I can see and sense things that others can't," she began, her voice a little shaky. Father Stephens was the only one she had ever told about her gift. It was risky sharing this secret with a relative stranger. But it was too late now. She had to warn him even if it meant risking her credibility.

"I know when evil is about, and I've sensed it strongly in this house since Father Stephens's death. That's why I warned you not to wander around here at night. It seems to draw power from the darkness."

"I see."

He seemed to be reflecting on something. Then it hit her: he felt it, too. She drew courage and went on.

"When I was sixteen, my family was in a terrible car accident. I was the only one to survive. But something happened to me, inside here." She tapped her head. "When I awoke in the hospital, I was changed."

"How?"

"It was as though a door had been opened into another dimension, one that surrounds all of us but few can see. After the accident, however, I could. First I sense the evil, and then if I allow this kind of spiritual eye to open, I can see it take form." She gave a nervous little laugh. "I'm sure you think I have a screw loose."

"No, I don't," he said. "Have you ever read any of the lives of the saints? Many of them had a similar gift. Padre Pio is the most recent one."

"Yes, I've read about him," she said. "But I certainly don't qualify for sainthood."

Rich smiled. "You're young," he said. "There's still time."

"Not if I have to continue to deal with my teenage daughter." She laughed, feeling the tension begin to ebb away. She really liked Father Rich. In fact, in some ways he reminded her of Father Stephens.

"I don't envy you," he said. "That's the great thing about being a priest. I don't have the parental issues you have. But, seriously, tell me more about this gift."

She shifted uncomfortably. How much could she tell him without the risk of losing what little of his acceptance she had just gained? But if she was to convince him of the danger that was resident here and save Vera from possible harm, she had to tell him everything.

"Once I passed a man and knew that he had raped and murdered a child," she said.

"Dear Lord. How awful!"

"But what could I do? No one was going to believe me." She slid out of her chair and stood by the mantel. "A few weeks later, this man's picture was all over the news. He had kidnapped and murdered seven children."

The priest closed his eyes against the image. "You're right. No one would have believed you. This gift must be quite a burden."

"Yes, it is," she said quietly. Emboldened by the way he seemed to understand, she went on. "Right now there's a man who comes into the café. A spirit envelops him like a dark vaporous cloud. It sweeps in with him every time he walks through the door. It makes my flesh crawl. Lately, that darkness has taken shape."

She paused briefly before concluding, "It's just a matter of time before his soul is lost forever. I can feel it, yet I'm powerless to do anything about it."

He rose, the firelight turning his blond hair bronze. "I think we need something stronger than sherry," he said. "How about some scotch?"

She watched him search the liquor cabinet. "Third shelf on the right," she said. "Scotch was Father Stephens's preferred drink."

"And Vera's, too," he said, studying the bottle. It had been almost full last night. Now it was half gone.

Jane couldn't help laughing. "I hope you don't hold it against her."

He looked up from pouring. "No, I like her too much. She reminds me of a feisty nun I once knew."

"I love her dearly. She and Myla were like mothers to me when I lost mine. I can't bear to think of anything happening to her, which is why I've come to try and persuade you and her to be careful, especially at night."

"I promise I'll make sure she leaves before dark." He handed her the scotch and sat on the arm of the sofa. Twirling the liquid around in his glass, he said, "I'm curious. Why didn't you warn the other priests?"

"The first one came while my family and I were away on vacation. We were down in Florida, visiting with my husband's parents. By the time we got back, he had already left."

"And the others?"

The second one was only here for one night, and the last one—"

"Father Braxton."

"Yes, Father Braxton," she said, sipping her drink. She smiled.

"What's so funny?"

"I have a confession to make. I deliberately didn't tell him."

"And the reason was . . ."

"He fired Marvin."

"The groundskeeper?"

"Marvin has worked here for over forty years. Where was he going to go? Right now, he's sleeping in his car. The hookers are all worried about him. In fact, I wanted to talk to you about reinstating him."

"To be honest, Jane, I think the fewer people there are milling around here right now, the better."

She thought on that. "Maybe you're right. We'll have to think of something else for him to do. So does that mean you believe me?"

"Every word."

"Why?"

"Someday I'll tell you my story, but for now I need your help. Come with me." He took her glass and placed it on a side table, then led her upstairs. Just outside Father Stephens's room, he paused and pointed to the wood-paneled door. It had been heavily gouged, as though claws had tried to rip through the wood. "This happened last night."

Jane felt a cold chill. "You're not safe here, and neither is Vera."

"I disagree," he said, glancing behind him as though searching the shadows. "Whatever is in this house isn't after Vera. It's been waiting for me, but rest assured. I'm taking the proper precautions until I can devise a plan to rid this house of it. In the interim, though, I think Vera should leave before dark and your hooking group should meet somewhere else."

seven

This was the sixth time the young couple, Barbara and Freddy Bartelli, had toured the small ranch (or what Realtors euphemistically call a "starter home"). It was the fourth house on the left on Circle Drive, where a row of similar homes were linked together by several acres of land, winding along the blue-collar neighborhood like a dime-store necklace. It had just come on the market this week, and was priced at under $150,000. Gail knew that it was going to get snatched up. She couldn't, however, convey this to the young couple, who seemed to want every relative and friend to offer their opinion.

Uncle Sammy, who had some loose connections to the construction business (he sold doorknobs for a manufacturer out of the Midwest), inspected the basement. Uncle Vito, who worked for the sanitation department in Bridgeport, thumped around the backyard in search of septic problems. Cousin Tony came to offer his advice about landscaping, and both sets of grandparents had spent hours testing doors, window sashes, and carpeting.

Today the couple had arrived with both sets of parents, which Gail took as the first hopeful sign. Parents were a primary source of down-payment moneys. If she could convince them that this was a good deal, she had a sale.

"I have the paperwork with me," she told the husband's father, who had arrived in a Lexus. This was also a good sign. If he had arrived in a beat-up Chevy, she would have packed her bags and gone home.

She followed him outside and watched as he crouched down and shined a flashlight underneath the front porch. "As I told your son and daughter-in-law, this house is not going to be on the market long," she said. "It's priced right, it's in a good location, and it has over an acre and a half of land. This kind of deal doesn't come along very often in today's housing market."

The man stood and brushed dried leaves off his trousers. "Yeah, I know. That's what all you Realtors say."

Why were people always so distrustful of Realtors? "I only say it when it's true," she said, not hiding her annoyance.

He shined the flashlight behind a shutter. "There's a wasp nest."

"I tell you what. If your son buys the house, I'll throw in a can of Raid."

He couldn't help smiling. They both knew what he was doing. The kids had settled on this house, and it was his job to uncover as many faults as possible in the hope of knocking down the price. She hated to disappoint him, but the buyers had made it clear that the price was non-negotiable.

"Listen, let's talk as parents," she said. "I know you want the best for your son and his wife. Today's housing market is crazy. Prices jump overnight. Deals like this are usually snatched up in a matter of days, not weeks. Is it a palace? No, but it's a good, solid little house, and a way for them to get into the housing market before they're completely priced out."

She could tell that he was mulling this over. Finally, the man folded his arms as he studied the exterior and asked, "So, what's the bottom line?"

She was just about to tell him the price was firm when her cell phone rang.

"I'm sorry. Would you please excuse me for just a moment?" She flipped open her cell phone and turned to face the road.

"Gail, this is Rose."

Her heart sank. Rose never called her at work unless one of the boys was in trouble.

"Who did what this time?"

"It's RJ. You'd better get over here right away. I've had to call the sheriff. I'm afraid he was caught dealing drugs."

"Go to your room," she told RJ as they stepped through the front door. "I need time to think."

She wished Ralph were here, but he had left yesterday on another one of his business trips.

"What about dinner?" RJ whined. "I haven't had anything to eat since breakfast."

"What about it?"

"I gotta eat."

"Yeah, and I've got to cool off. Go!"

For just a moment he hesitated, as though he were about to say something else, then changed his mind and raced upstairs. His bedroom door slammed shut as Gail threw her purse on the entry-hall table and stormed into the kitchen.

Jerry was stationed in his usual place in front of the television. Britney Spears was gyrating to a headache-inducing beat. Gail grabbed the remote and switched it off.

"Don't you have some homework to do," she snapped.

"Hey, that was the good part," he cried.

"Go!"

He was about to protest, then he saw the look on her face and wisely shuffled out of the room, mumbling something about its not being fair.

Chocolate. I need chocolate, she thought, hoping that the boys hadn't discovered her recent stash behind the cleaning supplies. She had felt confident that it was one of the last places they would ever think to look. She pulled out the bag of Lindt chocolates and embraced it like an old friend. Normally, two a day were her limit. She grabbed a handful. Two were definitely not going to cut it tonight. She popped one into her mouth. Wasn't it wonderful that science had finally caught up with what women had known all along? Chocolate is our friend. It certainly made for less guilt-ridden bingeing.

What was she going to do with RJ? She loved him as her own, but he was making her crazy. This time he had really stepped over the line. It was one thing to get suspended for some stupid practical joke, or even for being rude or unruly in class. But he had been caught selling marijuana. Bend Oaks High had a zero-tolerance drug policy, which meant immediate expulsion. Now what? She couldn't let him stay home and just vegetate. She'd probably have to find a tutor. She couldn't fathom where she'd get money for that. She'd already planned to take out a loan to pay for Jerry's braces.

She popped another chocolate into her mouth and let the velvety texture melt across her tongue. It was almost sensual. She walked over to the window, which looked out over the backyard, and pushed aside the curtain. An abandoned rake lay against the siding. She'd have to remind one of the boys to put it back in the garage. She stared into a ring of trees, letting her emotions settle like sediment on a lake after a storm. What would they do if the school decided to press charges? Rose said it was a distinct possibility. The school board felt that this would send a clear message to the other kids. Could RJ be sent to jail over this? The thought chilled her to the core. Why wasn't his father here to worry along with her?

She unwrapped another chocolate and made the decision to call Ralph. He hated being disturbed on business trips, but this was an emergency. She grabbed the kitchen wall phone and dialed. Seconds later, an automated voice answered and she was consigned to his voice mail. From past experience, she knew that he never checked his voice mail, so she called his secretary, Mavis.

"I'm sorry, Mrs. Honeychurch, I really don't know how to contact him," Mavis said. "He's on the road. But I will relay your message to call home if he should call in."

Damn him! Why didn't he let them know where to reach him in case of an emergency? One of the kids could have been hit by a car and needed blood. His mother could have had a stroke. You'd think a family man might consider the necessity of staying in touch throughout the day. But not Ralph.

Wine . . . she needed some wine to wash down the chocolate. There was a bottle in the fridge that she had opened last week for a pot roast. She pulled it out and held it in midair. It was nearly empty. Great! The boys must have gotten into it. Was there no end to her parenting woes today? She poured what was left into a glass and slugged it down, then went in search of more. Ralph kept the good stuff in the locked liquor cabinet. She grabbed her set of keys. Tonight's hookers' meeting had been moved to Jane's house, just up the block. She could easily walk from here if she was too drunk to drive, and if she could find another bottle she planned on getting sloshed.

Rap music seeped out of Jerry's headphones as he bounced back into the kitchen.

"I thought I told you to—"

"I know. Finish my homework. But I forgot to tell you that Grandma Vera called and said tonight's meeting had been moved back to the rectory and she wanted you to stop by the grocery store and pick up some chips and dip."

There went her plans for tying one on. She glanced at the clock above the sink. It was twenty past six. The meeting started at seven, and the rectory was clear across town. Even if she left now she'd never make it on time, and Myla hated it when anyone was late. She hurriedly stuffed several more chocolates into her red polyester jacket, which bore a mayonnaise stain from lunch, and grabbed her car keys. There was no time to change.

"There's a box of macaroni and cheese in the pantry and a pizza in the freezer," she told Jerry. "You and your brother are on your own for dinner. And, should your father call, tell him to get me on my cell phone . . . that is, if he still remembers the number."

The Z4 roadster maneuvered easily in and out of the rush-hour traffic leaving Boston. Kay Sprage loved its devilishly precise handling, the rev of the engine as it blasted through space going from zero to sixty in 5.9 seconds. She would have much preferred a country road, where she could open it up, feel the g-force suck her back into the seat, but for now she would settle for a game of skill as she wove through the thick mass of commuters heading out of the city.

A quick glance at the dashboard clock as she changed lanes told her she had a little over two hours to make it to Bend Oaks if she wanted to be on time for tonight's meeting. The hookers were a laid-back group in every way except punctuality. Myla ruled with an iron hand, expecting everyone to arrive on time.

She lowered the window on the driver's side, enjoying the wind in her hair. She would have rather driven with the top down, but rain was predicted later and she didn't relish being caught in a downpour, especially since she just had the car detailed. Kay lavished more love on her roadster than most women did on their husbands. Too bad Gail couldn't find an inanimate object of her own to love, Kay thought. Anything would be better than Ralph.

She and Gail had spoken earlier. Kay sensed that something was wrong. After some digging, Gail confessed that RJ had been arrested for selling drugs at school. "This is all my fault," she wailed. "If only I knew how to communicate with him better, but I've never had children. I have no background in child rearing."

If it were up to Kay, she'd communicate by applying the back of her hand to the back of his pants. What Gail really should do is turn the whole thing over to Ralph. After all, they were his kids.

Behind her, a tractor-trailer flashed its lights. She sped up. She had taken an instant dislike to the guy the first time she met him. Kay had invited Gail out to dinner in celebration of closing on the cottage, and Ralph tagged along. They had barely made it through the appetizers when Kay began hoping that he'd choke on one of the shrimp he was scarfing down at $3.75 a pop. The man could win a prize for biggest bore.

For the next two courses, she was subjected to a recitation of Ralph's sterling sales record, his "way" with clients, the clever tricks he used to close a deal, and how he "allowed" his clients to win at golf. Gail sat quietly, smiling while Ralph dominated the conversation, consulting her only when he felt confirmation was needed to give greater credence to one of his stories.

Kay wanted to kick him under the table. He had completely shunted Gail aside, ignoring the fact that they were there to celebrate her accomplishments, not his. By the time dinner was over, Kay had a splitting headache and great sympathy for Gail. How could anyone live with such a blowhard?

She and Gail had hit it off right from the start. Kay had been looking for a weekend house for months, but every place that she had been shown lacked charm. Then there were the monstrosities that could house an entire football team. What part of "she lived alone" didn't these Realtors understand? She wanted a *small* cottage, she repeated over and over. A place to escape to on the weekends. Something that wouldn't require a staff of servants or a full-time gardener to maintain.

Then one Sunday she happened upon a small ad in the *New York Times* real-estate section, listed under "Connecticut Vacation Homes": "It's a mess and needs lots of work, but for the visionary this lowly frog could be turned into a handsome prince. Only the stoic need inquire." Her interest piqued, she immediately placed a call to the number listed at the bottom of the ad. The woman who answered identified herself as Gail Honeychurch. They chatted for a while. Gail assured her that the house was large enough for an occasional overnight guest but small enough to discourage extended stays.

"Which I personally think is a good thing," Gail said. "It's like the old adage: 'Both fish and houseguests begin to stink after three days.'"

Kay laughed. She really liked this woman.

"But, honestly, this house needs a lot of work," Gail concluded.

Kay told her that was no problem—she had the resources to restore the cottage if it met her needs. She and Gail arranged to meet that following week, and the cottage was exactly as Gail had described it, including its state of disrepair.

The floors were rotted out. The kitchen was circa 1960s, with avocado appliances. The bathroom was drowning in mold and lacked even a basic heating system. But the view of the lake was spectacular. Kay made an offer, and together she and Gail scoured flea markets for furnishings. They discovered that they were both an only child—which accounted for their difficulty in sharing space—and their birthdays fell in the same month. Other than that, they were complete opposites. Kay lived a highly organized, jet-set life, whereas Gail had a laid-back, roll-with-the-punches style and felt that dinner at Applebee's and a movie was living the high life.

That fall, Gail asked Kay to a hookers' meeting. Not wanting to seem snobbish, she accepted, figuring it would be a onetime visit and she'd be through with it. After all, what could she possibly have in common with these women? But the evening had been filled with fun and laughter and a sense of warmth that suddenly made her life seem empty and shallow.

Unlike her jet-setting New York friends, these women were genuine. Oh, they may have lacked a certain social sophistication, but they had the kind of class that would never try to outshine a friend.

It wasn't about being prettier or smarter or more connected. They weren't interested in any of that. Their concerns centered on the bonds that connected them as women and as friends and neighbors in this small New England community. They lived authentic lives. They had no illusions of grandeur. They would never do anything that had worldwide impact, but what they accomplished as mothers, daughters, and sisters was held dear.

Kay must have been lost in thought for some time, because suddenly the Waterbury exit was looming up ahead. She threw on her blinker and moved over to the right-hand lane. Route 8 was just up ahead. She downshifted off the ramp, catching the reflection of the large illuminated cross in her rearview mirror. It stood on top of a huge outcropping in the southern portion of the town, part of a complex called Holy Land. The roadway grew dark. There were no streetlights along this stretch of highway. She switched on her brights. The traffic was light, and she allowed her thoughts to wander back to that afternoon's meeting in Boston, and to Ralph's surprise appearance.

Kay had been called to the Omni Parker Hotel by a prominent political family. A cousin had just been charged with the grisly killing of a college coed, and they wanted Kay to control the spin. She and the family, along with a bank of lawyers, had met upstairs in Suite 514, where they deliberated for most of the morning and into early afternoon, concluding that the best way to handle the situation was to distance this cousin from the clan. They discussed several ways in which that could be accomplished. Kay offered to set something down on paper, then submit it for their approval. Meanwhile, all comments to the press would be filtered through her office. They agreed, and the meeting broke up.

She had driven to Boston earlier that morning, skipped breakfast, and by two o'clock, when the meeting ended, was famished. Even so, she declined an offer to join the others downstairs for a leisurely lunch at the Parker Restaurant, though it was one of her favorites. She loved its quiet ambience—tall, wispy potted palms used as discrete barriers, separating tables into small, private enclaves. The walls were paneled in rich mahogany aged to a softly weathered glow. Everything harked back to a more gracious era. Even the cuisine remained as innovative as it had been in 1885, when the restaurant opened its doors to serve its first Parker House roll. Since then, such luminaries as Charles Dickens and Ralph Waldo Emerson had dined there. John F. Kennedy, who frequented the hotel throughout his adult life, was especially fond of its Boston Pie, which had been created by one of Parker's pastry chefs.

She headed toward the bar. Although the menu was limited, service was quick, and she planned to be on the road no later than three o'clock to avoid rush-hour traffic. With any luck, she'd be able to make the hookers' meeting at seven. She stepped off the elevator, the heels of her Pradas sinking into the deep-piled carpet. Crystal chandeliers and richly carved moldings gave the room a formal elegance. She felt slightly annoyed that she hadn't been able to move the meeting to Friday. She would have liked to stay the weekend. This grande dame was one of her favorite hotels, an elegant lady perched at the foot of Beacon Hill across from Boston Common. She never tired of coming here.

Normally she would have taken her time crossing the lobby, always on the lookout for prospective clients. Some of Boston's most powerful men and women frequented the hotel. But not today. She headed straight toward the bar, a richly paneled, stained-glass haven that served as a meeting place for some of Boston's social elite. She noticed Peter Rubins, president of a philanthropic group that helped alleviate the angst of accumulated wealth by directing money to various charities. He was seated off in a corner in deep conversation with Terry J. Titus, the philanthropic adviser to the younger Rockefellers. She had worked with Terry on several occasions. They were both on several high-profile nonprofit boards.

Terry saw her and waved. She nodded a curt greeting, wanting to avoid conversation, and settled in at a table tucked between a divider and a potted plant. She placed her Chanel bag on a side chair. It was a gift from a former boyfriend, who had said, "It's made of *caviar* leather, you know," as she unwrapped it—as though this brand of leather was somehow connected with fish eggs. She had always suspected him of being a victim of inbreeding. Their relationship had ended shortly thereafter. She grew tired of constantly having to explain things.

She ordered a salad and some Lakeland Willow Spring water at seventeen dollars a bottle. The waiter had just placed the slender green glass bottle on her table when a woman's shrill laughter shot, like a missile, across the room. Patrons discreetly turned in that direction. Loud noises were highly frowned upon in this hallowed place.

Kay sipped her water and sought out the epicenter of this social faux pas and nearly choked when her eyes fell on Ralph Honeychurch. He was seated nearly on top of a voluptuous blonde with thick lips that had been glossed to a high sheen. She was whispering something into his ear. Kay watched with rising anger as his lips curled into an expectant smile.

"Why, you slimeball," she said out loud, causing the waiter to ask if there was something she needed. She wanted to say a gun. She watched from behind a potted palm as the couple stole ardent kisses, acting like moronic high schoolers while making repeated toasts. She caught the label on the bottle of wine. She knew it well. It was one of her favorite Merlots and cost ninety dollars a bottle. And this was the guy who insisted that he had no money to hire a housekeeper for Gail, the woman who ran herself ragged taking care of *his* house and *his* kids!

Kay ordered coffee and a lemon tart, even though she never cared for dessert. She was stalling, not wanting to give up the table just yet. It offered a bird's eye view of the cheating, womanizing loser Ralph Honeychurch and his bimbo girlfriend. She toyed with the tart and ordered a second cup of coffee. Finally, Ralph signed for the check and the two left through the doorway that connected to the front lobby of the hotel. She didn't wait for her check. She threw four twenties on the table and followed the lovebirds as they made their way toward an elevator.

She knew the concierge and made some discreet inquiries. The "couple" were listed as Mr. and Mrs. Honeychurch, and had booked a room for the night. The dirty rat! He didn't even have the decency to book it under an assumed name. Probably thought he was above being found out.

Up ahead was the exit for Litchfield. Kay moved over to the slow lane and downshifted onto the ramp. She had another thirty-five minutes before arriving in Bend Oaks. Maybe by then she could decide whether to tell Gail.

Rich had told Vera to take the day off—with pay, of course, he added. He had an appointment with the archbishop and would be gone for most of the day. There was no need for her to hang around.

But she had come in at around ten anyway. The kitchen pantry needed cleaning out, and the front staircase could use a good coat of wax. When Father Rich was around, she couldn't get much accomplished. It seemed he was always underfoot, never more than a few steps away. She'd be happy to have the house to herself so she could get some real work done.

The day was uneventful, except that she kept misplacing things. She would have sworn that she had brought the duster into the library, only to find it back inside the kitchen closet hanging on its hook. The linens she had folded and thought she had put away upstairs were later found on the hall table. She had even managed to misplace her bike. She was certain that she had parked it right next to the back door, but she found it leaning on the front porch. Maybe she was finally losing her mind. She joked about it, but deep down it worried her. Her mother had suffered from dementia. In fact, it was her greatest fear—far worse than any fear of cancer or stroke.

As the day wore on, she thought about tonight's meeting at Jane's. It was the first time the hookers had ever met outside the rectory. Father Rich said he would prefer that they not meet when he wasn't home.

When Myla called to relay the message, it was obvious that her feathers had been ruffled. "I have a good mind to call the archbishop and complain," she said. "What's he afraid of? That we'll steal the cut crystal?"

At around five o'clock, Myla called to say that Vance had just phoned to say that Jane was going to be late and they should let themselves in. She had chaperoned one of Marilee's field trips and the bus was stuck in traffic somewhere near White Plains. Vance apologized for not being there to greet them, but he had to take Alex to a game.

"Why don't we just move the meeting back to the rectory?" Vera offered. "It would be a lot easier on everyone, and I'm already here. I'll call Gail and have her pick up some snacks on the way over. We'll deal with Father Rich when he gets home."

This sounded fine to Myla, so they called the others.

Vera glanced up at the kitchen clock. The women should be arriving shortly. She took down a fresh can of decaf, measured out enough for twelve cups, poured the appropriate amount of water into the coffeemaker's reservoir, and waited until she heard the water begin to drip into the carafe.

"Vera!" Myla called from the front hallway. "Come and help me get the rug out of my car."

"Coming . . ."

As the kitchen door closed softly behind her, the light on the coffeepot went out and the coffee that Vera had just made vanished.

Jane wrestled the cell phone out of her bag while the school bus inched along. Between the deafening roar of excited voices and the steady din from boom boxes, she was certain to be seriously hearing-impaired by the time they reached home.

By the look of the traffic, she still might not make it home on time. Vance would have to play host until she arrived. She pressed the power button and waited for the familiar musical ditty. As the screen lit up, she noticed that she had a voice message. She punched in her code and heard Vera's voice: "Jane, it's Vera. Myla and I have decided to move the meeting back to the rectory, so as soon as you get home come on over." Jane frantically dialed the rectory. She had to warn them to get out.

"What's wrong, Mom?" Marilee asked. "You look really awful. I told you not to eat those chili dogs."

Jane held the phone to her ear and felt her heart plummet down to her feet. The line was busy.

eight

Headlights were strung along Route 202, illuminating the night sky. Traffic was snared up ahead. Rich eased off the gas and crawled to a stop behind a Ford minivan. By the look of things, he'd be sitting here for a while. His frustration mounted.

It had been like this all day, one snafu after another. First he had driven an hour and a half to New Haven, where arrangements had been made weeks in advance at Yale for him to view the artifact around which his sabbatical was planned. Today's visit had been set to quickly authenticate it. He would return later to begin his extensive research. He should have been excited about the prospect of beginning a new project. Normally he was like a racehorse at the starting gate when he was about to view a new find, but his thoughts kept returning to the rectory.

Rich did not believe in a random universe. He had been sent to St. Francis Xavier for a reason, not by chance. As Father Malachi once said, our destinies act as magnets, drawing to us events, people, and circumstances that ultimately fashion the roles we were created to play. The thought of Malachi also called to mind the priest's prophecy that Rich had been called as an exorcist. It was a daunting statement, one that he had been trying to jettison for months. But what if Malachi was right? What if he had no choice, no say in the matter? What if the first leg in fulfilling that destiny lay within the rectory's walls?

Last night he had been awakened by footsteps marching up and down the hall outside his bedroom door, followed by three knocks on the front door that had shaken the house. It was clear that something was trying to get his attention. It was as though it were challenging him. But to what? He had called the bishop early this morning to set up an appointment to discuss his findings and, when asked, had confessed that something paranormal was, indeed, happening at the rectory.

"Then it's as I feared," the bishop said. "I can't talk further about this now. I'm on my way out, but when you come there's another matter I need to discuss with you. Father Stephens left a diary that might shed some light on this. No one knows of its existence but me. I only wish that I had given it to you earlier, but I didn't want to prejudice your assessment."

Rich had tried to get him to elaborate, but he refused.

"I'll tell you everything when you arrive," he said. "It's best that I explain it in person."

These thoughts circled round and round his head like birds of prey as he turned off Whaley Avenue and into the Yale campus. The head of the history department, Kenneth Fowler, was to have made arrangements for him to examine the artifact. Instead, Fowler was full of apologies. It seemed the family of alumnus Reginald Watson had petitioned the courts to have the artifact returned. A band of lawyers wielding a court order had arrived that very morning to have the artifact moved to a safe-deposit box until the dispute could be settled. Rich should have felt annoyed. This was the sole reason he had taken the sabbatical. But, surprisingly, he found his thoughts going back to what was happening in Bend Oaks.

Fowler, eager to make amends, insisted that Rich stay for lunch and meet the rest of the faculty. "We'd still like you to consider teaching here next semester as we discussed earlier," he said, trying to placate Rich. "Perhaps by then this muddle will have been ironed out."

Since there seemed no gracious way to decline the invitation, he acquiesced. It was midafternoon before he could extricate himself, and he headed straight for Hartford. As he approached the archdiocese, he noted a flood of reporters and news trucks stationed outside the complex. He slowed next to a police officer who was directing traffic and asked what had happened.

"The bishop had a heart attack," the officer said. "They just rushed him to St. Raphael Hospital."

The timing was too perfect to be a coincidence. The bishop was a healthy, robust man who jogged three miles every morning before Mass—not the kind of man who was likely to succumb to a heart attack without warning. Rich felt a gnawing suspicion deep in his gut that there was a direct link between the diary and the bishop's sudden illness. There was something in Father Stephens's writings that outside forces didn't want him to read and would go to any lengths to keep secret.

A horn blared away in the distance. Rich rubbed his temples. How long was this traffic tie-up going to last? Lack of sleep, coupled with a day filled with unanswered questions and frustrations, had whittled down his patience. He wanted to get back to the rectory as quickly as possible and begin digging through Father Stephens's bookshelves. If he couldn't get his hands on the old priest's diary, perhaps he'd find some answers elsewhere.

Up ahead, people were sliding out of their cars and congregating in small clusters. Rich turned off the ignition and got out. He might as well join them. Maybe someone knew a back road that skirted the congestion.

"What's the holdup?" he asked a man leaning against a pickup truck. He had the laid-back look of one of the locals.

The horn continued to blare in the distance.

"Old man Fredericks's sheep got out again," he said, sipping from a can of Budweiser.

"Is there another way to Bend Oaks from here?" Rich asked.

He nodded toward a turn off about a half mile up the road. "Take a right up there. It loops around some state land and then turns into an old dirt road. Stay on that for about a mile and you'll come to a fork. Veer left and it will bring you out about a quarter mile from town."

The horn blared on.

The man smiled, exposing a chipped front tooth. "The woman over there in that fancy car has been sitting on the horn for the last fifteen minutes. Someone should tell her that it won't make the sheep move any faster." Then, noting Rich's clerical garb, he suggested that he do it.

"Me? Don't let the getup fool you. I'm not much of a peacemaker," Rich conceded.

The man reached inside a cooler in the back of his truck and pulled out a Bud. "Here, this might help things a bit."

Rich shrugged and took the beer, thinking, What the heck. If she refused to be reasoned with, he'd drink it himself. He could use a cold beer about now. The car, he noticed, had New York license plates. That explained it, he thought. Nothing moved fast enough for New Yorkers. He edged over to the driver's side and tapped on the window. The eclectic motor made a soft whine as the window lowered, releasing a soft scent of very expensive perfume.

"Father Rich?" said Kay Sprage. "Don't tell me you're stuck in this mess, too?"

"Well, if it isn't one of the hookers. Small world." He nodded toward the road up ahead. "Looks like we're both stuck here for a while."

"What are sheep doing in the middle of the road?" she wanted to know. "I nearly ran one over."

He leaned easily against the car. "I guess it's one of the drawbacks of living out in the country."

"One?" she quipped. "I've been trying to call the hookers and tell them I'll be late, but there's no service here."

He handed her the beer, making a silent bet that she would refuse it. Kay Sprage did not look like the beer-drinking kind.

"Why, thanks," she said, expertly popping the tab with a perfectly manicured finger and taking a swig. "Nice vintage," she joked, studying the can. "I'll have to remember this label."

Rich laughed. How did someone as sophisticated as this women get involved with the rug hookers? They hardly seemed compatible.

"I hope Vera remembers to keep the lights on at the bottom of the rectory's driveway. I'm forever passing it by. Want some?" she asked, handing him the beer.

"You mean Jane's house, don't you? The ladies are meeting there tonight." He took a swig.

"No, I mean the rectory. We were supposed to meet at Jane's, but Vera called everyone and changed it."

"She what?" *Good God!* He threw the can on the ground and wrenched open the door. "Move over."

"Are you crazy? And pick up that can. You can't leave it there." He heaved her onto the passenger seat and moved in.

"Wait a minute! This is my car. *No* one drives my car but me."

"Fasten your seat belt."

"If you're in a hurry, I'll drive. After all, I am from New York."

He glanced out the window and expertly pulled out. "And I've spent the last five years driving in Rome."

Kay studied him for a second, then settled back in the seat. "You make a good point. You just better pray that we don't run into any-more sheep."

He downshifted into second gear and took the corner on two wheels. "I'm not worried," he said. "God is my copilot."

"That's all well and good, but I just hope he's licensed to drive New England's back roads."

The school bus had just rolled to a stop in front of the high school's main entrance when Jane pulled her daughter up out of her seat amid a hail of protests and practically hurled her outside.

"Mom! Stop! I forgot my bag," Marilee said, planting her feet solidly on the sidewalk.

Jane grabbed her arm and forced her forward. "We'll come back for it later."

"Someone will rip it off. It has all my stuff in it."

"Then I'll buy you new stuff, which will give you a legitimate reason to go to the mall," Jane said, racing through the parking lot. She flipped off the car's alarm. Lights flashed in the distance. "Hurry up, Marilee."

"Mom, you're acting crazy."

"Get into this car now!"

"All right! Geez . . ." She slid over to the passenger side.

Within minutes, Jane had threaded the SUV through a crowd of parents and students. The main road was just a few feet up ahead. She gave a cursory glance both ways, then floored the accelerator. The car lurched forward, tires squealing, a cloud of dust rising from beneath the wheels.

"Mom, you're really scaring me," Marilee said, holding on to the dashboard with both hands.

"Grab my cell phone and call the rectory."

"I'm calling Dad," Marilee said, punching in their home number. "You're acting too weird."

Jane snatched the phone back. "Call the rectory first and tell the hookers to get out of there now."

"Why?" Marilee had never seen her mother like this before.

"I'll explain later, but for now we have to warn them." Jane recited the phone number.

"It's busy."

Jane was consumed with a growing sense of foreboding. Why had Vera changed the meeting place? She should have told her what she had sensed and warned her that it wasn't safe, especially after dark. And where was Father Rich? Why hadn't he stopped them?

The road to the rectory wound along narrow country lanes. Having grown up here, she knew every bump, every turn in the road. The speed limit was thirty along this stretch, but she was flying at fifty on the straightaways, slowing down as they neared dangerous curves, and praying that no deer would decide to cross their path. One had run out in front of her a few years back. It was like hitting a brick wall.

She made the fifteen-minute ride in less than eight. The rectory gates stood open. She took the turn on two wheels.

Marilee screamed, "You're going to kill us."

Jane rocketed down the driveway, gravel shooting out from under the tires like shrapnel. The rectory was shrouded in darkness. She had a sinking feeling. For one brief second, she hoped that the hookers had decided to meet at her place after all. But then she saw the cars parked alongside the portico. She came to a screeching stop and reached behind her to search for a flashlight.

"Listen to me," she told her daughter, halfway out of the car. "I'm going in, but I want you to stay here, inside this car. Lock the doors. And under *no* circumstances—and I mean *no* circumstances—are you to get out. You got that? If I'm not back in ten minutes call the police, then your father."

The rug was taking shape, Myla thought, studying the design as it lay draped over the library table. Of all the rugs they had hooked down through the years, this definitely was her favorite. Kay was right. This rug would generate a lot of raffle ticket sales even among the locals.

She ran a hand over the mermaids that swam among sea horses of soft coral and tall-masted ships. She had hoped to finish the details in the center portion this evening, which is why she was slightly put off by the absence of two of the club's members. The background would take the longest to complete, but before they could start that all the details had to be done.

"I'm sure Jane will get here as soon as she can," Gail offered, filling in a sea urchin with a bright coral strand of wool.

"All I can say is it's a good thing Vera moved our meeting back here. If we had to wait for Jane to get home, we'd be even further behind."

"Now, Myla," Rose said, hooking a perfectly even row of sea-foam-green wool. "We have all winter to finish this. Relax."

"Easy for you to say. If it's not finished in time for the festival, it's my head on the chopping block."

"We haven't missed a deadline yet," Vera reminded her. "You know, Myla, there are other things in life besides rug hooking. You should travel more. Broaden your mind."

"I like my mind just where it is, thank you very much," Myla said, snipping off a strand of wool. "There—the lighthouse is finished."

Everyone bent forward to study it—each loop was perfectly even. No one could surpass Myla's hooking.

Rose caught something in the air. "Does anyone smell that?"

The others paused, inhaling deeply.

"My God, what is that awful smell?" Myla asked, clamping a hand over her nose. "It smells like rotten cabbage."

"Or sewage," Gail offered.

"Ugh!" the others wailed.

"Where's it coming from?" Vera asked, getting up to inspect the room. "Here's the source. It's coming from the heating vents."

"Could be the septic is backed up downstairs," Gail said, putting aside her rug hook. "I'll go and have a look."

Vera opened the windows. Curtains blew into the room like ghostly apparitions. "You want me to go with you?"

"No," Gail yelled back, already halfway down the hall. "I do this sort of thing all the time."

The basement felt as though it were below zero. Gail shivered, wishing she had grabbed her jacket. She ran the flashlight beam across the floor. Nothing seemed to be amiss, but the smell was definitely coming from down here.

The oil burner came on with a bang, forcing the metal door open. Gail nearly jumped out of her skin. The flames from the burner cast a strange orange light that reflected along the cement wall like sharp, pointed fingers in some primitive dance. The place gave her the willies, and for a moment she wondered whether she should go back upstairs and call a serviceman. She didn't relish the thought of investigating the rest of the cavernous space alone. There was something about the dark corners that sent a cold chill up her spine.

"Snap out of it," she chided herself. What was wrong with her? Criminy, it was just an old basement. She had explored hundreds like it before. The flames drew her attention. She studied the fire, something she had never done before. It was fascinating. It was as if it were alive, beckoning her. She was overcome with a strange sense of detachment. It was as if she were standing outside herself, an observer watching her movements from some distant place.

She inched over toward the flame, overcome with the irrational need to caress it. Tongues of fire swayed in a primitive dance. Then she heard it, calling to her.

"*Touch the flames,*" it said.

She inched closer. Its warmth reached out and touched her cheek in a lover's embrace. Her heart raced with anticipation. It was like being enveloped by something erotically primitive. She drew nearer. Something wonderful was about to happen. Her body tingled with excitement.

The closer she drew, the clearer the voice became. It was soft, cajoling. It made promises of sensual pleasures beyond her wildest imaginings. A core part of her tried to pull away, but she didn't have the strength. She had become ensnared in its spell. An image of Homer's epic flashed through her mind. Was this how it had been for those lost within the Siren's song? She reached out her hand tentatively, drawing steadily nearer. The heat intensified. She felt its touch, hot and probing.

Upstairs, a window crashed closed. The sudden noise snapped her out of the trance. She recoiled in horror. What had she almost done? Her heart beat fast, like the wings of a moth caught inside a glass jar.

"Gail . . ."

This was no imagined voice. "Who's there?"

The wind was picking up outside, the shutters rattling against the outside of the house.

"Gail . . ."

Adrenaline surged through her body, urging her to flee. She raced toward the staircase. Halfway across the damp earth floor, her flashlight went out, pitching the basement into total darkness. She flipped on the switch—on and off, on and off—then banged it against her hand. Nothing. She was stranded in total darkness. Her mind went into overdrive as her need to flee intensified. She'd have to feel her way. She reached into the darkness. The thought filled her with dread. It would be like plunging her hands into a dark, cavernous cistern. She swallowed hard, reached out a hand, and took a step forward. Something brushed across her fingertips.

"We've been waiting for you."
She screamed.

Jane reached the front porch just as a car raced down the driveway. She recognized it instantly. It was Kay's roadster. It roared to an abrupt stop as terrified screams issued from inside the house.

"Hurry!" Jane urged, waving them on.

"What's happened?" Kay asked, racing up the stairs, Rich close at her heels.

"I don't know," Jane said. "I just got here myself."

Rich tried the front door. It wouldn't budge. "Lend a hand," he said, shouldering the wood panel. "On the count of three. One, two, three . . ."

They each gave it all they had as they bounced against the door. It gave way under their combined weight, and they crashed inside.

"Help!" Myla screamed. "Get us out!"

"It's coming from behind the library door," Jane said.

"Hold on. We're coming," Rich shouted. "Jane, get me something I can jam between the doors."

"There's a poker by the fireplace in the study." Jane took off at a run.

"Gail's downstairs in the basement," Vera called through a crack in the door. "We heard her scream. Please, check and make sure she's all right."

"I'll get her," Kay offered, pulling a penlight out of her pocket.

Rich grabbed her wrist. "No! Stay here and help Jane. I'll go."

Jane had reappeared with the poker.

"I wish someone would tell me what's going on here!" Kay said, helping Jane leverage the iron rod in between the pocket doors.

"Push," Jane instructed.

Both women gave it their all. Suddenly the doors gave way. Myla tumbled into Kay's arms, sobbing hysterically. Rose and Vera were pasty white.

"What happened?" Kay asked, trying to console Myla.

"I'm not sure," Rose said, looking as though she'd just escaped the fires of hell. "We smelled something putrid coming from the basement and Gail went to investigate. Then the lights went out. And the windows and doors slammed shut. It was eerie."

"Then we heard Gail scream," Myla added. "It sounded as though something awful had happened down there."

The basement door squeaked open. Father Rich appeared first. The women held their breath.

"It did," Gail said, coming up right behind him. She dusted the cobwebs from her jacket. "I saw a rat."

The next day Vera stood in the center hall with the light streaming in from the overhead skylight and tried to figure out what had sent three perfectly sane women into fits of hysterics. To hear them screaming and carrying on, you would have thought they were a bunch of silly schoolgirls, while there was a perfectly logical explanation for everything that had happened. The window sashes were old, probably rotted through, and had given way under the strong wind streaming into the room, and the library doors had swelled shut owing to dampness. They just needed a good planing to set them right, that's all. It was an old house. These things happened.

Of course, Gail's scream didn't help any. A rat, my goodness! To hear her screams you would have thought she had encountered the Devil himself. Good thing she never took one of those trips to the Amazon. Why, in some of those places there were spiders as large as miniature poodles. Vera should know—once she found one inside her sleeping bag.

Well, there was cleaning to do. She couldn't waste all day trying to figure out what had happened here last night. She set her cleaning supplies on the second-floor landing and arranged them in order. She liked to have things systematically lined up when she tackled a project like this. It saved time. The banister needed a good polishing, and it was just the kind of labor-intensive work to get her mind back to practical matters.

She snapped open the can of Butcher's Wax and tore one of Ralph's old T-shirts (which she had taken out of the laundry basket this morning) into several strips. She dipped a corner of one into the wax, then spread a thin layer along several spindles. She was careful not to allow the wax to build up, especially inside the crevices; it was murder to get out when it dried. As soon as the wax had dried to a white film, she took a soft chamois and began to buff. Within seconds, the dull, lifeless wood began to glow. She studied her work. "That's more like it," she said out loud. There was no better feeling than the satisfaction of a job well done.

The large arched window was at her back. She continued along. Sunlight poured through the glass, but, strangely, it gave off no warmth. Maybe the windows needed re-caulking. Wind was probably coming in through the cracks. She decided that after this section of spindles she would go downstairs, make a cup of tea, and search for her sweater. Then she'd write a note to Father Rich asking him to have someone look over those windows. With the winter coming, they needed to take care of things like this.

Occasionally a soft breeze lifted a branch of the horse chestnut tree that stood near the window, casting its thin, spidery shadows along a far wall. Strange images of ghostly, grotesque shapes rose from the shadows. She felt a shiver of fear. What was wrong with her? She didn't spook easily. She averted her eyes and concentrated on her work. She heard something move downstairs.

"Is that you, Father Rich? I'm up here."

She had left him working in the study. She waited for a response, but there was only silence. Suddenly she got the strangest feeling that she wasn't alone. It was as if something were watching her from the shadows. In her mind's eye she saw a withered hand reach out from behind her. She spun around, but the space was empty.

Maybe the fumes from the wax were getting to her. She snapped the lid of the can closed. She definitely needed that cup of tea. Her nerves were still shaken from last night. She would come back to this later. She figured that since she was going back downstairs she'd gather up the dirty rags and throw them into the laundry basket. She planned to run a towel load later. May as well add these to the pile. She went to pick them up, but they were gone.

"Now how can that be? They were here just a moment ago," she said, taking comfort in the sound of her own voice. It made her feel less alone in the empty house. She ran a hand along the crimson carpet, as though she could possibly have overlooked several white cloths. "Strange . . ."

Alzheimer's . . . dementia . . .

No . . . no . . . no. She *knew* they had been here just seconds ago. Maybe they had slipped through the spindles and onto the foyer. She leaned over the banister. A sea of marble stretched below. Was that them down below? She leaned farther. She could almost make something out. What was it? She leaned over even farther.

She felt a set of hands grab her by the waist and push. She was being lifted up over the railing. She reached out blindly for some purchase but found none. Her screams echoed through the house.

"Vera! Good God, woman," Rich shouted, wrenching her back seconds before she would have plunged to the floor below. "What in heaven's name are you doing? You could have fallen and broken your neck."

She was trembling, both from fear and from the icy chill that filled the stairwell. Rich felt it, too. What had Malachi told him that night in Rome as they stood inside the upstairs room that was as cold as a meat locker? Demons absorbed the heat generated by humans as an energy source to manifest themselves in this dimension.

"I misplaced my polishing rags," Vera was saying, her eyes bug-eyed with fear. "I was trying to see if they had fallen below."

"You mean those?" he asked.

Neatly folded alongside the can of Butcher's Wax were the three white rags.

Kay arrived back in New York City the night of the ill-fated hook-in and was immediately submerged in work for the next few days. All thoughts of what had transpired fled. One of her top clients was in need of damage control. He was a backer of one of those ubiquitous reality shows. A woman contestant had quit in a huff, complaining of unfair treatment and hinting at sexual misconduct by one of the producers. She was threatening to sue the show. The claim was, of course, bogus. The contestant had even gone so far as to hint that for a tidy sum she would withdraw her complaint. Kay's client feared that if any of this was leaked to the press the story would spin a backlash of negative publicity, something he hated more than poor ratings.

It was three days before Kay found the time to try and piece together what had happened that night, beginning with Father Rich practically carjacking her roadster, followed by what they had discovered at the rectory. It all seemed so peculiar. He was hiding something. She could feel it—it felt like fear. But of what? It seemed improbable that a man of his ilk could seriously give credence to those ghost stories that were circulating, or could he?

She finally had plenty of time to mull over the incident while she was stuck in traffic on Seventh Avenue. She was seated in the back of her limousine, which smelled of rich Italian leather and the Fleurissimo worn by her last client, whom she had just dropped off at her West Side penthouse. Kay would recognize that scent anywhere. Jackie O. had once favored it, making it her signature fragrance. It had been created by the famous perfumer Olivier Creed for Grace Kelly, as one of Prince Rainier's wedding gifts, but Jackie had appropriated the scent and made it her own.

This was the first peaceful moment she'd had since returning to the city. She stared out the window at the hordes of pedestrians lining the sidewalks and thought about the scene she and Father Rich had encountered when they arrived. Myla, Vera, and Rose all seemed badly shaken. Jane was nearly manic, acting as though the women were in imminent danger and had to be rescued. Father Rich displayed the same urgency, racing through the countryside like an Indy 500 driver. It certainly was strange.

And how did the women get locked inside the library? The doors were jammed shut, as though someone or something had slammed them with enough force to fuse them in place. The windows inside the library were sealed just as tightly. Kay had tried to get Vera to talk about it, but she said everything had happened so fast that she was at a loss to explain it. Myla was badly shaken and insisted on being driven home. Rose offered to take her.

Her gut told her something had happened inside that room that no one wanted to talk about. And why had Father Rich insisted on having the meeting relocated to Jane's house in the first place? Maybe the rumors of ghosts were true? Yeah, and there really was an Easter Bunny. Kay didn't believe in ghosts. But she had to admit that something strange was going on, and she planned to find out what it was. As soon as she could reschedule some appointments, she was driving back to Bend Oaks. Maybe Gail could fill her in on what had happened.

nine

Rich stood staring out the library windows as a soft breeze tipped with autumn gently fluttered into the room, bringing with it the scent of warm earth and wet leaves. Outside, a riotous profusion of mahoganies, clarets, ochers, and sunshine yellows painted the landscape, lending a sense of vitality to the cloudless sky and the balmy day. His eyes fell briefly on a section of the stone walk that encircled the rectory. Several stones had been disturbed and now lay off to one side. Vance had mentioned the need for repairs the last time Rich visited the Sit and Sip.

"As soon as I get a chance, I'll send some men over to fix the pathway by the porte cochere," Vance said. "The hearse that came to get Father Stephens's body tore it up pretty bad."

For one fleeting moment, Rich considered throwing on a pair of sweatpants and tackling the job himself. He had helped to lay stonework on a dig once in Rome, and he certainly could use some physical exercise. It was, after all, a day meant to be savored. The winter rains would come early enough, stripping the countryside of all color, all life, and shrouding autumn's bright palette in somber shades of gray.

The window sash brought his thoughts back to the events of the other night. What had caused the windows to slam shut and seal the hookers inside? He ran his hand along the panels, checking for some defect. He found none. Then, although he had repeatedly opened and shut the windows a half dozen times before, he did it again. The sash lifted easily. Nothing caught or dragged. Everything appeared to be in perfect working order. There was no evidence that the wood had swelled owing to condensation. The paint looked as though it had just been applied with a soft sable brush—not a nick anywhere.

He folded his arms across his chest and leaned his chin into his hand. There was absolutely no logical reason that they had suddenly closed and then refused to open. The same was true of the pocket doors. The tracks were clean, the rollers oiled, and the lock mechanism worked properly. Although he was no engineer, Rich felt fairly certain that there was no mechanical reason that the doors had closed on their own volition and locked shut.

He studied the room with an eye to catching some flaw, some discrepancy that might explain what had happened here. On the surface, it appeared to be an ordinary room kept in good order—even more so since Vera had come aboard as housekeeper. His gaze flitted over the tall library shelves filled with leather-bound books, the horsehair sofa swathed in its original green silk, the pair of Chippendale leather-tufted chairs flanking the fireplace. To the natural eye, everything was as it should be. Then what could have terrified the women? What had turned an ordinary room—a place where the hookers had met for decades—into a space that evoked mass hysteria? Had the rumors of ghosts and haunting that had been circulating caused their imaginations to go into overdrive, or had they experienced the paranormal—a touch of what had sent the other priests fleeing?

He would bet a year's salary that this event had nothing to do with overactive imaginations. These women were too grounded for that. He was also willing to bet that whatever force walked these halls at night and caused priests to flee and perfectly sane women to act like scared children was but a precursor of something more frightening yet to come. He had heard it wandering the halls the past few nights, felt it trying to affect his mind. It had attacked the bishop. He was certain of that now. It would go to any lengths to prevent him from uncovering anything that might stop its destructive path.

It was building like a storm cloud. Jane was right. Whatever Father Stephens had once contained had been unleashed. Now these women and he were somehow involved. He was certain that it had already tried to kill Vera. He would have to find something at the church that she might do. It was no longer safe for her to work here, not even during the day.

He sank down onto one of the leather chairs and glanced across the room at the window and into the gathering dusk. Part of him wanted to flee. Since the parchment he had originally come to decipher was now the center of a legal battle, he could cancel his sabbatical, call the dean at the University of Rome, and tell him that he was suddenly free to teach the winter session. The dean would be thrilled.

But what would happen to the women? If he left, who would protect them? He supposed the archdiocese could board up the house, lock the gates, and throw away the key. Build a new church rectory, miles from this place. But what if it got loose and infected other homes? Although he was far from being an expert on the occult, he had done sufficient reading on the subject to know that entire communities had been destroyed by the kinds of entities that currently infected this place.

Father Stephens had realized its potential evil. According to Jane, he had tried to vanquish it, but he wasn't powerful enough. He did, however, find a way to contain it. Interesting. What was the secret that he had taken with him to the grave? And how had it been unleashed again after all this time? Did it have something to do with the priest's death?

If only he could get his hands on Father Stephens's diary. Perhaps it held the key. But the bishop was still in intensive care, and his assistant denied any knowledge of a diary. Thankfully, he was out of danger, but it would be a while before he could receive visitors.

The shadows were thickening. Until now, the evil had not sought an open confrontation, but he knew that was coming. It was only a matter of time. The sense of destiny that Malachi had prophesized was unfolding.

Exorcist . . .

The term still made him shudder. He got up and walked into his study. The sound of his footfalls echoed against the marble floor. He paused halfway through the foyer. What could turn such an incredibly beautiful architectural space into a reservoir for evil? He hurried into the study and poured a large glass of brandy, downing it in one swig.

He felt liquid heat course down his chest, tempering his thoughts of unrest. Vera had laid a fire. He checked to make certain the flue was open, then took a box of matches down from the mantel and lit the fire. It was a well-built fireplace with a strong draft. The fire caught instantly, filling the room with the sounds of wood snapping and hissing under the orange flame.

The fact was, he could deny it all he wanted to, but Malachi was right. He could feel it. His destiny was about to be revealed. It was not one he would ever have chosen for himself, but now that it had been thrust upon him he felt it his priestly duty to sally forth. May God have mercy on his soul.

But what if he didn't possess the spiritual stamina, the power, to take on this formidable adversary? He had seen what it could do to both body and soul. It was clever and cunning. Not only was he at risk but the women were now part of this. He poured another brandy and lifted his glass: *If it is possible, may this cup be taken from me. Yet not as I will, but as you will.* His thoughts traveled back to Rome. It was there that the odyssey had begun. If he had known what was to follow, he would have run.

It had been a beautiful summer day in Rome, the kind of day when the air is sweet with the smell of jasmine and the light is tinged with that special golden ocher that's indigenous to Italy, casting its glow over the famous city until it looked as though the rooftops were gilded, the streets bathed in magic. This was the light that had drawn artists down through the centuries.

Rich never tired of viewing this light from the balcony of his Vatican apartment. But on this day his revelry was interrupted by the Pope's assistant, who had brought an urgent request. Would he travel to the north of the city, to a compound where a cloistered group of priests resided, and decipher an ancient parchment that had recently come into their possession? The assistant emphasized that it was a most urgent and highly secretive matter.

Rich was considered an expert on ancient manuscripts and had accepted hundreds of similar requests through the Vatican. This was the first time, however, that he had been asked to pay a house call. But, given that the request had come directly from the Pope, he could hardly refuse. He assured the assistant that he would have someone else take over his classes and headed out.

And so he had started out that fateful day, with the sun beating down across his shoulders, a book bag heavy with reference material slung over his back, never suspecting that what he was about to encounter would forever alter his life.

Rich headed up the tightly woven cobblestoned path that wound past a row of houses whose paint had been faded by the sun. Wash hung outside the windows, and the smell of garlic and freshly baked breads permeated the air. From inside one of the apartments, a piano played softly. He caught snatches of Verdi as he bent into the climb. The grade along the road at this point steeply increased.

The early-July, hot Roman sun beat down relentlessly. His black shirt soaked up the rays like a sponge, and the heat coming up through the stones burned his feet. Sweat poured down his back until his shirt was soaked through and stuck to him like freshly hung wallpaper. Several times, he had to stop, drop the heavy canvas bag, and catch his breath.

It took him nearly fifteen minutes to reach the front gate, which was embossed with an intricately designed wreath. A knotted strand of rope was attached to a small bell. He gave it a tug and waited. A reed-thin young man with sober eyes appeared, dressed in a long, flowing robe with a knotted belt, his feet clad in sandals. He ushered Rich into the compound and down a path that wound through several gardens and a maze of tall boxwoods that completely sheltered the villa from the street. Finally, they entered a small courtyard. A stone bench hewed from granite was positioned in front of the statue of Mary and Child. Its sides were slightly worn, as though many anxious hands had sought purchase there, beseeching the Holy Mother's intervention.

The priest motioned for Rich to stay, then soundlessly disappeared behind a row of arches that stretched the length of the villa. Rich dropped the canvas bag and flexed his aching fingers. He'd have blisters tomorrow for sure; he studied his thumb, where one was already forming in the weblike flesh between his fingers. Oh, well . . . he'd tend to it when he got home. Meanwhile, he decided to take a little stroll around the property while waiting for his host to appear.

The view was amazing. From this vantage point, Rich could see all of Rome. The grounds had been graded. The house and the out-buildings were perched on a high knoll, and the gardens sloped down, spreading out like a lady's fine gown. A nine-foot masonry wall painted the color of aged sienna surrounded the compound. Leafy strands of bougainvillea, intertwined with jasmine, arched over its entire expanse. Occasionally, a whiff of air would carry the jasmine's soft, gentle fragrance on a breeze. Rich closed his eyes and breathed in.

He never tired of Italy's particular blend of scents. The smell of herbs, garden ripe tomatoes, and pungent grapes seemed to have impregnated the very stones. To walk along any of Rome's streets was to experience a symphony of aromas so intoxicating that it was easy to be carried away in search of their origins. Small restaurants proliferated throughout this section of Rome, as well as private homes that set out small round tables on the sidewalks. For a minimal charge, one could enjoy a home-cooked meal.

It seemed to Rich that all of Rome was a canvas that artists had spent centuries painting. Everything was created with an eye to beauty—even the simplest items, like the decorative details on paper used to wrap a floral bouquet, the bags that held crusty fresh-baked bread, or the label on a slim bottle of olive oil.

And the sounds of Rome were unlike those of any other city. Unlike the clamor of New York, here the sounds of city life resonated with a more gentle timbre, as though the brassiness of commerce had been filed away. That seemed especially true here at the priest's villa. In fact, there seemed to be a complete absence of sound. Not even a bee buzzed among the profusion of jasmine. But how was that possible?

"There you are," a strong voice called out behind him. "This is my favorite spot, too," the man said, taking in the view as though for the first time. He offered his hand. "I'm Father Malachi. You must be Father Rich Melo."

Rich noticed him staring at his crescent-shaped birthmark. He shifted uncomfortably under the gaze.

"I noticed your bag filled with some rather ponderous-looking books by the statuary," the priest said rather hastily. "I see that you've come prepared to work."

"That I have," Rich said, studying the man's face. He appeared to be in his early sixties.

"Why don't we go in out of this hot sun? A room has been prepared downstairs where you can work."

Rich followed him indoors. The villa was as cool as a sylvan glen. Together they walked through a maze of rooms until they came to a narrow space with tall arched windows that sat at the rear of the house. A large table in the center of the floor held two ornate candlesticks and an earthenware pitcher of water, around the base of which condensation had gathered.

"Will this do?" Father Malachi asked.

"It will do just fine," Rich said. He got the impression that Malachi was anxious for him to begin, so he wasted no time. "Why don't you tell me a little about this parchment that you want me to decipher. What do you know about its origins?"

Malachi motioned for him to sit down. Rich pulled out one of the tall-back wooden chairs at the table and waited for his host to join him. The older priest settled his thick black robe around his spindly legs and began. "Upstairs is a young girl. In fact, today is her twelfth birthday. Her name is Louisa. Until two months ago, she was a normal child. Her family lives in a small fishing village about twenty miles from here. Her father is a merchant. He sells imports— mostly stoneware, some antiques. That pitcher was a gift from him."

Both men glanced at the table.

"Louisa has two younger sisters and four older brothers. All are devout Catholics who attend St. Clare. I've talked to their pastor, who assures me that they are good, simple people. Not prone to flights of fancy."

Malachi leaned forward slightly and clasped his hands. "One day Louisa's father received a crate of old vases and earthenware jars from a merchant in Tunis, and he asked his daughter if she would like to help him unwrap its contents and set them out so that he could assess their value. She had done this dozens of times before and he knew she would be careful, so when some customers came in he left her to the task.

Malachi gazed softly out at the garden as he conjured the scene in his mind. "Inside one of the large urns, Louisa found a small piece of parchment about this big." Malachi indicated an area of approximately six by seven inches. "When I later interviewed Mariana, her younger sister, she said that Louisa immediately became obsessed with the need to possess it. She hid it from her father and made her sister swear that she would never tell. Mariana agreed, but later when she asked to see the parchment Louisa became extremely agitated and said it had been sent to her alone. No one else was to look at it but her."

Rich's interest heightened. During the past few years, several important finds had found their way out of the back alleyways of Tunis. Its proximity to the Mediterranean, and its complete lack of ethics concerning the handling of ancient artifacts, had made Tunis a natural repository for those wishing to trade on the black market. Last year, a piece of basalt bearing a single inscription had been traced to a Tunis merchant, who later admitted that he had bought it from a Bedouin in Negev. The lettering was Aramaic and mentioned the military victory over *Bth-Dwd*—"the House of David." Later, it was authenticated as having been written in 1045 BC, during King David's reign.

"Almost immediately, Louisa began to separate herself from the family. Her mother was the first to notice. Louisa had always enjoyed working in her father's shop, but she now spent hours alone, wandering the maze of hills behind their house. One day the mother sent Mariana to fetch Louisa home for dinner. She found Louisa sitting by a cliff, her eyes closed, the parchment spread out across her lap. Mariana said that she appeared to be tracing the symbols with her hand. And when the young sister drew nearer she heard Louisa speaking in a strange language, one that she had never heard before. The girl was startled when Mariana called her name. She quickly rolled up the parchment and put it aside, then accused her of spying on 'us.' "

"Was there anyone else around?" Rich asked.

Malachi shook his head. "The sister said she was alone."

Clouds had gathered in the west, casting the room in shadow. Malachi reached over toward a lamp, whose shade was tilted at an odd angle. Rich found it unsettling that he hadn't straightened the shade before switching on the lamp. A pool of limpid yellow light shone ineffectively in a corner. The room remained cast in a gray pall.

"Then the family began to notice that strange things happened whenever Louisa was in the house."

"What kind of things?"

"Scratching sounds behind the walls. Doors and windows that refused to stay open. Electrical appliances going off and on by themselves."

"All of which could have perfectly natural explanations," Rich suggested.

"Yes, they could. But soon things began to occur that defied logic," Malachi said. "Most of the activity took place at night, between the hours of nine PM and three AM."

Rich sat up straighter in his chair. That seemingly insignificant statement drew his full attention. This time element was known as the "physic hours." In all the cases concerning demonic activity, the disturbances always took place between nine in the evening and three in the morning. It was meant to be a mockery of the time that Christ had spent on the Cross. It was a classic demonic signature. He was suddenly very intrigued.

Malachi continued, "It began with what seemed like an innocuous event. Mariana awakened her parents, complaining that the girls' room was freezing. The father followed his small daughter into the bedroom and said it was like entering a walk-in freezer. The next day the father called in a heating specialist and had the heating system checked out, but nothing was amiss. The problem continued for weeks, and the mechanic was recalled repeatedly, but each time the system was found to be in good working order. In frustration, the father ordered a new oil burner installed, but this, too, did nothing to stop the sudden drops in temperature. At this point, the mechanic was at a loss to explain it.

"Then one night Louisa fell asleep on the living room sofa. The parents decided to leave her there and went to bed. A few hours later, the mother got up to use the bathroom and went in to check on Louisa. The air in the room had turned to ice. The girls' bedroom remained normal. It was then that the family realized the temperature fluctuations occurred only in the room that Louisa occupied."

"Interesting. Then what happened?" Rich prompted.

"The nighttime disturbances began to escalate. One night Mariana awakened to feel what she described as the air being sucked out of the room. She couldn't breathe and started for the door, calling out for her sister as she raced into the hall. When Louisa didn't follow, she ran back into the room and saw her sister's body levitating several feet off the bed. Her screams brought her parents running. The father raced over and pulled Louisa's blankets off, thinking that perhaps it was some kind of trick, but he fell back in shock. It was no trick. His daughter's body was floating in midair."

"And what was Louisa doing while all of this was happening?" Rich wanted to know.

"Ah . . . that was the worse part, according to her parents. The child was writhing in a state of sexual ecstasy. The father became so distraught that he finally grabbed her by the arm and yanked, but she didn't budge. He told me that it was as if her body were made of granite. Then Louisa began to speak, only it wasn't her voice they heard. It said, 'Leave her, she's ours! We are not finished having our pleasure with her yet.' The scene was repeated nightly for several weeks.

"The parents were soon terrified, both for themselves and for their daughters. Theirs was a small town. Gossip was the primary source of entertainment, so they decided to restrict Louisa to the house. But the child soon developed almost superhuman strength, and no one, not even the father, could restrain her. Several times she broke out. They found her later roaming the village completely naked, making lewd and perverse comments to people in the street.

"Finally, the police became involved. The people in the village demanded that something be done to contain the child. If the parents didn't comply, the officers said, she would be committed. Meanwhile, the father's business suffered."

"Guilt by association," Rich offered.

"That and the undercurrent of rumors that insisted the child's behavior was a reflection of the home life."

"How did you get involved?"

"The local priest was sent to me through the office here in Rome."

"Do you take on many of these kinds of cases?"

"No, just those that have wide-reaching implications."

Rich's face reflected his confusion. "You mean against the Church?"

"No. I mean that if the power of the demonic attack is not contained or abolished, it could have ongoing consequences."

"I don't understand."

"Think of this as a deadly virus that, if left unchecked, could infect hundreds, perhaps thousands, of innocent victims."

"I assume that you believe all of this has something to do with the artifact the child discovered."

"I'm certain of it, which is why I must ask you what might seem on the surface as a very personal question."

"Which is?"

"How is the present state of your soul?"

"My soul? You mean, am I in a state of grace?"

Malachi nodded.

"No disrespect intended, Father Malachi, but the state of my soul is between me and God."

"Not here, it isn't." His eyes grew small, probing. "You must understand the gravity of this situation. Demonic creatures are very clever. They've been spreading hate and derision since the advent of man. All they need is one flaw, one crack in a person's soul, and they can gain entry, much the way bacteria seeps into the bloodstream through an open wound. And once they gain entry they quickly take over until the soul is shrouded in blackness, devoid of all God's light. And their actions don't stop there.

"Next, they attach themselves to the people surrounding the victim—parents, siblings, friends, spouses. They do it through a campaign of fear and discouragement. Their mission is to discredit God's love, make the victims believe they are all alone in this fight. Wherever you see despair, you know that Satan has been fast at work."

Rich slid back casually in his chair and rested his elbows on the arms of the chair. He studied the older priest over clasped hands. "You're talking about the physical reality of evil."

"You say that as though you don't believe evil is real."

"The Catholic doctrine says that I must. But do I have any modern-day corroborating evidence of the type of demonic possession that is spoken about in the New Testament? No. Don't get me wrong. I think it's an interesting study, but I'm not sure it's relevant for today."

Malachi's face turned grave. Color left his cheeks as he rose from his chair. "Come with me. You need to understand the full gravity of the task I'm about to ask you to undertake. I want you to meet Louisa."

Rich set his drink aside and followed him upstairs.

Malachi stopped in front of a doorway at the end of the hall. Another priest was stationed outside the door. He knelt before a straight-backed chair and was reciting the rosary. His mouth moved soundlessly as he fingered each bead. Beside him was a small table on which there was a bottle of holy water, a crucifix, and several religious medals. Rich recognized St. Ignatius and Our Lady of Fatima among them.

Malachi opened the bedroom door. The two men stepped inside.

The first thing Rich noticed was the stench, an odor so foul that it made him gag. He grabbed for his handkerchief and covered his nostrils.

The room was shrouded in total darkness except for a bank of candles that burned in front of a makeshift altar that held a statue of the Madonna and Child. A second priest, who was heavily clothed, sat praying beside a small stone fireplace. A fire blazed, yet the temperature in the room was well below freezing. Rich remembered what Malachi had said about the cold following Louisa. It certainly was evident here.

Malachi motioned for Rich to come closer to the child. Lying on the bed was a small body, swathed in a sheet formed like an infant's swaddling clothes; arms and legs were bound within the layers of cloth. Rich stared down at the sleeping figure and drew in a sharp breath. The child's face was completely distorted. The skin was white, transparent, paper-thin, and stretched like a death mask across the face. It gave the impression that it might rip apart at any moment, revealing bone and sinew.

"Dear God . . ." he murmured.

At the mention of God, the creature jerked its head in Rich's direction. The eyes turned as black as coal and stared into his face. For a moment, he felt all the heat leave his body and a cold hand wind its way around his heart. He watched with a mix of fascination and repulsion as the child's mouth opened and emitted a chorus of voices that began to speak in a singsong voice.

"We know what your daddy did . . .

"We know what your daddy did . . .

"You weren't good enough, were you, Rich? Your daddy dropped you off one day and never came back. Poor little Rich. . . ."

"How could you know that?"

"Don't engage it in conversation," Malachi cautioned.

"You have no power here, Father Rich Melos. Go away before I call upon my master. He will send another legion marked just for you."

"Be silent!" Malachi commanded, removing a vial of holy water from his pocket and sprinkling it on the bed. With each droplet, the demon inside the child screamed in agony. "St. Michael the Archangel, defend us in battle," he intoned. "Be our protection against the wickedness and snares of the Devil."

As the priest made the sign of the cross, the girl's body flipped up into a standing position, the blankets ripped from her body, and she slowly began to rise. Rich stared in disbelief. What he was witnessing was impossible, yet there was no denying that the fine line that he had always believed existed between the spiritual and the natural world was dissolving. No rational explanation could account for what he was witnessing.

A grimace stretched across the creature's face as it began to advance, floating inches above the bed. It was headed toward him. Its hands, the shape of talons, reached for his throat.

Two younger priests stormed into the room, shoved Rich aside, and tackled the creature to the floor.

"Get out!" Malachi screamed, pushing Rich into the hallway and slamming the door shut behind him.

ten

"Do you believe in evil now, Father Rich?" Malachi asked, stepping back inside the downstairs room.

Rich noticed that in their absence someone had unpacked his canvas bag and carefully laid out his books. "I don't know what I believe," he confessed, running a hand over a leather binding. "How did she . . . ? How did it know . . . ?"

"I think we both could use a drink," Malachi said. He dug inside the deep pocket of his robe, removing several wads of tissue before unearthing a small skeleton key. This he used to open a chestnut wood cabinet that sat beneath a window looking out over a side garden.

"Will this do?" he asked, holding up a bottle of Napoleon brandy.

"That will do just fine," Rich said, studying the label.

"I apologize for not warning you," Malachi said, handing Rich a glass before settling down in a leather chair. "But, as you just experienced, no amount of warning could properly prepare anyone."

"What was that upstairs?"

"Louisa. God have mercy on her soul," he answered quietly, and made the sign of the cross. He took up a photo from a small marble-topped credenza and handed it to Rich. "This was taken about three months ago."

The child in the photo looked nothing like the one who was imprisoned in the room upstairs. Here she was a smiling young girl, her blue eyes sparkling with life. Locks of curly brown hair cascaded down her back like a waterfall.

"It's hard to believe that's the same child."

"Yes, I know," Malachi said. His words were weighted with sadness. "I've seen evil in various forms throughout my many years as an exorcist. But this case is the most virulent I've ever witnessed. The intensity of the demonic powers that possess this child is unprecedented. I began the Ritual of Exorcism about six weeks ago, but we're no closer to deliverance than we were when I started." He drained his glass and went to pour another. "I don't know how much more the child's physical body can endure. I fear that if we're not successful soon, she may die.

"That's why I'm in dire need of your expertise. Whatever is on that piece of parchment holds the key. I've only held it once, but I could feel a darkness pulling at my soul. It's only with the greatest self-will that I was able to resist." Malachi studied the amber liquid in his glass. "No wonder the child was without defenses. It seems to cling to any residue of sin, or unforgiveness, using it as a conduit to possession."

"Is that why you insisted that I be in a state of grace before you would allow me to examine it?"

Malachi nodded. "Just because you're a priest doesn't make you immune to possession. I fear if you carry any trace of sin, your immortal soul could be at risk. I can't allow that, no matter how much I wish to save Louisa. I hope now that you understand what's at stake you'll agree to help. In turn, I will do everything within my power to protect you."

Rich glanced up at the ceiling, the horrors that he had witnessed still fresh in his mind. "And if I refuse?"

"I would not hold it against you."

"But the child . . . ?"

"The demon has compromised her immortality. Unless we can find a way of delivering her soul, she will be consigned to spend eternity as you have seen her now."

The thought was too horrific to contemplate. "And you feel that the key to freeing her is somehow connected to the parchment."

"Yes," Malachi said emphatically, placing his empty glass on a side table. "I must know its origins and, especially, its name. Without it, I am powerless to release her."

Rich rose silently and walked over to the open French doors. The sun was setting and the landscape shimmered under the ocher-tinted light. But the beauty of the scene was lost on him. Instead, he stood deeply regretting his earlier cavalier attitude toward Malachi. A sudden swell of humility washed over him. A spiritual war the likes of which he had never witnessed before raged directly overhead. Rich, like most people, had always considered evil to be more of a concept than a reality. Well, that had changed. He had seen evil in its physical form. Would he ever forget the tormented creature upstairs?

He turned and walked back toward the priest, then knelt humbly before him on the cold ceramic tiles. Looking up into Malachi's tired old eyes, he asked with deep sincerity, "Father, would you hear my confession?"

Rich was granted absolution for his sins. The room was then blessed with holy water, and the protection of St. Michael and the Blessed Mother was invoked on Rich's behalf. Minutes later one of the priests appeared, carrying a locked metal box.

Malachi cleared a section of the long wooden table, which still bore droplets of the holy water. Taking the box from the younger man, he dismissed him with a nod, then reached inside his robes and withdrew a tiny silver key. He hesitated briefly before inserting it into the lock. Rich heard a small click.

Malachi opened the lid, laying it gently against the table, then made the sign of the cross before reaching inside and withdrawing a rolled parchment that had been covered in a piece of black cloth. He studied Rich's face for any sign of hesitancy. Seeing none, he placed the parchment on the table.

"I'll leave you, then. The others and I will be in continuous prayer while you work on the text. If you begin to experience anything strange, you are to call me immediately. Do you understand?"

Rich nodded, his eyes fixed on the ancient artifact. How many similar parchments had he deciphered over the years? A hundred, perhaps. Normally, he felt a rush of excitement at this point: the thrill of examining words written by someone who had lived thousands of years ago. It was a time capsule, a direct link to a world long lost. But this time he felt only foreboding. Were the contents of this parchment responsible for what he had seen upstairs?

He was barely cognizant of Malachi's departure until he heard the door close behind him. He removed a pair of white cotton gloves from his canvas sack, a magnifying glass, and several small orbs of cotton, which, if needed, would be used to clean small areas. As he prepared the work area, he remembered Malachi's warning: "Evil can only enter an empty house. Fill your mind with the things of God. Remember his sacrifice on your behalf. He turned a crown of thorns into a crown of glory. Focus on his crown."

Before commencing, Rich closed his eyes, centered his thoughts on the Savior whom he had sworn to serve, then took a deep breath; he carefully removed the black cloth, which revealed a leather parchment. It had been tightly rolled around a piece of olive wood that was almost fossilized. Both smelled heavily of sulfur.

He studied its shape and size, searching for any signs of instability, but the papyrus appeared in good shape, with only a few dark areas along its edges and a small lower portion that had been torn away. Inside his canvas bag were four leaded weights, which he used to anchor the four corners, allowing him to view the text as a whole.

Large sections appeared to be covered in a thin layer of ash. He took a soft piece of cotton damped with oil and lightly swabbed the upper right-hand portion, making small, circular motions. As if by magic, writing began to appear. His excitement grew. The text had been written in Ugaritic, a blend of cuneiform and Hebrew script popular during the reign of King David. That would date the papyrus to around 1055 BC.

The text was decorated with pentagrams, which flanked the top; in between the pentagrams rested a crude six-sided star that had been created with two pyramids. The bottom of the parchment contained a drawing of Dagon—half man, half fish. Dagon was part of a pantheon of idols worshipped by the Philistines and the Canaanites during that period.

The light in the room was dimming, and Rich was too absorbed in his work to get up and search for a switch. Instead, he grabbed the two candlesticks that were on the table. Placing them on either side of the text, he struck a match. A cloud of sulfur rose like incense. He waited for the wick to catch and blew out the match. The candlelight gave a mystical quality to the text. He could almost imagine himself as the author bent over the piece of leather, a lighted vessel of oil the only source of illumination in the room.

Rich settled back into his chair and began to read, occasionally glancing at a reference book to better understand the subtleties of certain symbols, such as a bird or a swallow, which was often used to indicate a word that had the *wr* sound as one of its syllables. Although he was conversant in ancient Hebrew, there were several archaic passages that required hours of research, especially those that were linked with the cuneiform. The lined pad on which he had been recording his findings was soon filled with notations as each word, each symbol, was painstakingly translated. Several times he had to scratch out an entire line of text when he discovered a change in form or meaning. But slowly, as the sun continued in its heavenly course and night descended, the story written on the parchment began to take shape.

At six o'clock, there was a light knock on the door.

"Yes?" he asked, never lifting his eyes from the text. "What is it?"

"Father Malachi has asked if you would like some dinner," the priest who had entered the room said.

"No, I want to finish this first."

"It's growing too late to return to the Vatican. The buses would have stopped running by now. We'll make up a room for you."

"Fine," he said, going back to his work.

"When you're done here, just pull on that bell cord above the fireplace. Father Malachi doesn't like anyone wandering around here at night alone."

Their eyes met. No explanation was needed. Rich nodded and went back to his work.

The hours ticked away and the shadows deepened. He had been at this for ten straight hours. His back hurt. His eyes were bleary from the dim candlelight, but he couldn't draw himself away until it was finished. The story that was unfolding held him captive.

Finally, the last symbol had been deciphered. He threw down his pencil, brought his hands behind his head, and stretched. In all the years that he had been deciphering ancient manuscripts, he had never uncovered a tale quite like this. Although some of it was closely aligned with the biblical account of that period, other portions could be attributed to superstition or myths. Or was the story it contained pertinent to the evil that had enslaved the child upstairs? Rich paused to consider the ramifications if this proved to be true.

The story began during the reign of David. A famine had struck the Israelites and King David sought its cause. The Lord answered,

"It is on account of Saul and his blood-stained house; it is because he put the Gibeonites to death." The Gibeonites were survivors of the Amorites, mercenaries used by Israel whom David's predecessor, Saul, had sworn to protect. But Saul failed to honor his promise and, in fact, tried to annihilate them.

Wanting to end the famine that was bringing devastation to his people, David sought the Gibeonite leaders in an effort to ameliorate this travesty. The leaders were ushered before David's throne and asked what would appease them. They replied, "We demand that seven of Saul's male descendants be handed over for execution."

Miphah was an Amorite woman who had been taken as a spoil of war when she was a young girl and later made one of Saul's concubines. This liaison had resulted in the birth of seven sons. Since these men were not of a direct lineage, David singled them out to be sacrificed.

Miphah raced to intercede for her sons' lives, but to no avail. Watching from the palace gates, she witnessed all seven being tortured, pleading for death to come and end their torment. Her wish was finally granted. Overcome with grief, she sought out the Gibeonite leaders to ask for her sons' bodies. They refused her request, insisting that the bodies be left to rot under the relentless sun. She then sought David's intervention, but was denied an audience with the King.

Then, in a final act of infamy, the Gibeonites tied ropes around the seven decaying corpses, strung them to their horses, and raced through the sands, spreading the rotting flesh and entrails along the desert floor.

Miphah combed the desert in search of her sons' remains, swearing revenge on the House of David. Although she had lived among the Israelites, she had never truly forsaken her ancestral gods. Now, in a white heat of rage, she unearthed the pagan image of Dagon that she had buried decades ago beneath the floor of her house.

"Pack some bread and water," she told her servant. Under cover of night, Miphah left the city gates and traveled several days into the desert, then waited for the sign of the Scorpion to appear clearly in the night sky.

In ancient cultures, the scorpion symbolized death, destructive forces, and darkness. It was seen as a creature that crept stealthily along, apparently harmless, as it overcame or circumvented obstacles while in search of its victim. Because of its diminutive size, it was able to conceal itself and work its sorcery without risk. It was just the type of symbol Miphah needed to invoke retribution against the House of David.

She waited a fortnight, until the red star of Antares (the heart of the celestial Scorpion) was clearly visible overhead, then began her ceremony. In exchange for her soul and the souls of her sons, she made a pact with the Devil against the House of David. The pact was written on seven pieces of parchment and sealed with the blood of both Miphah and Dagon. For each seal that was opened, a corresponding portal would be opened, releasing all manner of foul, demonic powers into the world.

Before this evening, Rich would have dismissed all of this as nothing more than ancient folklore governed by superstition. But after having seen the child upstairs and felt the power that seemed to emanate from the piece of ancient leather that he now held in his hands, he wasn't so sure. What if this was real? What if the pact that Miphah had made had continued down through the centuries? What if it held the power to infect anyone who came upon one of these parchments? It was a chilling thought, yet one that he felt might have some basis in truth. And if that was so? He pushed back his chair. A flood of terror washed over his soul. He must warn Malachi.

Then, as though the powers of hell discerned his intent, a terrifying scream issued from the upstairs room. Rich recognized it at once. It was Malachi.

———

"Hurry. The door is sealed shut," a young priest shouted as Rich bolted up the stairs. "Father Malachi is locked inside alone."

Suddenly the floor beneath their feet began to shake, and the sound of wood and plaster crumbling thundered through the hallway.

"What's happening?" Rich yelled above the noise.

"I don't know," the priest said, trying to steady himself.

It felt as though the entire building would crash down around their ears. Slate roof tiles could be heard overhead sliding down the eaves and crashing onto the courtyard below.

"We've got to get in there," Rich shouted, shouldering the door. "Lend me a hand. On the count of three."

Another priest had appeared seemingly out of nowhere. Together, all three rammed the door with all their might. The wood buckled under their combined weight and they crashed inside.

"Dear Jesus . . ." Rich said. One of the priests made the sign of the cross.

Father Malachi had been nailed to the wall in a mock crucifixion. His body was suspended several feet above the floor and his face was covered in blood. The wooden crucifix that he kept tucked in his belt had splintered and the halves were now impaled in his wrists. What had once been the child Louisa stood in front of him, issuing a string of obscenities in a voice that sounded straight from the bowels of hell and a language that Rich recognized as ancient Aramaic.

"And so you think you know how to banish me," it taunted. "But you know nothing. I am more powerful than all the priests in your whore the Church. I will rip out your souls and personally carry them down with me into hell."

One of the priests grabbed for her waist, but an invisible force propelled him across the room. He landed with a thud against the wall.

Slowly, the child's body began to rotate like a pinwheel. "You all are condemned," the voice said. "You have no power over me. I am all-powerful. See how I can torment you at will."

"Father Melo," Malachi called, his voice failing. "Tell me its name before it's too late."

The creature paused in mid-rotation. Its lifeless eyes settled on Rich's face. Suddenly it was as if a great fog had washed over his brain. His eyes grew heavy and his mind felt as though it were being dragged down into a black void.

"St. Michael, come to our aid," Rich prayed. "Defend us in battle, be our protector against the wickedness and snares of the Devil."

The demon laughed. "Go ahead, call him. He will not come. Others have detained him."

"Don't believe it," Malachi shouted. "The Devil is a liar."

The crescent-shaped mark on Rich's neck began to burn something fierce. He cried out in pain. It was as if he were being branded. At the same time, he felt a strange sense of power, like an electrical charge, pulsating through his body. Without his volition, his hands rose toward the heavens and words began to tumble from his lips. He felt helpless to stop them. He had become a conduit through which the spirit of God in His infinite power would save the damned.

"Dear Jesus, Savior of the lost, defender of the helpless, victor over evil, send your Holy Spirit to demolish Satan's weapons and set the captives free."

The creature's body slowly drifted back toward the floor.

Rich caught a glimpse of fear in its eyes. His voice was charged with authority as he mandated the Devil to leave. The air crackled with the power of his words. "I command you in the name of Jesus, the highest sovereign God, who by his blood spilled at Calvary was given authority over all things, including principalities and powers of darkness. . . ."

The words had a physical effect, repelling the creature back toward the opposite side of the room.

"Stop." It was a child's voice that spoke now, filled with sweetness. "You're hurting me, Father Rich. Please don't let it hurt me. Stop and it will go away."

"Don't listen to it," Malachi warned. "It's just a ploy."

But Rich had listened, and his rational mind was now engaged. How could he continue? he questioned. This was a child. He hesitated.

"Thank you, Father Rich, for saving me," the voice continued. "I'm so hungry. Won't you please give me something to eat? We could share something. Perhaps a piece of fruit."

"Keep going," Malachi shouted. "It's a trick! Banish it. Say its name!"

"Don't listen to him," the creature said in a hypnotic voice. Once again, a feeling of great heaviness settled over Rich.

"I'm just a little child. You don't want to hurt a child, do you? Let's go for a walk in the garden. The flowers smell so lovely at night."

Malachi had worked his hands free and fell with a thud to the floor. Ignoring the pain that racked his body, he rushed toward the creature and placed a rosary around its neck and tightened the strand like a noose. It screamed out in pain and spit out a string of obscenities.

"Keep going! Don't stop." Malachi fought to contain the creature.

Rich called for the Holy Spirit's intercession and felt an immediate sense of release. He pointed a hand at the creature and commanded it to deliver its name and be gone. For a moment, it seemed as though all the hosts of heaven and hell were poised on the edge of some great abyss. A strong wind rattled the closed windows.

"Say your name. I command you!"

The windows burst open. The wind ripped through the room.

"Say it! I command you in the name of Jesus to obey!"

The creature's body began to vibrate off the floor like a jackhammer. The eyes rolled back into its head and it began to make curdling, choking sounds.

"My name . . . my name . . ."

"Say it!"

"Its name is Artemian, servant of Dagon," Rich shouted.

The creature's eyes bored into his soul.

"You may banish me, but there are others, and they will find you no matter where you go."

eleven

Gail sat at her new vanity table on her new velvet-cushioned backless chair, which had been purchased with no money down and no payments or interest for one full year. It had been delivered the very next day by two short, stocky Latino men who on the surface appeared as if they might have trouble lifting an armchair, let alone the heavy vanity table, but who had moved with the fluid ease of trained weight lifters.

The veneered semi-curved vanity table had fit perfectly against the wall between the pair of windows that looked out over the backyard. Gail had eyed it critically as the men carefully maneuvered it around the king-size bed. For a brief moment, she felt a hot poker of regret. She didn't really *need* a vanity table. What little makeup she wore was easily applied standing in front of the bathroom sink, and she never spent more than five minutes with the hair dryer each morning. And the cost—$2,500! She had never paid that much for any piece of furniture in her life. She must have gone temporarily insane.

The men settled it in place and made her sign the paper attached to a metal clipboard. Suddenly she was filled with regret. Heck, the darn thing didn't even fit in with the rest of the decor. It was an elaborate affair with a three-sided arched mirror and a double set of drawers hidden behind panels that bore hand-painted bouquets of violets. In a room dominated by Ralph's preference for ultramodern leather and chrome, it looked like a beached anachronism.

"*You're worth it,*" a voice whispered.

Instantly, all uncertainties fled. The voice was right. It was exactly what she had always wanted. She could see that now. Besides, wasn't it time she treated herself to something she enjoyed instead of always deferring to Ralph's taste? She studied the vanity with a critical eye and concluded that she deserved it. In fact, she deserved a lot of things that she had denied herself—and for what? For those spoiled, moronic stepsons and a husband who treated her like a nanny and a housemaid?

No . . . no. She felt a mental tug-of-war go on inside her brain. That wasn't right. She loved Ralph and the boys.

The voice returned with vigor. "*Forget about them. Do things your way. Start by taking better care of yourself. You deserve it.*"

Her misgivings melted away under the heat of the repartee. The voice was right. Look at Kay Sprage. They were both the same age, yet Gail looked ten years older which is why she had driven to Macy's and charged eight hundred dollars' worth of skin-care products.

RJ had caught her a couple of times in her new nightly ritual, which included exfoliating, mud masks, and slick coats of moisturizing cream before retiring. The boy had looked at her as though she had been replaced by an alien.

"You never did that stuff before," he said, scrunching up his forehead in a frown. "How come you're doing it now? You look okay just the way you are."

There was the problem. She looked just "okay." Not fabulous or sexy. That, however, was about to change, owing, in part, to the vast array of expensive elixirs that now topped her vanity, each filled with the promise of eternal youth and a new, rejuvenated Gail Honeychurch. Lined across her new vanity table like an arsenal of war were shapely bottles of Lancôme's Ablutia Fraîcheur purifying gel; high-definition mascara guaranteed to give length and lift to one's lashes; crayoned pencils—one for lining the eyes, the other for shaping the brows; bronzing powders; shimmering blushes in several hues; concealers, liquid foundation, and pressed powder; nineteen tubes of lipstick; replenishing creams and antiwrinkle creams that promised to lift, firm, and make lines and wrinkles magically fade; and enough Frederic Fekkai hair products to open a salon.

Gail applied a light coat of Serenity eye shadow under her brows, Bermuda Sunrise to her lids, then worked Spice Island into the corners as the salesgirl at Macy's had instructed. According to the girl, when applied in just this way it was guaranteed to make her eyes appear bigger, more luminous. She studied the effects and had a moment of great uncertainty. Perhaps she had applied a tad too much. She leaned closer into the mirror. Maybe she'd better go back to her favored blue shadow.

She was about to wipe it off and start again when she heard an argument brewing outside her bedroom door. RJ's and Jerry's voices were rising. She put down her makeup brush and started to get up. If she didn't intervene now, it would escalate into a full-blown fistfight.

"They're not your sons," the voice reminded her. *"Let them battle it out. This is your time. You deserve to pamper yourself."*

A body crashed against a wall. Her bedroom door vibrated. Next, a piece of china shattered. Silence followed. She imagined both boys suspended in mid-fight, waiting for her bedroom door to fly open.

As always, the voice was right. What concern was it of hers? Let Ralph deal with it when he came home. She waited, a makeup brush hovering in midair. There were a few harsh accusatory whispers, followed by footsteps, as the boys bounded down the stairs.

Good. They had gone.

She searched her reflection in the mirror for any flaws. What was she being so indecisive about? She looked great! She applied a covering of blush across the upper portions of her cheeks. The salesgirl had commented that she possessed wonderful, chiseled cheekbones. She studied their contour in the mirror.

"Very sophisticated," the girl had added. "Fashion models would kill for them."

Yes, Gail agreed. They were rather attractive.

The boys had taken their fight outside onto the patio, their voices rising louder and louder through the open bedroom window. Two metal chairs scraped across the flagstone among a hail of insults.

She glanced at her new Movado watch, with its black museum dial. She brought it closer to her face and tried to puzzle out the time. Who would invent a watch that didn't have any numbers? Still, it was very attractive. The school bus arrived promptly at seven-forty-five, and it was already nearly seven-thirty. If Jerry didn't stop messing around he'd miss it for sure.

RJ said something to Jerry in a surly voice, which resulted in another round of verbal exchanges. She got up and closed the window. She caught RJ looking up, poised in mid-insult. His face registered surprise that she hadn't hurled any threats at them.

Gail walked into the bathroom and studied her outline in the full-length mirror. She turned this way and that, admiring the way the black mesh chemise lent her figure a provocative curve. The lacy garters and mesh stockings completed the lingerie ensemble nicely. In fact, for the first time in years she actually felt sexy.

The hall clock downstairs chimed seven-thirty. Shoot! She had an eight o'clock closing in Waterbury. She raced back into her bedroom and quickly slid into the silk cherry-red suit she had purchased yesterday at Nordstrom's in Hartford for fifteen hundred dollars. She gasped at the price when she first saw it. But the voice convinced her that it would give her career a boost.

"You need to look professional," it said.

She had to admit that it was stunning, and rushed back into the bathroom for a final look. The voice was right. Besides, it was time for a new image. If only she could do something with her hair. It

shaped her head like a football helmet. In a rare moment of inspira-
tion, she turned toward the sink and rummaged through the medi-
cine cabinet, where Ralph kept a tube of hair gel. She had no idea
how much one was supposed to use, so she squeezed a puddle into the
palm of her hand and smoothed it through her hair. Not bad, she
thought, studying the effect. *Très chic.* She heard the school bus rumble past outside as she walked back into the bedroom.

"Hey! Wait up!" Jerry shouted.

Oh, well . . . he would have to walk, she thought, sliding into
her new Prada crocodile four-inch pumps. Then, grabbing a matching purse, she headed downstairs just as Ralph announced his arrival
home.

"Where in God's name are you going dressed like that?" Ralph asked,
gaping at her as she descended the staircase. He dropped his suitcase
on the floor as his eyes traveled down her camisole, stopping at her
ample cleavage. His face flamed red.

"No wife of mine is leaving this house looking like that," he declared like a man from the Victorian age.

"Like what, Ralph?"

He stammered, "Looking like . . ."

"Attractive?" she said, the corner of her mouth turned up in
what could have been interpreted as either a smirk or a seductive
smile.

Vera raced in, a piece of toast between her teeth as she battled
with the sleeve of an oversize cardigan. "Nice outfit," she mumbled,
crumbs flying out of her mouth. "Oh, hello, Ralph."

"Mother."

"Are you going past the church this morning?" she asked Gail.
"Father Rich wants me to sort through the linens in the sacristy."

"I thought you worked at the rectory," Ralph said, looking
confused.

"Not anymore. Too many strange things are happening over there."

"Strange things? What strange things?"

"The rectory is haunted."

He looked at his mother and then at his wife as though they had both lost their minds. "What's happened while I was away?"

"I can give you a ride if you hurry," Gail told Vera, completely ignoring Ralph's query. She grabbed her car keys. "Oh, and in case you're interested, Ralph, your sons are in the backyard. One has been suspended from school for selling drugs; the other has deliberately missed the bus for the third day in a row. Take care of it."

"Me? What am I supposed to do?"

"You could try being a father," she suggested.

Vera giggled. She really wanted to cheer, "You go girl!" It was about time Gail told him a thing or two.

"What the hell has gotten into everyone?" he raged. "I'm gone for a few days and when I come back all hell's broke loose. Kid's charged with selling drugs. You're dressed like some kind of . . . well, hell, I don't know what you're dressed like. And my mother is talking about a church building being haunted."

"Maybe if you stuck around more you wouldn't be so confused," Gail said sweetly, and walked out the door.

"Marilee, pickup," Jane shouted over the normal early-morning din at the café. She watched to see if her daughter would respond, while taking the next order hanging from the circular metal clipboard and expertly turning the sheriff's three eggs over easy.

"Marilee. Pickup." This time the command held a little more edge.

Marilee, tall, lithe, soft chestnut curls framing a perfectly oval face, a bud of womanhood on the verge of full bloom, moved between the tightly packed tables with the grace of a gazelle. A table filled with the men in her father's crew eyed her tightly cut jeans while keeping a careful watch on Vance, who was seated at the counter with his back to their table, reading the morning paper.

Marilee stomped over to the grill. She had made it very clear several times this morning that she resented being pulled into servitude, as she called it. Just because both of Jane's waitresses hadn't shown up for work shouldn't mean that she had to pitch in. There was no time to change afterward, which meant that she'd have to go to school smelling like grease. Yuck! She added another order to the metal clipboard, then grabbed two plates of home fries and an order of French toast for table number 3, making certain that Jane noticed the scowl. "You'd better tell Alex to get off his butt and clean the table by the window," she groused. "I just saw the town crew pull up."

Jane cracked two more eggs. The grill sizzled. "Alex, let's get with the program this morning," she yelled.

Alex never heard a word. His attention was focused entirely on the display window of his handheld game.

"Earth to Alex," Jane called.

Vance glanced up from his newspaper. "Alex, do as your mother tells you."

"Just a minute. I've almost topped my best score."

"Now," Vance said with a finality that the kids knew would brook no more delays.

Marilee swung around the counter. A smug look covered her face. If she had to sling bacon and eggs to the local behemoths, then Alex should suffer, too. Several home fries slid into a customer's lap as she set the plate in place.

"Hey! I prefer to eat them, not wear them."

"Sorrrrryyy . . ." she said, not at all concerned that her attitude was hardly customer-friendly. In fact, she wished they'd all take offense and go home. Just because her mother wanted to spend her days serving up piles of food didn't mean that she wanted to.

"Marilee . . . pickup . . ."

She noticed a grease stain on her new blouse. Ugh! God, she hated her life. She stomped back to the grill.

Her father grabbed her arm as she rounded the corner. "Change the attitude," he said quietly, never taking his eyes off the paper.

The threat was clear. She could either buck up and do as her mother asked or he would make certain that her life as she knew it was radically altered. "Sorry, Daddy," she said, eyes cast down. She planted a kiss on his cheek. She waited until she saw him smile. *Godddd*, he was such a pushover. But she had to placate him. She couldn't risk any parental interference right now.

Tonight she had a secret date. His name was Tye. He was a nineteen-year-old college freshman whom her parents had forbidden her to see, which is why she had told them that she was meeting with her science lab partner after school and would be late getting home.

The bell above the front door rang. Gail walked in. Marilee could hardly believe her eyes. She had never seen anyone look so lame. What was she thinking, with all that makeup? And her hair. Ugh! Thank God Gail wasn't her mother.

Could that possibly be Gail? Jane wondered as she caught her best friend's reflection in the mirror above the grill.

"Hi, Jane," Gail called out.

"Hi, Gail," she said, waving a spatula above her head.

The café grew very quiet as Gail sauntered up to the counter. "I just stopped in for a quick cup of coffee and a blueberry muffin," she said, hiking up her skirt and sliding onto a stool. She locked her four-inch heels through the metal runner and tried to balance her weight. "I've got a closing. I'm already late, but you said you wanted to talk to me. I'm afraid you're going to have to make it quick."

Jane poured some coffee into a Styrofoam cup. "You're certainly dressed to the nines. These must be some pretty impressive buyers."

"Mom, the bus is here!" Marilee shouted, bouncing plates of food onto the counter and scrambling for her backpack. She bolted through the front door like a prisoner granted parole before Jane could utter a word.

"I'll take over," Vance said, taking a final sip of his coffee and nearly gagging. He had just caught sight of Gail. He looked searchingly at Jane. She shrugged.

"Nice outfit," he told Gail. He grabbed the orders and held them aloft so that everyone could see. "All right, who gets these?"

The town crew raised their hands.

"So? In three words or less, what's up?" Gail asked as Jane slid a mug of coffee across the counter.

Jane couldn't seem to force her eyes away from Gail's hairdo.

"Jane?"

"Sorry, your new image kind of threw me."

"You like the suit? Kay Unger. I bought it at Nordstrom's. And look at this." She pushed up her sleeve. "Movado. I've always wanted one. What do you think?"

Jane was really confused. They had just spoken last week about the dire state of Gail's finances. In fact, Gail had confided that they might have to take out a second mortgage on the house just to cover RJ's legal fees. So what had changed? Had she found out about Ralph's affair and decided to try and win him back with a makeover? If that was true, poor Gail. The bum wasn't worth it. Kay Sprage had called Jane earlier in the week for advice after spying Ralph and his lady friend in Boston.

"You've known her much longer than I have," Kay had said over her cell phone en route to one appointment in a day filled with celebrity meetings. "Is she the type that would want to know, or does she subscribe to the belief that ignorance is bliss?"

Jane had suggested that they wait. Gail had enough on her plate at the moment, she said. There was RJ's mess at school. And Vera's return, not that her mother-in-law was a bother. The two women enjoyed each other's company. Still, a certain amount of privacy was bound to be lost with Vera in the house. On top of all that, things at the office had slowed to a crawl.

Jane studied her friend now. Gail looked more as if she were dressed for a costume party than for the office, but who was she to judge? Suddenly she realized that Gail was still waiting for a response. "I think the watch is great," she said. "In fact, I think this whole new look is . . . great. It suits you."

Gail's face lit up with genuine delight. She reached over and gave Jane a hug. "Thanks, girlfriend. I think so, too." She twisted her wrist one way then the other, admiring the watch. "Ralph was a little put off by my new look."

At the mention of Ralph's name, Jane found herself treading carefully as she slid Gail's coffee and muffin into a white paper bag bearing the Sit and Sip logo. "Oh?" she said.

"Throw in a couple of extra jellies, will you? He thinks things have gone to hell in a handbasket while he was away."

"Maybe he should spend more time at home," Jane said hotly in defense of her friend. How she wished she could add "instead of bedding down his mistress."

"That's exactly what I told him."

"Good for you."

"Look at the time. I really do have to fly. So what was it you wanted to tell me?" She carefully dismounted the stool and fished inside her purse for some change. When Jane opened the café, all of her friends made it a steadfast rule that *nothing* was ever to be given away free of charge.

"Father Rich wants us all to meet at the rectory tonight. He's saying a special Mass."

"What for?"

"It's a blessing. On the rectory," she said simply. There was no sense in going into the details now. "We're meeting a little before seven. Kay's driving up from the city. I spoke with her last night. She said she'd meet you at your house and pick you up on her way into town."

"Sounds fine," Gail said. "I'll call her later and confirm. See you later." She grabbed her take-out order and sailed toward the front door.

Jane watched her go, suddenly overwhelmed with a sense of foreboding.

"Two more orders of eggs over easy," Vance said, handing her the slip. "Jane? You okay?"

"Fine," she said, cracking open an egg. She would think more about Gail's problems later. Right now she had a business to run. "Thanks for helping out."

"No problem. We're a team. Next time one of my guys calls in sick, you'll lend a hand digging ditches, right?"

She laughed, playfully giving him a punch in the ribs.

"Can you handle this all by yourself?"

"Sure. Things slow down now until lunch, and by then I'll have pulled someone off the street to help."

"All right, I'll see you later," he said, planting a wet kiss on her cheek and heading out.

Jane went back to work and began to scrape down the grill, clearing blackened bits of burned potatoes. Her thoughts went back to Gail. Something wasn't right. Granted, she could have found out about Ralph's affair, which would account for the strange vibes Jane was picking up, but there was something else—something strangely familiar and chilling.

What had Gail really encountered that night down in the rectory's basement? Had she inadvertently tapped into the presence that had sent three priests running in fear and had Father Rich so concerned that he was performing a special Mass in hopes of vanquishing it? It was a frightening prospect.

There was one way to find out, although it had been years since she had allowed herself to go there. The restaurant was empty, and customers seldom dropped by at this time of the morning. It would only take a few moments.

She made certain everything was in order, then walked back into the kitchen and leaned heavily against the door. Closing her eyes, she slowly allowed her mind to drift into that place of special knowing. She focused on Gail until she could see her image clearly. Gail was driving to work. The familiar countryside flashed by outside the car windows. A radio played softly. She caught snatches of a country-and-western song. Gail leaned forward to turn up the volume just as a black mist began to rise, blocking out all light and encasing her in a dark vortex.

Jane's eyes snapped open. No . . . it couldn't be.

twelve

It was six-fifteen by the time Gail finished her last phone call of the day. She hurriedly tidied up her desk. Kay was due at her house in less than thirty minutes. She had called earlier from New York and they had confirmed arrangements to meet at Gail's house.

Gail hoped there would be time for her to change. What had she been thinking when she dressed this morning? Her two employees had been eyeing her strangely all day. Maybe she was having a mild nervous breakdown. Isn't that what people do when they've reached the end of their tether? RJ's lawyer had called earlier, demanding a $2,500 retainer. They'd definitely have to take out a second mortgage on their home to cover the expenses—no doubt about it. If only Ralph would ask for a raise. Why was he so reluctant? There couldn't be anyone in the company who worked harder than her husband. My God, he traveled three weeks out of the month.

Thoughts of Ralph made her hurry. She could picture him now, reading his newspaper and scowling at the clock, wondering where she was and why dinner wasn't on the table.

"*Let him wait,*" the voice intoned.

What was wrong with her? She had never thought things like this before. She adored Ralph and at times still couldn't believe that he was her husband. She saw the way other women looked at him whenever they were together. Ralph was an incredibly sexy man in a rumpled kind of way. He had a great smile and a wry sense of humor that always caught her off guard, making her laugh out loud. Aside from the fact that he traveled too much, was a terrible father, and often treated her like a maid, he was a great guy. At least that's what she had always thought until now. So what had changed her perceptions?

Where were those darn shoes? She had kicked them off under the desk. How did Kay walk on those things? She groped blindly beneath the desk. The phone rang just as she felt the tip of a heel. She reached for the receiver.

"Where the hell are you?" Ralph exploded. "That friend of yours Kay is here. She said you're going out to Mass over at the rectory. Who goes to Mass at night anyway?"

"Father Rich—" she tried to explain, slipping her feet into the shoes.

"—and what about dinner?"

From out of nowhere, anger ripped through her voice like a power surge. "What about it?"

"What did you say?"

"You've got two hands. Make something."

She slammed down the receiver, thinking, Boy that felt good. So good, in fact, that she was completely unaware that she had put the Pradas on the wrong feet.

Kay sat on the kitchen stool watching a microcosm of American domesticity and felt a wave of gratitude that she had managed to stay unattached.

Ralph was making a pretense of searching for something for dinner. RJ wandered up and down the room, a cell phone pinned to his ear like an earring. The other boy (What was his name? She could never remember) was at least making an attempt at doing his home-work against the senseless roar of MTV.

"Put that down!" Ralph bellowed, slamming a cabinet door. He was not having a good day. "Can't hear myself think."

For the umpteenth time, she wondered how Gail put up with all of this. The kids were serial killers in the making; the husband had all the charm of Saddam Hussein; plus she was expected to run a full-time business and a house without any household help.

Last Christmas the hookers had played Secret Santa. Kay had drawn Gail's name. Her gift had been a cleaning service, paid in full for an entire year. Not that it did much good, she thought, looking around. The place still looked as if it was under siege. Sweatshirts, coats, and other grungy, smelly attire were thrown over the back of the couch. Candy wrappers and empty cereal boxes cluttered up counters and tables. And the bathroom . . .

Kay sipped wine from a goblet she had found in the dish rack and rewashed herself. Over the rim of her glass she watched Ralph star-ing into the phone's receiver as though he couldn't believe what he had just heard. Kay suppressed a smile. I wonder if Gail has finally told him where to shove it, she thought wryly.

Of course, this was highly unlikely. From what she'd seen, Gail would take anything this family dished out. For some unfathomable reason, she loved this motley crew. She was heavily into the "sanc-tity of the family," which probably had something to do with her par-ents' divorce. Her father had moved out of state shortly afterward and she seldom saw him.

She continued to watch Ralph, knowing her stares would un-nerve him. He turned away and assumed the wounded, martyred look of a saint assigned penance for another's sin. He had managed to find a can of Campbell's Tomato and Rice soup and was now read-ing the can.

You idiot, she thought. Just pour it into a pot, add a can of water, and heat it up. Even a child could do it. Well, there you had it. First he needed the IQ of a child. Meanwhile, he was acting as though it required an instructional video.

"Never done this before," he explained, giving her that "I'm a mariner lost at sea and need help" look.

It's not working on me, buddy, she thought. She slipped off the stool and headed toward the fridge. Ralph stepped aside with an air of expectancy, like a runner ready to pass the baton, which in this case was a red-and-white can of soup. She ignored him—walked right past and experienced a delicious sense of accomplishment, feeling his penetrating stare filled with equal parts disappointment and rage.

She pulled open the fridge door and reached for a bottle of cheap Pinot Grigio. She really did have to send Gail a case of the white Bordeaux she'd bought in Provence. Ralph was still poring over the soup label as she refilled her glass. What in God's name did Gail see in this clown? Sure, the guy had tight buns and great pecs and was reasonably handsome, but Kay found his arrogance—that "I'm God's gift to women" sort of thing—a massive turnoff. Apparently, however, some women found it attractive. Hence the small harem of poor, misguided females who had been uncovered by the private investigator she had hired at a cost of five hundred dollars an hour to trail the SOB. Business trips, my foot!

If looks could kill, the one he had just shot her would have been fatal. Apparently, Ralph wasn't accustomed to being ignored. He had seriously expected her to come to his rescue. Fat chance! Back to the stool and more open observation. She was really getting on his nerves. It was wonderful.

From the start of her and Gail's friendship, Ralph had made no secret of how he felt about Kay. From their infamous dinner, she had pegged him as a self-centered male chauvinist and, in accordance with that title, had afforded him the same courtesy she did all such specimens: she dismissed him. But men like Ralph didn't like to be ignored. They were threatened by women they couldn't dominate.

In response, they became rude, obnoxious boors. That's the way to win us over, Kay thought. Show us how very right we are.

Ralph was trying hard to ignore her with as much distaste as he could muster. She didn't take offense. In fact, she rather enjoyed watching a primate at work. First he made a big deal over searching for a pot: he exhaled loudly, pulled open cabinet doors and slammed them shut, ransacked the contents. The pots were hung over the center island. He finally looked up. A light went on. He knew she was watching him. His face flushed red.

"You staying for supper?" he asked, his voice dripping with sarcasm as he tried to unhook a pot handle. Instead of lifting it up, he tried to shake it loose. Pots banged against each other. The rack swayed as though it were caught in a strong wind. Several utensils clattered onto the granite countertop along with the pot.

"No, I don't think so," she said, trying hard to keep a straight face. Yet the stifled laughter hung in the air like a vapor. Ralph got a whiff and duly registered the affront. His eyes turned cold. He slammed the pot down on the stove.

Temper . . . temper . . . She liked pissing him off. She especially liked pissing him off now that she knew he was cheating on her friend. She drained half the glass of wine in one slug. If only she could let Gail in on the secret. She had thought about what Jane said—Gail already had enough to deal with—and had come up with a much better plan.

"Tell your brother to get in here and help set the table," Ralph barked at Jerry. "And turn off that goddamned TV."

Something in his father's voice told the teenager he had better obey. Jerry got up and turned off the set, then left the room in search of his brother.

The room grew strangely quiet. The refrigerator motor rumbled on.

"So, Ralph . . . how was Boston?"

His head jerked around as though he had just been doused with a cold glass of water.

"Boston?"

"It's a great time of year for a trip to Boston. Great scenery. Wonderful food. How did you like your meal at the Parker? I thought the lamb was a little dry that day. What about you and your . . . er . . . friend?"

He chuckled and turned up the jet under the soup. "I think you'd better lay off the wine. That wasn't me you saw, toots."

Toots? Could you be any more annoying? Kay, however, was a master at maintaining her cool when dealing with Neanderthals. "Reaaaallly?"

A dark cloud crossed his face. Stormy weather ahead, she mused. This was going to be fun.

"I don't know what the hell you're up to, but I really don't have time to listen to it, so why don't you take your classy ass out of my kitchen and wait for Gail in some other part of the house, like on the front porch, while I make dinner?"

"Is that what you call dinner? A can of soup? Interesting."

He gave the pot a stir and shook his head, mumbling under his breath. "Gail can sure pick 'em."

"And so, apparently, can you. But I can't say much for your taste. Your companion—the one you were rubbing up against like a cat on a scratching post—she seemed like a cheap set of goods."

Bingo! The expression on his face was priceless. She could tell by the look in his eyes that he was searching for a plausible explanation.

"Oh . . . that?" He turned his back on her and took three bowls out of the cabinet. "I had a deal I had been working on for a couple months, and the company finally decided to give it the okay. I didn't want to lose the deal, so I flew in. I was supposed to meet with the company president. He couldn't make it. The woman was his secretary. She brought the papers over."

"I see. Which called for a celebration, right?"

"Right," he said a little too quickly.

"Funny . . ."

"What's that?"

"You never told Gail about this side trip."

"I don't tell her everything that happens at work." He was growing defensive again.

"Wasn't that the day RJ got kicked out of school? Yes, I believe it was. Dealing drugs is a pretty serious charge. I know if my son had just been arrested I would have liked to be notified. You carry a cell phone, right?"

"What's this? Some kind of shakedown?" He smiled, trying to make light of it, only Kay wasn't laughing.

"Do you?"

"Do I what?"

"Carry a cell phone?"

"Yeah, I carry one."

"Don't you check your voice mail? Gail was frantic. She called me at work. I offered to drive down, but she said she'd keep trying to reach you. I know she left several messages. Why wouldn't you return her calls?"

"What are you, Dick Tracy? I don't have to answer to you. You're not my wife."

"Could it be you didn't want to be disturbed? Maybe Sandy— that's her name, right?"

His eyes filled with uncertainty.

"Yes, I remember the private eye I hired to tail you said her name was definitely Sandy. Oh, and the one in North Carolina—her name is Carol. Then there's always good old dependable Joanna here in the main office. I suppose you keep her around in case you need a little quickie while Gail's busy at the office."

She met his steely gaze, thinking that if looks could kill she was dead meat. His nostrils were flaring. He looked like a bull about to charge, only she was an expert with a red cape.

"Business trips my foot, you deadbeat. You are some piece of work," she concluded, taking another sip of wine.

Gravel crunched outside. Headlights flashed across the kitchen wall. Gail was home. She beeped three times. Ralph glared at Kay. He was trapped and he knew it.

"I can't believe you hired a private eye to tail me."

"You'd be surprised what they can uncover in a short period of time," she told him. "Like a person's credit-card bills. The ones they have sent to a secret P.O. box. You know, until now I never understood how you could work so many long hours and make so little money. All that time spent away from home. Those bills explained a lot. Three-hundred-dollar dinners for two. Jewelry. You even took one of your mistresses on a cruise to the Bahamas, you slimeball."

Kay causally slipped into her silk jacket and adjusted the collar and sleeves. "Gail is a dear friend. I hate how you've dumped on her. You've been using her as a babysitter and housemaid while you flit from one affair to another having a grand old time."

He walked around the counter to face her. "What are you going to do? If you tell her it will kill her."

She laughed in his face. "You really have the most exaggerated opinion of yourself of any man I've ever met. No, Ralph, she won't die. She'll be hurt, but she'll rebound. In case you haven't noticed, she's made of pretty strong stuff. She'd have to be to put up with all this and not complain."

"So what are you going to do—tell her tonight? If so, you'd better let me know so I can be out of here when she gets back." He looked nervously over his shoulder toward the driveway.

"That's exactly what I'd expect from you. Coward." Kay could see him planning it all out. He'd call one of his ubiquitous girlfriends and play on her sympathy. She would invite him to stay with her while he sorted things out at home. Oh, no, he didn't! She went in for the kill. "If you leave, you'll have to take your sons with you. After all, they are *your* children, not Gail's."

Kay watched with amusement as Ralph assimilated this newest threat. A girlfriend might take in a man who had been thrown out on the street by his wife, but taking in a man with two teenage boys was a whole other ball of wax.

"What if I decided not to tell Gail?" Kay said, playing with the band of her Cartier watch.

"Why would you do that?" he asked warily.

"Because I want Gail to be happy, and for some unfathomable reason she feels marriage to you fills that bill. Look, I'm willing to leave you with just a warning. This time," she amended, grabbing her purse as the pot of soup boiled over.

"But remember, I'll be watching you. And if you ever cheat on her again, I will make it my business to see that she gets the best divorce lawyer money can buy, which means she'll get the house and every last dime you ever make for the rest of your miserable life."

Neither of them had heard Gail slip into the mudroom that was connected to the kitchen by way of the garage. She had come in search of a more comfortable pair of shoes. She slipped quietly out the back door as Kay turned to leave.

"Oh, and one more thing," Kay said. "Of course, you'll get sole custody of the kids."

Rich glanced out the tall windows in the study. The hookers had arrived. Car doors slammed, and the women's voices rose like wind chimes.

God, he hoped this worked. His didn't want to consider what must be done next if it didn't. Once again, his thoughts returned to that strange night at the villa in Rome. Malachi was plumped up against a bank of pillows, his wrists heavily bandaged. The doctor had just left. He was amazed that the priest hadn't bled to death and insisted that he be hospitalized. Malachi refused and then, with great effort, waved a hand dismissing everyone from his bedroom. Everyone, that was, except Rich.

Malachi motioned toward a chair. "Pull that up closer to the bed," he said. His voice was thick with exhaustion, and Rich could sense that the effort to speak was draining what remained of his strength.

"Perhaps it would be better if we waited until you've had time to recuperate," Rich said.

Malachi's face grew tight with impatience. "No. What I need to say must be said tonight, and you need to hear it."

"All right. If you insist."

"Only once every century does the Church see someone with your gift emerge."

"Gift? What gift?"

"I saw it displayed in there." He nodded toward the room at the end of the hall. "You gave the command to one of the most powerful entities I have ever encountered. I've conducted hundreds of exorcisms over the last forty years. Twice, I was this close . . ." He pinched his fingers together. The movement cost him dearly, and he winced in pain. ". . . to losing my life. The entity that held that child captive upstairs was more powerful than all of them combined. Yet as soon as you gave the command to be vanquished, it obeyed. It responded because it had encountered a channel for God's power far superior to itself."

He collapsed heavily against the pillows. "You have received a divine weapon that has been fashioned for this day and age, a time when evil is growing at an unprecedented rate," he went on. "If ever the world was in need of your skills, it's now. Don't turn your back on the gift that you've been given. The world is in need of it now more than ever before."

The curtain that separates memory from the present closed. He watched the women approach the house with an overwhelming sense of predestination overlaid with trepidation.

Why him? Why now? There was absolutely nothing in his past that had prepared him for this task. He was a scholar, a teacher, not some archaic exorcist—a role almost forgotten in today's society. It had gone the way of the Latin Mass and crying statues and apparitions. Although the modern Church acknowledged that evil existed, it leaned more toward reasoning and looked to psychology for answers. Devils and demons had gone the way of other superstitions and old wives' tales. Still, he could not dismiss what he had experienced.

He heard the front door open and the women call out his name. He had left the front gates open. "I'm in the library," he answered.

What if he was wrong? What if he should never have included them in this? But something deep in his soul knew that they were an integral part of this transition—a transition that he felt was not just for him but for them as well. He didn't quite understand how or why, but somehow they were all caught up in this together.

thirteen

It was nearing seven o'clock and Vance still wasn't home. Jane pushed aside the curtains and stared out the kitchen window. Darkness hung like a shroud, obscuring even the two-story, mammoth barn Vance used to store his equipment only twenty feet away. Of all the nights for him to be late, she thought, chewing her lip. He had warned her this morning that it might happen.

"It looks like I might have to work some overtime tonight," he said, bagging his lunch. "There's an early frost predicted this weekend and the project manager on that job we're working on over in Bristol wants to pour the foundations tomorrow morning, which means the excavating has to be completed today."

"But Father Rich is saying Mass at the rectory tonight," she reminded him.

"Take the kids with you," he suggested.

"I can't." She couldn't risk exposing her children to whatever roamed the halls of St. Francis Xavier's rectory.

Vance was staring at her, expecting an explanation. She realized that for the first time in their marriage she was going to have to lie to him.

"It's a special Mass," she said. "It might go long. You know how restless the kids can get."

"Then have Marilee watch Alex until I get home," he told her, planting a quick kiss on her cheek before bustling out the door.

The deception had haunted her the rest of the day.

Her breath sent billows of fog against the window as she strained to make out any hint of headlights coming down the road. Marilee had been due home an hour ago. She had told Jane that she and her lab partner had to stay after school to work on a science project, and that when they were finished the girl's mother would drive her home. Marilee had promised to be home by six-thirty. She knew that Jane had to leave.

She released the curtain, which fell back into place with a soft whoosh, grabbed a sponge, and began wiping the counters, which she had cleaned only a few minutes ago. This was all her fault. She had been distracted when Marilee rolled off the details this morning. She had been on the phone with Father Rich, making plans for this evening. Why hadn't she made Marilee write everything down? Her mind seemed in a fog lately. What was the name of the lab partner— Ericka? Or was it Katrin? She couldn't remember. Some parent she was.

She reached for the kitchen wall phone and punched in Marilee's cell-phone number. It rang half a dozen times before dumping her into voice mail. "Darn her!" Jane said, slamming the phone hard on the counter. A piece of plastic broke off and went sailing across the kitchen floor. "Oh, great!" She found it wedged beneath the front of the dishwasher.

Wait until she got home, Jane fumed silently. Marilee had really crossed the line this time. All privileges, including her phone, would be suspended. That should make her think twice before pulling something like this again. It wasn't as if she didn't know how important tonight's Mass was to Jane. They had discussed it at the dinner table last night. Marilee was doing this deliberately. Jane knew it. It was payback for the incident the other night involving that horrible boy, Tye. Good God, where did she find him? Jane wondered.

They had met the infamous Tye for the first time last week. Vance had been reading the sports section in the *Bend Oaks Gazette*, and Jane was spending a rare free moment hooking a small rug for the front door when a car entered their driveway with the radio blaring and the horn blasting.

"Who the heck is that?" Vance asked Jane, setting aside the paper and dashing to the front window. When it came to his daughter, he was like a guard dog in his wariness of strangers.

"It's my date," Marilee called out, sailing past them both and out the front door. "Don't wait up."

"Date? What date?" Vance said in disbelief. "Who is this kid? Do you know him?"

"No," Jane said, quick on her daughter's heels. "And if she's not introducing us there must be something about him that she knows we won't approve of."

The couple barreled outside, Vance shouting over the din at Marilee to wait a minute before getting into the car.

"Dad . . . I'm going to be late," she whined.

"I sincerely hope that your date's father is driving that van or you're in serious trouble, young lady," Vance said. "Anyone old enough to drive is too old for you to date. You know that. We've had this discussion before." He headed straight for the driver's side of the van.

"Daddy! Don't!" she called after him, her voice tight with panic. He rapped on the window.

The window eased down, revealing a boy several years older than his daughter with massive tattoos and a nose ring. "Hey, man, what's up?" the youth said, his eyes hidden behind a pair of dark sunglasses.

Vance cut to the chase. "How old are you?"

"Nineteen."

"Now, that's a problem. My daughter is only fourteen."

"No kidding? She told me she was seventeen," he said, smiling as though it was a great joke.

"Marilee!" Jane said, pinching her daughter's arm.

"Ouch!" She jerked her arm away. "I hate you! I hate you both!" she screamed, and ran into the house.

Vance leaned in a little closer. "I don't ever want to see you hanging around my daughter again, got it?"

"What are you, like, the Nazi father?" he said, laughing at his own cleverness.

Vance grabbed his nose ring.

"Ouch!" he cried, arching his head.

"If you ever come near her again, I promise that I will hunt you down and rip this thing out of your nose. Got it?"

"Yeah, man, I got it," he said, all bravado suddenly vaporized.

"Now, get out of here before I call the cops," Vance said.

Tye mumbled something under his breath, then threw the van in reverse. Tires squealed as he slammed out of the driveway. He paused by the road long enough to align Vance in his sights, then gave him the finger.

Vance charged down the driveway, but the boy sped away, burning rubber.

"I'm never talking to either of you again as long as I live! You treat me like I'm a child," Marilee shouted from her bedroom as Vance and Jane stepped inside.

Since then, both parents had become the enemy.

Alex looked up from his bowl of Froot Loops.

"Mom, go to your meeting. I'll be all right by myself," he said, shoveling spoonfuls of cereal and milk into his mouth.

Jane felt her heart melt. He was growing up so quickly. The chubby toddler she once balanced on her hip had been replaced by a young boy who was already several inches taller than she and whose childhood features were fast giving way to a rugged handsomeness. He looked so much like his dad. It was just a matter of time before girls began calling.

"Are you sure you don't mind staying here alone?"

"*Mommmm* . . ." Alex moaned, aiming the remote at the DVD player. *The Incredibles* sprang to life.

"All right, I'm going," she told him. "You have my cell number if you need me, and in an emergency there's Mrs. Whitehouse next door."

She could tell he was only half listening. She ran over and quickly gave him a kiss on the head, then grabbed her car keys off the counter.

"Have your sister call me the minute she gets home," she said.

Alex looked up with unconcealed glee. "She's really in trouble this time, isn't she?"

Jane rushed across town, her anger toward Marilee quickly replaced by fears for her friends. She hoped Father Rich's plan worked.

She was especially concerned for Gail. What she sensed this morning had deeply troubled her. She had tried to contact Gail several times throughout the day but was told by the receptionist that Gail was out with clients. She'd left a message requesting that Gail call her back. But Gail never returned her call, which was so unlike her. One of Gail's pet peeves was people who never returned phone calls.

Jane looked out over the landscape, which was already shrouded in inky blackness. Evil drew its powers from darkness, which made the Mass that was being held tonight at the rectory even more dangerous. But Father Rich said it was imperative that the service be conducted when the paranormal activities were most active. She just hoped that those gathered there tonight would be safe.

Jane came to a shortcut the locals used to circumvent the more heavily traveled Route 202. It was an old dirt road that ran through a section of the state forest. She had no qualms about using the road during the day, but at night it turned into a dark and lonely stretch of highway. She slowed the car, hesitating. It would cut the distance between here and the rectory in half—time that she could use to discuss her concerns and what she had detected about Gail with Father Rich.

She flicked on her directional signal and began the lonely trek. The high beams cut a narrow tunnel through the darkness. On the shoulder of the road, she spied an occasional pair of eyes. Deer and coyotes roamed freely through these woods. So did bears and bobcats. None of that bothered her, however. She loved all kinds of wildlife. Still, it was a little eerie seeing specks of light stare out from behind the bushes.

Outside, the wind picked up. Branches swung in the breeze, casting ghoulish shadows across the road. Suddenly every horror film she had ever seen flooded her imagination. Men with hooked arms, trying to pry their way in. Ghouls with plastic masks and manic eyes wielding chain saws. The road farther up ahead and the woods on either side were cast in deep shadow. Anything could be hiding out there.

The corner of her headlights caught a large section of the road that had been washed out by the summer rains. She slowed to a crawl and eased the vehicle around it. Last thing she needed was to end up in a ditch. So much for saving some time.

The interior of the car had turned chilly. She used her left hand to check the electric window panel. Everything was closed. She flicked on the heater, heard the fan engage, and waited for the accustomed stream of hot air to take off the chill. That was one thing she liked about her SUV. It never took long to heat up—a real plus in the dead of winter. But for some reason nothing was happening. In fact, it was getting colder. She shoved the temperature gauge all the way over to high and ran her hands over the vents. That was peculiar. Hot air was flowing freely. Then why wasn't the car heating up?

Oh, well. She'd be at the rectory soon enough, but she made a mental note to call the service station first thing in the morning. Winter was only a few months away—whatever was wrong needed fixing. Her thoughts were still focused on the heat problem when she got the strangest sensation that she was no longer alone. A chill, which had nothing to do with the temperature, ran up her spine. She kept her eyes locked on the road up ahead, deliberately avoiding the rearview mirror, afraid of what she might see.

All right. You have to get a grip, she cautioned herself. Her nerves were a little on edge, that was all. Hadn't she checked the backseat before getting in, as she always did? Vance was always making fun of her for it. "Afraid that a thrasher might be hiding in the backseat," he teased.

But it wasn't what could be seen with the human eye that now filled her with dread. Gripping the steering wheel tightly, as though it could somehow ground her, she forced herself to turn around. The backseat was empty. She sighed with relief. I really have to cut back on my coffee consumption, she thought.

Streetlights were visible in the distance. In a matter of minutes, she would come to the main road. Well, one thing was certain. She was never going to take this shortcut again at night. Feeling almost light-headed with relief, she glanced at the rearview mirror and gasped.

A thick black mass was filling the backseat. She watched in frozen terror as it began to take shape. A face was forming, dark and sinister, with eyes like red orbs that pulsated in the darkness. Her first thought was to jam on the brakes, jump out, and run. But what if there were even more horrible creatures lying in wait, ready to drag her into the heavy forest? But if she stayed . . . ?

A cold breath, devoid of all life, blew against the nape of her neck. She could feel her mind beginning to shut down. It was only a matter of seconds before it overtook her. Her children's faces swam before her. No . . . she would not let this thing win. Then she remembered that she had some holy water in her purse. She grabbed the purse and gave it a good shake. Her wallet, wads of crumpled tissue, small blue envelopes of NutraSweet, and hair clips all went flying.

A hand reached across the back of her seat and rested on her shoulder. She screamed and floored the accelerator. The SUV leaped forward. Her right hand searched blindly for the holy water. Finally, she felt something smooth and cold: the vial. She pulled it free and tore off the cap with her teeth.

"Be gone in the name of Jesus," she intoned, throwing its contents over her shoulder. It was the last thing she remembered before the air bag exploded as the SUV crashed into a lamppost.

"Where is Jane?" Kay whispered as the group of women gathered to begin the Mass.

They were assembled in the library. The table they normally used for rug hooking had been turned into a makeshift altar and a row of metal folding chairs was lined up in front.

Rose shrugged. "Maybe something came up at home."

Kay doubted that anything "at home" could have kept Jane away. This was too important. And not for one moment did she buy into the notion that the Mass was being said to bless the rectory. What kind of fool did they take her for? She might be the least religious person among them, but it didn't take a saint to know that something was going on inside this house and this Mass was being said in response to it. She knew that it was sometimes used to vanquish evil spirits.

Evil spirits . . . listen to me, she thought. Really! Still, she had to admit that there were a lot of unexplained events that had recently taken place in the rectory. Three priests had left without a word to anyone and refused to return. Then there was that incident the other night. It was like coming upon a scene from a horror movie. Windows and doors sealed shut. Her friends, whom she considered pretty levelheaded, screaming as if they were being chased by the Devil himself. And Gail . . . What had happened down in the basement?

She glanced over at Gail now. Something was different about her since that night, and it wasn't just her new fashion sense. She studied Father Rich, seated behind the altar. For a well-educated and seemingly erudite man, he certainly was behaving strangely. She remembered the way he reacted when he learned that the hookers had changed their meeting place to the rectory. Something akin to fear had entered his eyes. And what about that madcap race through the countryside? It was as if he had known that what they encountered would take place. Could St. Francis Xavier's new pastor be experiencing the same paranormal activities that had chased his predecessors away? she wondered.

Paranormal? Evil spirits? Bah! Humbug. She didn't believe in that sort of thing. Granted, the house was a little dark and filled with museumlike furniture—but haunted? She glanced at Gail again. Maybe she had found out about Ralph. That would account for her sudden un-Gail-like behavior. Maybe Jane knew what was going on. She checked her watch. Where was she?

"Something must have happened to detain Jane," Father Rich said as he stood up. "I think we'd better not wait any longer. Let us begin. In the name of the Father, the Son, and the Holy Ghost . . ."

Kay hadn't attended a Mass since she was a child, when it was recited in Latin. She was surprised to see Myla walk up to the lectern and begin the readings. Much, apparently, had changed since then.

"A reading from the Second Book of Chronicles," Myla said, clearing her throat. "Lord, there is no one like you to help the powerless against the mighty—"

BOOM! BOOM! BOOM! Something was hammering hard against the front door.

"Should someone get that?" Myla asked.

"Ignore it," Father Rich said.

"What if it's Jane?"

"It's not. Continue."

Myla looked at the others for some kind of explanation. Rose shrugged. She went back to the readings.

"Help us, O Lord our God, for we rely on you, and in your name we have come against this vast army. O Lord, you are our God: do not let evil prevail against you—"

BANG! BANG! BANG!

This time the noise emanated from inside the walls and shook the room.

"What in heaven's name—?" Myla said, looking out into the library.

"Probably air in the heating system," Vera offered.

"Maybe so, but what's that over there," Rose said, pointing to an area behind the altar where letters were forming.

"L E A V E"

All right, this was spooky, Kay thought. Still unwilling to accept the paranormal, however, she frantically searched for a plausible explanation. She was busy scouring her memory for some scientific reason behind what she was seeing when a rumble like the sound of an approaching train erupted from beneath the floorboards. Planks buckled. The metal chairs they were sitting on began to move.

The women got up and ran toward the altar for safety. Just as they reached Father Rich, the candlesticks burning on either side of the altar went out. An eerie silence followed. Everyone froze.

"Why do I get the feeling that we're waiting for the other shoe to drop?" Rose said.

The chalice filled with wine tipped over with a thud. The group watched in silence as it covered the floor. A blood-red stain seeped into the white linen altar cloth.

"What is going on here?" Rose asked, her voice a pitch higher than normal.

"That's what I'd like to know," Kay said.

"Well, one thing is for sure," Vera said. "I'm pretty certain it hasn't got anything to do with the pipes."

Like a concert maestro, an invisible hand swept across the room, commanding the symphony to continue. The walls shook with a deafening beat. Across the room, floorboards lifted and fell like piano keys. Meanwhile, the set of leather chairs flanking the fireplace began an eerie dance.

"I think we'd better get out of here," Vera offered sagely.

"I'm with you," Kay said, heading for the door. "I'm beginning to feel like I'm in a Harry Potter movie. The next thing you know, we'll have floating pumpkins and enchanted ceilings."

"Vera's right. You'd better get out," Father Rich told them.

Everyone made a mad dash for the door as books flew off the shelves like missiles. Something was being scraped across the floor. Kay turned to see the heavy damask sofa, which only moments ago had sat beneath the front windows, traveling across the room on its own.

"Watch out!" she screamed, pushing Myla out of its path.

It landed with a thud, wedging itself inside the archway and blocking their exit.

"Oh, not again . . ." Myla moaned. "We're trapped."

Rich rushed in front of the women and tried to move the heavy couch, but it wouldn't budge.

"You're going to have to climb over it," he instructed them.

Meanwhile, the pounding grew louder, as though a monster of mythic proportions were trying to break free from inside the walls. The wall sconces began to rotate, shooting sparks like Fourth of July fireworks out into the room.

"I think we'd better hurry," Kay said. "You go first, Myla."

"Rose, get on the other side and help her over," Rich directed.

Rose hopped over in one fluid movement. Her ample bosom threatened to spill out of her low-cut blouse, and she made some hasty adjustments before offering Myla her hand.

"Come on. Hurry," she urged.

But Myla wasn't moving. She studied first the couch and then her skirt.

Vera immediately sized up the problem. In order for Myla to climb over the sofa, she would have to hike up her skirt. "Oh, for Pete's sake, Myla," she admonished. "This is no time for modesty."

Another earthshaking bang vibrated across the room. That was all the prodding Myla needed. She pulled up her skirt, exposing a pair of leopard-spotted underwear, and scooted over the sofa. Rose helped her safely into the foyer.

Only Kay and Rich remained.

"You go first," he told her.

"Wait. Where's Gail?" Kay asked. She had lost track of her during all the chaos. Then she spied her standing beneath the heavy bronze chandelier in the center of the room. It swayed as though it were caught in a strong wind. Her eyes traveled toward the ceiling. The chain was slowly detaching itself from the mounting. Any minute now, it would come crashing down. She gasped.

Rich flew across the room, grabbed Gail by the shoulders, and hurled her out of the way seconds before the chandelier crashed to the floor in an explosion of metal and glass, littering the room like confetti.

He and Gail had slid across the polished floor, landing next to the fireplace.

Kay raced over. "Gail? Are you all right?"

There was no response. Kay bent down. Gail's eyes were closed and a bright trail of blood was oozing through her hairline.

fourteen

The ambulance made its way through the darkened streets under a steady blare of sirens. Folks along the route pried themselves out of their comfortable after-supper chairs to press their noses up against their front windows and wonder what poor soul had been singled out by fate. They wouldn't have long to wonder. Bend Oaks averaged only two emergency calls a month (much to the chagrin of the local EMTs, who had just purchased a new state-of-the-art rig), so whoever was being rushed to the hospital tonight would be headline news by morning.

Rich sat beside the stretcher with Vera, who held her daughter-in-law's hand tenaciously.

"She's going to be all right, isn't she?" she asked the emergency medical technician, her face tight with strain.

"Charlotte Hungerford Hospital is one of the best in the state. She'll be in good hands," he assured her.

The sirens stopped just outside the hospital zone. A few more turns and the vehicle's backup buzzer sounded as the driver maneuvered the three-ton rig into an empty bay. Seconds later, the back door was thrust open by two hospital attendants dressed in Pepsi-blue scrubs. With practiced efficiency, they rolled out the stretcher, snapped the legs into position, and whisked Gail through the double doors.

"Go in with her," Rich told Vera. "I'll wait here for the others."

Myla, Rose, and Kay had stayed behind to fill out the sheriff's report.

The air, cold and damp like a sodden sponge, settled along his shoulders, but he was oblivious to the discomfort. His mind was fixed on what had taken place at the rectory. The ritual of the Mass was one of the most powerful forms of deliverance in cases where satanic forces were suspected of being at play. Then why hadn't it worked? Since that night in Rome, he had done a lot of reading on cases of possession and demonic infestation, but the power behind tonight's display was unlike anything he had studied.

Since his arrival, it seemed to have stepped up its malevolence. At night, the house was filled with strange whisperings and footsteps walking overhead and along the corridors, accompanied by a crypt-like cold that flooded the rooms. He had taken to reading Father Stephens's books late at night. He was finding them quite a source of information. One such book had mentioned the cold phenomenon associated with demonic disturbances, confirming what he already knew. Demons used body heat as a form of energy through which they could affect the physical world. He had witnessed this lately. The room would grow icy cold. Then something paranormal would happen, like a piece of furniture suddenly vanishing, then reappearing in another part of the house. One night he saw a table levitating in the hallway.

All of this was intended to scare and intimidate. As Father Malachi had said, demons were clever beings. They knew that Rich possessed the power to do them harm and were intent on chasing him away. But since he hadn't fled they had increased their efforts. Most disturbing were the marks outside his bedroom door. Whatever was creating them was growing more determined to break in. The paneled door now looked like shredded confetti. No wonder the other priests had fled.

But he wasn't going anywhere. Not until he had figured out why this presence had resurfaced after years of lying dormant. Was it directed specifically at him, in an effort to dissuade him from taking on the role of exorcist? Perhaps it figured that if it could intimidate and frighten him enough, he would abandon any pursuits in that direction.

He stamped his feet. They felt like blocks of ice. The wind had picked up and the temperature was dropping. Even though it was only mid-October, he wouldn't be a bit surprised if they saw snow before the week was out. He looked out over the parking lot and wondered what had become of Jane. She had promised to be there tonight. What had happened? Was she afraid of confronting the demons that had once plagued her? He would make a point of getting her alone tomorrow to find out. But one thing was certain. Those who had been there were lucky not to have gotten killed. He had tackled Gail only seconds before the chandelier came crashing down. Unfortunately, his act of heroism had also resulted in her injury.

Rich thrust his hands inside his wool coat, watching a car pull alongside the entranceway and deposit a young woman, clutching a child in her arms. She raced through the hospital doors, her eyes wide with fear. Minutes later, a young man led an elderly woman through the parking lot. The woman leaned heavily on his arm as though her strength had been spent. Rich marveled at the human drama that must play itself out here every day.

An icy drizzle began to fall. He tucked himself into a corner by the side of the building to continue his vigil. He had given up smoking years ago, but right now he'd give his eyeteeth for a Marlboro. Strange how old habits rose out of nowhere when you were under duress. He had worked hard to attain his academic standing, avoiding anything that hinted of controversy. If his colleagues ever caught wind of what he was involved in now, he could kiss his hopes of a department chair goodbye.

Darn Malachi! He was the one who had opened up this can of worms. Rich couldn't help thinking that life had been relatively sane until he met the exorcist. *Exorcist*—the word seemed archaic in today's high-tech, we-can-explain-anything society, yet there was no denying that there were forces out there that defied rational explanation. He had seen them in Rome and again tonight. So had the women. He felt a flush of anger. The Mass hadn't worked. If anything, it seemed to have made matters worse. Now what was he supposed to do?

He searched the parking lot and wondered how long it would be before the hookers got there. That term still made him smile even in the midst of this madness. If nothing else, this assignment had allowed him to meet this great fraternity of women. He was especially taken with Kay and her tough-as-nails, quintessential New York attitude and quick wit. "I feel like I'm in a Harry Potter movie," she'd said.

The memory made him smile. These women were something. Even with all that had happened, they offered to stay behind to help the sheriff with his report. But he got the feeling that if Lucifer himself were to show up they'd be unimpressed. They were some tough cookies.

They were also good people, and for their sake he would see this thing through, despite the repercussions. For the first time in his life he felt himself to be part of a larger family, and family didn't desert each other in times of crisis.

The EMT who had worked on Gail walked through the automatic doors and headed toward the rig.

"How is she?" Rich called after him.

"Looks like a mild concussion," he shouted back. "They'll probably keep her overnight, but she's going to be okay."

"Thanks for everything," Rich said, then resumed his vigil as he waited for the others to share the good news.

"If you want something, you're going to have to speak," the nurse told Marvin, growing increasingly more annoyed. A line of patients stretched out behind him waiting to be triaged.

He looked at her with baleful eyes but remained silent. That's how the evil one tricked you. Father Stephens had told him so. The priest said that evil gained entrance to a man's soul by two routes: through his words, or through his actions. Marvin could contain his actions, but he had never been certain about his words. As a safety measure, he had simply decided to stop speaking.

He whistled and pointed toward the parking lot.

"Stand over there," the nurse told him, exasperated.

"Fred, come here. See if you can figure out what this man wants," she said to a young security guard.

Fred walked over, his leather gun holster squeaking, and gave Marvin the once-over. A mixture of impatience and distrust flooded his eyes. "Let's go outside," he said, hustling Marvin none too gently through the automatic doors and onto the sidewalk. He waited until the area was empty before issuing a stern warning.

"I know all about your kind. You're looking for a free handout, but it's not going to happen on my shift. You stay out of there," he said, nodding toward the emergency room. "And I'm warning you. If you come back again, I'll call the police and have you hauled away for disturbing the peace. You got that?"

Marvin nodded, his eyes as big as hubcaps. He wanted to ask the man why he was so mad, but he was afraid. He hadn't done anything wrong. He was just trying to get help for Jane.

"Good. Now get going." He gave Marvin a shove.

Marvin disappeared like liquid mercury behind a row of parked cars.

"And don't come back," he yelled after him.

Rich had watched the exchange from behind a stone column. Wasn't that Marvin, the rectory's former groundskeeper? he wondered. The guard had been a little hard on him. He wondered if Marvin was in need of help. Maybe he needed a place to stay the night, or a hot meal. He followed him into the parking lot. Maybe there was something he could do. Bringing him back to the rectory was definitely not an option, but maybe he could set him up in a motel for the night.

Several rows down, he spied the interior light flash on Marvin's rusted-out station wagon. And in the dim light he recognized Jane's pained face.

"What the—?" He raced over.

"Father Rich . . ." Jane said, smiling weakly as soon as she saw him. "What are you doing here?"

"I could ask you the same question," he said. "What happened?"

"I crashed the SUV against a tree and hurt my ankle," she said. "I also managed to leave my cell phone at home. Lucky for me, Marvin came along when he did or I'd still be sitting there." Just the thought of it gave her the chills.

"Let me help you get inside," Rich said. "Marvin, go back and ask one of the attendants for a wheelchair."

Marvin glanced back at the emergency entrance sign and shook his head no.

"Oh, yeah. The guard. Wait here. I'll go get someone."

"That's not necessary," Jane insisted. "If I could just lean on you, I'm sure I can make it. It's not that far."

He decided not to argue and offered his arm.

"Would you mind getting my purse? My insurance card is inside."

"Here, hold on to her," he told Marvin.

He found the purse wedged between the front console and the windshield. He pried it loose, then paused to have a look around. Incredible. The interior of Marvin's car was decorated like a shrine.

Crucifixes, medallions, statues, and pictures of the saints blanketed the ceiling and walls. Stationed between the two front bucket seats was a statue of St. Michael.

"Father, I don't know how much longer I can stand here," Jane called.

"Sorry." He backed out, hitting his head on the doorframe. "Blast it." He rubbed his scalp and handed her the purse.

"Jane! Father Rich!" The hookers' voices rang across the parking lot, Rose's spike heels clicking like castanets on the asphalt.

"The sheriff took enough notes to write a book," Kay complained. Then, spying Jane's swollen foot, she grew concerned. "What happened to you?"

"I had a little accident."

"That means two hookers are down tonight?"

"What do you mean?"

"Gail was just rushed here in an ambulance."

The fire crackling in the fieldstone fireplace did little to dispel the chill that had settled around the group huddled in the Edwells' family room. Vera was spending the night with Gail at the hospital. As the EMT had predicted, they were keeping her for observation.

Jane, with her ankle heavily bandaged, lounged on the couch, her foot propped up on a pillow. Fortunately, nothing was broken. The doctor said it was just a sprain and sent her home with an Ace bandage, a pair of crutches, and some painkillers. She had forgone the pills in favor of a hot mug of decaf heavily spiked with Jack Daniel's.

Vance was busy playing host. Myla had kicked off her shoes and taken over Vance's leather recliner. Kay and Rose had pulled in a pair of straight-backed chairs from the dining room, and Father Rich sat on an ottoman with his back to the fireplace.

The Thomaston grandfather clock in the front hall, a wedding present from Father Stephens, struck midnight. No one spoke, as though each was afraid to broach the question paramount on everyone's mind: what had they witnessed tonight at the rectory? Two weeks ago, they had been frightened when windows crashed shut and doors locked by themselves. Tonight, however, they had been terrified.

"Mom, is there anything else I can get you before I go to bed?" Marilee asked, fussing with the pillow behind her mother's head.

"No, I'm fine, dear," Jane said, smiling up into her daughter's worried face. She ran a hand along Marilee's dark curly mane of hair. "If I need anything your father can take care of it."

"Are you sure?"

The anxious look on her daughter's face tugged at her heart. She hated to be the cause of it, yet she had to admit that Marilee's concern was a wonderful change from her usual indifference.

"You could do one thing for me," Jane said.

"Anything."

"Check on Alex and make sure he's okay. Sometimes he throws off his covers."

"Sure, Mom. I'll take care of it."

The group fell silent, waiting for Marilee to leave the room. Rose was the first to speak. "Father, would you please tell us what happened tonight? I'm confused. I thought the purpose of this Mass was to clear the house of any—"

"Irregularities," Myla offered.

Rich stared into the empty coffee mug. "It's a long story."

"Lucky for you I have about six hours before I'm due at work," Rose quipped.

"We'd all like to know," Kay said. "Anymore coffee?"

Vance lifted the empty carafe. "I could make more."

"That's okay. It wasn't the coffee portion of this concoction that I was interested in," Kay said.

Vance grabbed the half-empty bottle of whiskey and went around topping everyone's mug.

"The Church doesn't speak much about the Devil or demons anymore," Rich began hesitantly.

"Demons?" Myla asked.

"As outrageous as it might sound, I'm afraid so, yes."

"Thank God that's all it was. I thought I had seriously overmedicated."

Kay's and Vance's laughter set off a chain reaction. When it subsided, they all eased back in their chairs, tension fading away like an echo.

"Before I go any further, you all must give me your solemn word that what's said in this room will stay in this room, agreed?"

"Sure," Rose said. The others nodded.

"I was asked by the archbishop to investigate reports of a haunting at St. Francis Xavier. The three priests before me had all reported paranormal activity at the rectory."

"So the rumors were true," Myla said. "They *were* all frightened away."

"What made the archbishop think that it wouldn't send you running as it had the others?" Rose wanted to know.

"I had some experience along these lines back in Rome, and because of my background he asked me to quietly investigate."

"What kind of experience?" Kay asked, incredibly curious.

"I had worked with an exorcist."

"You mean like in the movie?"

Myla felt a chill run up her spine. "My husband took me to see that thing. I couldn't sleep for weeks. Thoughts of it still give me the willies."

"Are you telling us that exorcisms still take place?" asked Vance.

"More frequently than you know," Rich said.

"I'm confused," Kay said. "We're talking about a building. Can a house or a building be possessed? I thought they could only be haunted."

"That's a good question, but in either case we're talking about some kind of entity," Rich said, leaning his elbows on his knees. "Ghosts are associated with hauntings. They're human spirits who, for whatever reason, are earthbound. They make noise, scare people a bit, but are basically benign."

"And possession?"

"Possession occurs when an inhuman spirit that we call a demon or a devil takes over a space like a building or a home or attaches itself to an object like a doll, a parchment, even a pet—anything of a physical nature. It uses this as a kind of host until a soul comes along that is outside God's grace."

"Then what?" Vance asked.

"Then it takes possession."

"This is getting creepy," Myla said. "I definitely don't want to be alone tonight."

"We have a spare room," Vance offered.

"You're welcome to stay," Jane added.

"I might just take you up on that," Myla said.

"How does that happen?" Vance asked, throwing an arm over the back of the sofa. Jane snuggled closer. "I mean, how does something like this begin?"

"First it has to be given an entryway."

"How?"

"Well . . . there are a few ways. The most common approach is by dabbling in forms of the occult, like séances or Ouija boards."

"Ouija boards? You mean those things anyone can buy at the local toy store?" Rose asked, setting her mug on the coffee table. "There must be half a dozen of those circulating around our building. They sure keep the kids quiet on rainy days."

"I strongly suggest that you gather them up and burn them," Rich said, his voice hard-edged.

"You can't be serious?"

"I'm dead serious."

"But how did the rectory get . . . infected?" Kay asked. "I would have thought that rectories were immune to this kind of thing. You know, hallowed halls and all that."

"I'm afraid not," Rich answered. "But I've never heard of anything quite like what we encountered this evening. Hauntings are cases of things going bump in the night. This energy was malevolent and seemed intent on causing physical harm. Like tonight with Gail."

"But why?" Rose asked.

"I don't know," he answered simply.

The room grew quiet as everyone reflected on the discussion. Finally, Kay broke the silence by asking about Jane's accident. Everyone's attention shifted to Jane, who looked pale and fragile as she glanced up into her husband's face.

"Before I answer your question, Kay . . ." She turned to Vance. "Honey, there's something I should have told you a long time ago. It's about . . . gifts that I developed after my parents' accident," she began hesitantly.

"You mean how you can see things other people can't?" he asked.

"You know about this?"

"I've known from the beginning. Only a half-wit wouldn't have sensed something different about you after your family's accident. I talked it over with Father Stephens. He explained that certain traumas can cause psychic channels to open."

"And you were all right with that?"

He hugged her close. "I married you, didn't I?"

She threw her arms around his neck and buried her face in the soft folds of his skin, feeling a heavy weight lift from her soul. "I've wanted to tell you for many years, but I didn't know how."

"And I wanted to tell you that I knew, but Father Stephens said I was to wait until you were ready to tell me yourself." He smiled and kissed the top of her head. "You sure waited for a strange moment to tell me."

"It's only going to get stranger," she predicted.

"Wait a minute, wait a minute," Rose interrupted. "Are you saying that you're a psychic, like, 'I can see into the future'?"

"More like 'I can see into the realms of evil,'" Jane said. She swallowed hard, then told them what she encountered in the car moments before the crash.

"It sounds like it wanted to stop you from attending the Mass, but why?" Kay asked.

"It perceived her as a threat," Rich explained. "We're dealing with a highly evolved entity. It's clever, manipulative, and knows how to instill enough fear to make people back away, especially the ones who might interfere with its plans."

"That's the thing that still confuses me," Rose confessed. "What plans? What's its motive?"

"Ultimately, to take possession of someone's soul," Rich answered.

"That's rather a chilling thought," Myla said.

"But it could have done that aeons ago," Rose insisted. "Why didn't it try to possess Father Stephens, or you, Jane? You lived there for several years. Why wait until now?"

"Father Stephens had learned to contain it," Jane offered.

"But he didn't vanquish it," Kay said.

"He didn't have the power," Jane answered.

"So what set it loose again at this time?" Rose asked. "Father Stephens's death?"

"No, I don't think that had anything to do with it," Rich said, then looked over at Vance. "I think that you might inadvertently have set it loose."

"Me?" Vance said, nearly spilling his drink.

"What does Vance have to do with this?" Jane asked defensively.

"You did some excavation work a few months ago along the back of the property, right?" Rich asked.

"Yeah. The Piedmonts were putting in a pool. Unfortunately, there was a bed of shale right where they wanted to put it. We set off a couple of blasts of dynamite to clear the way for excavation."

"I'm betting that the blast did more than loosen some bedrock. My guess is that it loosened a vault in the downstairs basement."

"I'd almost forgotten about that," Myla said. "It was installed when the house was built, but as far as I know it's never been used."

"What's a vault got to do with this?" Rose asked.

Rich explained. "While you were all inside the hospital, I stepped back outside and talked to Marvin."

"You *talked* to Marvin," Myla asked. "How? He hasn't uttered a word in over fifty years."

"It was a creative conversation," Rich said with a smirk. Then he went on to relate the story that Marvin had shared with him.

Rich began by saying that Marvin reminded him of a boy he had known while growing up in the orphanage. His name was Billie and, like Rich, he had been dropped off like last week's laundry on the steps of St. Bridget's Home when he was five years old. From that day on, the boy never spoke another word.

He and Rich soon became fast friends, devising an innovative combination of hand signals and charadelike motions with which to communicate. It was this form of communication that Rich used with Marvin this evening to discover what might be the key to the paranormal activity taking place at the rectory.

"According to Marvin, it can all be traced back to Charles Whitcomb II," Rich began. "On the day before his wedding, Charles received a package from an antiquities dealer, someone from the Middle East. Apparently, he had met the man on his grand tour a few years back. As you might know, this was an era when Egyptian archaeological finds had sparked an intense interest in collecting ancient artifacts.

"From what I remember reading about that era, the competition grew heated among these men of privilege and soon they were going to any lengths to possess something rare, even hiring cat burglars to steal pieces from rival collectors. So when Charles received this rare parchment on the eve of his marriage, he probably thought it prudent to lock it away in the vault in the basement of his new home."

Myla interrupted to say, "That was the night he was killed."

"Does anyone know how he died?" Rose asked.

Myla's face grew pale. "It was quite grisly. My grandparents spent a small fortune keeping the coroner's report quiet."

"What did they find?"

"His body had literally been pulled apart," Myla said with a shudder. "Vance, do you have any more of that whiskey?" She watched Vance refill her mug. "That's why they boarded up the house and refused to visit the property."

"And so things remained quiet until the estate was bequeathed to the Church and it was turned into a residence," Rich continued.

"I heard that the first priest who lived in the house died. Is that correct?" Rose asked Myla.

"Yes, he and his assistant."

"You'd think someone might have figured out that something strange was happening at the house and torched the place," Kay offered.

"The men died of heart attacks. I guess the coroner saw nothing strange about their deaths," Myla said. "Anyway, the house was closed again until Father Stephens came along."

"Why didn't it chase him away?" Rose asked.

"Apparently, it tried," Rich said. "According to Marvin, Father Stephens had the same experiences we've had over the last few weeks."

"And he stayed?" Kay asked. "Brave man."

"He didn't have a choice. The archdiocese wouldn't give him permission to close the house for fear of having to report what was happening. He was instructed to quietly do whatever he could to contain it."

"Why didn't the Church offer him some help?" Kay asked. "Doesn't the Church have priests who handle those kinds of things?" She found this insight into the workings of the Church hierarchy fascinating.

"Like an exorcist?"

She nodded. "They're still out there, aren't they?"

"It's not something that the Church likes to talk about, and I suspect at the time there just wasn't anyone around who had that type of background," Rich explained. "But from what little I've been able to learn about Father Stephens by talking with parishioners and folks around town, he was a deeply spiritual man."

"That's true," Jane said quietly.

"His core beliefs must have given him access to spiritual powers the others lacked."

"I'm still not clear on the connection between this artifact and the paranormal events taking place at the rectory," Myla confessed. "How did Father Stephens know they were connected?"

"Your uncle did some of the plumbing at the rectory, didn't he?" Rich asked Vance.

"Yeah, in the early days, when he first started out in business, he was kind of a jack-of-all-trades. Later, he focused on excavating."

"Were you there the day the basement flooded when the main broke?"

"Where was I?" Jane asked Vance.

"You and Gail were away at the Cape visiting with Father Stephens's friends, but yes, I remember that. The main shutoff valve that connects the water supply from the well to the house burst. Gallons of water came flooding into the basement. My uncle and I went over to fix it."

"And you discovered the vault," Rich said.

"What vault?" Jane asked.

"It was hidden behind a false wall in the basement," Vance said. "The only reason we discovered it was because the pipe leading outside threaded right through it. To get to the main water valve, we had to take down the wall."

"But according to Marvin, Father Stephens called in a locksmith and had it opened. That's when he found the parchment."

Kay turned to the priest and asked, "The one that Charles had the night he was killed?"

"The same one," Rich said. "Marvin doesn't remember the particulars, but apparently after it was discovered Father Stephens made a hasty visit to Yale University and had it deciphered. Apparently, whatever it contained only confirmed his suspicions that it was the root cause of all the evil that was manifesting itself inside the house."

"What did he do with it?" Rose asked.

"He brought it back to the rectory and locked it in the vault."

"Why didn't he just burn it—get rid of it?" Kay asked, realizing for the first time that she was talking about the paranormal as though these things were everyday events.

"Things of this nature cannot be destroyed by physical means," Rich explained. "So he probably figured that it was safer to bring it back here and contain it, rather than risk allowing it to fall into the wrong hands."

"So the question is, how did Father Stephens contain it?" Rose said.

"I don't know, but there might be a way to find out," Rich answered.

"How?" Jane asked.

"Father Stephens left a diary. The bishop has it. I got the impression that it chronicles that period. It's highly possible that it contains the information that we're lacking."

"But according to today's newspaper the bishop is still in intensive care," Rose said. "How are you going to get it?"

Rich put his head in his hands. "I don't know. I've made a

couple of calls to his secretary. He promised me he'd try to get the bishop's permission to hand it over. But in the interim I'll just have to wait."

"You know what strikes me as strange?" Kay said, pouring herself another drink. "The bishop has a heart attack right at this time, just when we need access to a diary that's in his possession and that might hold the key to all this. It seems rather coincidental, doesn't it?"

"I don't believe in coincidences," Myla said sagely.

"Neither do I," Rich said.

"So what's next?" Rose asked.

"I'm going back to the rectory and see if I can find that parchment. I'll decipher it, and perhaps it will offer us some insights into what we're dealing with."

"You'll find the combination in the upper right-hand drawer of Father Stephens's desk," Jane said.

"I'll go with you—you'll need a backup," Kay offered, digging in her purse for her car keys. She handed them to Rich. "You'll have to drive. I've had way too much to drink."

"You sure you want to go back there?"

"I began my career by handling rock groups," Kay said, slipping into her cashmere coat and adjusting the collar. "Demons are just one notch down."

"What is that smell?" Kay clamped a hand over her nose. "It's absolutely vile."

"Evil," Rich said simply. He shined the flashlight against the far wall. "Vance said the vault was behind a false wall."

"There." Kay pointed toward an area cast in deep shadow. "It looks as though a section of wall has moved away from the foundation."

They cleared away the cobwebs and found a loose panel.

"Here, give me a hand," Rich said to Kay.

"I feel like Nancy Drew," she quipped, helping him shift the panel to one side.

Rich laughed. "Doesn't anything faze you?"

"Polyester. Unless it's being worn by Gail." Kay grew quiet. She wondered how Gail was doing. Vera had called before they left to report that Gail's cut had needed ten stitches to close. Poor Gail, she thought. Maybe I'll stay over at the cottage tonight and pay her a visit in the morning before rushing back to the city.

The panel creaked and groaned like a human in pain. Finally, a thick metal doorway was revealed.

"Hold this," Rich said. He handed her his flashlight and pulled out a rumpled piece of paper. Kay steadied the beam of light on the paper while Rich carefully entered the combination, twisting and turning the lock mechanism. On the last entry, he felt the tumblers click into place.

"Here goes," he said, pushing down hard on the handle. The door swung open easily.

"Give me the light," he said, stepping into the vault. Kay passed it over and followed him inside.

As he ran the beam over a row of shelves, she let out a soft whistle. "Wow. Look at all this stuff. It looks as though it belongs in a museum."

Pieces of Egyptian pottery that Rich recognized as dating from the Middle Kingdom lined an entire shelf. Bronze pieces—intricately detailed and no doubt Byzantine—and rich European medieval tapestries filled other shelves.

He whistled. "This collection must be worth millions."

"What's that over there?" Kay asked, pointing to an intricately inlaid wooden box the size of an attaché case.

He studied the carvings. "This could be it."

He tried to open the box, but it was locked. Now what? It was a valuable artifact, one he didn't want to damage.

"Hold this," Kay said, handing him the flashlight. From the small purse slung around her neck, she produced a thin, reedlike piece of metal. She slid it into the lock and twisted. The lid popped open.

"Is there something you'd like to confess?" Rich asked suspiciously.

"I have a colorful range of clients," she explained, lifting the lid.

"This is it," Rich said, carefully removing the yellowed papyrus.

"Shine the light here," he told her. He quietly studied its contents for several seconds without comment.

"Well? What does it say?" Kay asked, peering over his shoulder.

He looked at her, his face tight with disbelief. It couldn't be, yet it was. Inside the box was an exact replica of the parchment that he had deciphered for Father Malachi in Rome—one of the six that Miphah had used several millennia ago to make her pact with Satan.

fifteen

Gail glanced briefly over at Jerry and gave him a look that sent shivers up the boy's spine. He tried to ignore the stare, hot as a branding iron, that was aimed at the puddle of spilled milk coursing dangerously close to the edge of the granite counter. A primal fear rose like a flashing road sign portending a dangerous curve, and sent him scurrying for a roll of paper towels.

Jerry eyed her warily. Ever since she had returned home from the hospital, their doormat of a stepmother had gotten really weird, almost scary. She hadn't said two words since she was released from the hospital, which in itself was weird. Gail liked to talk and talk. She was always giving advice, warning them to wear warm clothes, asking about school and homework. Now it was as if they didn't exist. Even her looks were different. There was something about her eyes that creeped him out.

"Turn that blasted television down," Ralph grumbled. "I can't hear myself think."

"The control's right next to you. You turn it off," Jerry said, downing the last drop of cold cereal and milk. His father had been on his tail ever since he had gotten home. He was all bent out of shape because he had to take a week off from work to care for Gail.

The doctor said that she'd suffered a serious concussion and shouldn't be left alone. He had tried to get his mother to take care of her, but she was helping Mrs. Edwell down at the Sit and Sip Café since Father Rich was away in Rome.

"Gail, find the remote and turn that thing off," Ralph said. The woman had bumped her head, that was all. Why was everyone acting as though she had had a leg amputated? He went back to his newspaper.

Gail grabbed the television remote and walked over to Ralph, then waited until he looked up.

"Yeah? What do you want?"

She pointed the remote between his eyes and hit the off button.

"You're the one I'd like to turn off," she said, then burst out laughing.

Jerry could tell by the look in his dad's eyes that even he was a little scared. She had never talked to him like that before.

"Don't you have to meet the bus?" Gail asked Jerry.

"Yes, ma'am," he said, eager to get out of there.

He grabbed his backpack off the counter and shot out the back door like a missile. It was the first time this year that he made it to the bus stop on time.

The seat-belt light went on seconds after the turbulence began to rock the Delta 763 with enough force to shake the passengers' fillings loose and for the fifth time since leaving JFK the captain's voice worked to assure the passengers that everything was under control. "This is Captain Richards speaking," he said. "It seems as though we've hit another pocket of turbulence. We're on the radio now asking to be rerouted."

The plane was rocked by another thunderous air current that sent an equally powerful current of fear rippling through the cabin. What remained of their meager microwavable dinner plates went sailing. Several attendant lights flashed on, illuminating the darkened cabin like a marquee on Broadway.

"Sorry about that, folks," the captain went on. "I have to tell you that in my twenty years of flying I've never encountered a weather system quite like this one. Even the folks back in Houston, who track our course, can't find it on any of their meteorological maps. But until we can find our way around it I'm asking that passengers remain seated."

The man next to Rich reached out to tag a flight attendant as she raced past. "Another rum and coke."

"I'm sorry, sir, the captain has ordered all food service stopped until we're safely through this mess."

"Then just give me a couple of those bottles of plain rum," he whined, nearing a meltdown.

"I'm sorry, sir, that includes all alcoholic beverages as well." She scurried toward the rear of the cabin, where a small child had vomited in the aisle.

"Wait until we get on the ground," he swore under his breath. "My company will never use this airline again."

They had left JFK at eight-fifteen this evening and were six hours into the flight. Rich had one of the prize seats—the first row in economy, right behind first class. It provided plenty of legroom to stretch out during the thirteen-hour flight, which included a short layover at Heathrow before catching the next leg of the flight to Rome. Malachi was waiting for him. Rich planned to show him the parchment and persuade him to travel back with him to Connecticut.

He had tried to settle in and catch some sleep, but the combination of turbulence and his neighbor's anxiety had made sleeping nearly impossible. The man continued to harass the overtaxed stewardesses for more booze. Rich was almost tempted to intercede on his behalf just to shut him up.

The plane gave another jolt. The man swore. Several elderly ladies a few aisles back screamed with fright. Rich looked out into the blackness, a perfect backdrop for the images that ran through his thoughts like a movie reel: the rectory's dark history, the more recent disturbances, Vera nearly toppling over the banister, the events during the Mass. The power he had witnessed unleashed that night had convinced him of the gravity of the situation. That, coupled with the discovery of the second parchment, deeply concerned him. Something more sinister than he had originally suspected was happening in that house—something beyond his ability to handle alone. That had become quite evident on the night of the Mass. It was by God's grace that the women hadn't been killed.

Thunder rumbled outside, accompanied by strong gusts of wind that tossed the plane around like a toy. A jolt of lightning lit up the night sky, and for just a second Rich thought that he saw something move alongside the wing. He leaned in closer. Another thunderbolt rocked the plane. Moments later, a jolt of electricity danced along the wing. The nose of the plane dipped dangerously. The engines whined as the pilot fought to keep the plane steady. Passengers' terrified screams bounced off the cabin walls, quieted only by the oxygen masks that had fallen from the overhead compartments and were now being fitted over their faces.

Rich glanced at an attendant as she made certain that everyone knew what to do and saw the look of fear etched clearly across her face. The plane felt as though a giant hand were bouncing it from one hand to the other. The interior lights went out. The man beside Rich fainted.

The glow of the floor lights reflected off the windows. Rich leaned in closer to get a better look outside. Something was out there. He could feel it, and it was staring back at him. Another round of lightning flashed outside the cabin windows, illuminating the wing, where an ancient creature—part of the pantheon of heathen gods—remained mounted. Red orbs of light emanated from its eyes, and its tongue, filled with maggots, flickered against the glass. For a moment, Rich thought he was the only one who had seen it, but then other passengers began pointing toward the windows and screaming. Pandemonium broke loose. Some people wept; others prayed. Some released their seat belts and rushed through the aisle as though they could somehow escape.

Rich remained calm and studied the creature intensely, unafraid. Beneath his feet lay an attaché case that held the parchment. As long as it survived, so would the evil that it contained, and Rich knew that it would not allow him or this plane to be destroyed. He made the sign of the cross and pulled down the blind. Seconds later, the plane leveled out. The storm was over, leaving those aboard to wonder if their terrifying ordeal had been caused by mass hallucinations.

The sun's rays, dusted in ambers and tinged with sienna, warmed the terra-cotta tiles that ringed the patio outside Father Malachi's villa. Rich had come directly from the airport and was badly in need of a shave and a shower, but he declined a young priest's offer to freshen up. He had more important things on his mind.

He was shown into the same room that he had occupied once before. Moments later, Malachi stepped in and, without preamble, said simply, "Where is it?" Rich removed the parchment and handed it over to him. The older priest uttered a prayer of protection before unrolling it. He settled his reading glasses on the tip of his nose and began to study the text. Meanwhile, Rich brought him up to speed, briefing him on the rectory's history and the rash of paranormal events that had taken place since Father Stephens's death.

"At first I couldn't understand why the Mass hadn't stopped the paranormal activity. Then I learned about this," he said, indicating the parchment.

"Yes, that would explain its ineffectiveness," Malachi concurred. "You were right to bring it here. It's imperative that it be kept in a safe place. I am, however, deeply concerned for the safety of your—what did you call them?"

"Hookers."

"I know my English is a little rusty, but doesn't that mean . . . ?"

Rich smiled. "Not in this case. They're rug hookers."

"Rug hookers?"

"I'll explain later."

"Yes . . . well, I'm very concerned for them. Just being exposed to the parchment could have jeopardized their immortal souls. You witnessed what happened to the child."

"That's why I came," Rich said. "I need your help."

Malachi adjusted his glasses and studied the symbols. "You're certain that this is a sister to the other?"

"Yes, I'm positive. I never considered that the others might have survived when I was translating the one you have locked away." His voice grew sober. "If these two have made it down through the years intact, perhaps the other five are out there somewhere."

"Dear Lord, have mercy on us," Malachi intoned, removing his glasses and sinking into a chair.

"I've come to ask for your help," Rich said. "I suspect that one of the women is being used as a host. We'll need to perform an exorcism and close the portal before it's too late. I don't believe the demon has complete possession of the woman just yet, so there's still time, but it's imperative that we act quickly."

"How do you know this?"

"One of the hookers has the gift of second sight. She can see into the realm of evil. She senses that something is happening to her friend but feels it hasn't taken complete possession of her yet, which means we still have some time left."

"But not much," Malachi concluded. He frowned. "I thought you told me when you last left here that you'd never get involved in another exorcism. Something about not wanting to risk your career or . . . what did you call it? Oh, yes . . . your validity among your peers."

"Yes, I know," Rich said, studying the tiled floor.

"And what changed your mind?"

"These women. They're exasperating and totally without restraint, and they pretty much run the parish and the priests. God help the permanent pastor who has to deal with them in the end."

"But—?"

"I've been thinking a lot about that question on the ride over here," Rich said. He looked at Malachi and smiled gently. "For the first time since taking my vows, I feel like a real shepherd. I've sidestepped relationships of any sort all my life. I suppose it has something to do with the fact that my father abandoned me as a child. But since meeting these women I've learned what friendship and family and servitude are all about."

"May I also make a confession?"

Rich looked at him quizzically.

"I said you were destined to be a great exorcist, but there was one major component missing."

"What was that?"

"A shepherd's heart. Apparently, these women have helped you find that."

"So, now what?" Rich asked, leaning forward and resting his elbows on his knees.

A cloud moved over the landscape, casting the patio in shadow. Malachi glanced out the window. "It all depends on whether you're willing to take on the role God has assigned you."

"As an exorcist? No. I'm still not convinced that's the role I was meant to play."

"Then why are you here?"

"I came to give you the parchment for safekeeping, and to ask you to come back with me so that *you* can perform the exorcism."

Malachi sank back in his chair. "No."

"No?" Rich asked in disbelief. "What do you mean, no?"

"Just what I said. Whether you wish to believe it or not, this is your time. As I told you before, the present world is badly in need of your skills."

Rich jumped up from his chair. "Listen, at this juncture I'm ready to go along with your prophecy that maybe—just maybe—I've been called and someday I might be equipped to handle this new role. But right now these women's lives are at stake. I've never conducted an exorcism before. I've seen what you went through with Louisa. I can't imagine coming up against that without proper instruction."

"You don't get it, do you, Rich?"

"Get what?"

"You don't need instruction." He got up and tilted Rich's head to one side, exposing the crescent-shaped scar. "You've had this since birth, haven't you?"

"Yes, but what does that—"

"It's the mark of a powerful priesthood. An ancient order not often spoken about in the confines of the Church, yet its power continues to transcend time. Its role down through the millennia has been to shield innocent souls from evil."

Rich rubbed his neck, watching Malachi uncork a jug of wine and pour the ruby liquid into two glass goblets. He walked over and handed one to Rich.

"I've never read anything about this order," Rich said, taking the glass.

"Not many know about it. It's a secret society begun thousands of years ago. Someday I'll tell you more, but right now let's concentrate on the situation at hand." He opened the glass doors that led to the patio and stepped through, then beckoned to Rich to follow. The sun felt good, cleansing against his cheeks.

"You have the Ritual of Exorcism as written by the Church," Malachi reminded him. "Follow it to the letter. Fasting and prayer before you begin—it's a powerful weapon against the Devil, and you'll need all the weapons you can muster. I feel the women are part of this arsenal. They each possess a skill of their own that will aid in this fight. Combined, you make a powerful force against the armies of hell. And don't forget for one moment that it is a fight. A fight to the death." He lifted his glass in a salute. "And to the victor goes the soul of man."

"And what happens if the women are caught in the cross fire? They're not trained in this any more than I am. I saw what it did to Louisa. What if I fail?"

"Then don't," Malachi said simply, sipping his wine.

Rich paced up and down the flagstones, his temper flaring. "But how can I prevent it without your help?"

"You have a gift, Rich. A powerful gift. Believe in it, and in the One who stands beside you. Satan knows his time on earth is short," Malachi continued. "He's using every ploy he can to ensnare souls. First he convinces the world that he does not exist. It reminds me of that scene in the *Wizard of Oz* where the professor is stationed behind the curtain, working levers and running the show, and, when he is discovered, shouts, 'Ignore that man behind the curtain.'

"Unlike any other moment in time, Satan's power is growing. How? It feeds on man's disbelief, both of his kingdom and of God. People like you and these women are major threats to his campaign, because you possess the power to prove to the world that both exist. That also means, however, that you are all extremely vulnerable to attack. So be careful, Rich."

"I don't understand why we would be singled out."

"Think about it, Rich. You have the gift of banishment. I saw it displayed that day upstairs. You came up against one of the most powerful forms of evil I have ever encountered and yet, at your command, it was vanquished. And remember, those parchments contain the means of opening portals, conduits to hell. Imagine the suffering that would be unleashed should that be allowed to happen."

Rich ran a hand through his wavy blond hair. "I don't know. All of this sounds so far-fetched. If it weren't for the fact that I witnessed what happened upstairs—"

"You say that one of the women has the gift of discernment. Her skills will be invaluable to you in this campaign. She can ferret out their movements, see into their realm, and possibly unveil their plans. The other women . . . ?" He spread out his hands. "Perhaps their bond of friendship is so strong that it can weave an impregnable wall against these dark forces. I simply don't know. But like all things, this, too, will be revealed in time.

"At the moment, all you need know is this: together, you create a powerful weapon of mass destruction against the Devil's strongholds. But be warned. Satan is not going to simply slink away without putting up a fight."

Rich glanced at Malachi, who spoke so freely of demons and Satan and devils. Was this, too, to be his future?

"What if I refuse to take him on?"

Malachi looked at him sadly. "You don't have a choice, Rich. Even if you try to turn your back on this, he will hunt you down. You and the women. As I said before, your gifts make you all a liability."

"In other words," Rich said, "I'm damned if I do, and I'm damned if I don't."

"I'm afraid so."

The men fell silent, their heads tilted skyward as they watched a group of blackcaps. They would be migrating to Africa at this time of year, Rich thought. He remembered the Roman superstitions that were associated with birds. In early Rome, a text called the Sibylline Books was filled with omens revolving around birds and what they signified. What type of bird, where they had been, how high they were flying, and where they were bound all portended the viewer's fate. Now, if he were a Roman back in 114 BC, how might he interpret this omen?

Blackcaps were common birds aligned with the common people, like those he had been asked to shepherd. They were flying high, bound for a journey, and so was he. The flock was headed west toward Africa, where they would stay for the winter. The journey would be arduous. Many would fall by the wayside.

He drained the goblet. So, based on this ancient form of superstition, the birds flying overhead indicated that he was to shepherd his flock on a dangerous journey, and as their leader he must be extremely careful or some would be lost. The flock of birds disappeared into the setting sun, their loud calls breaking the relative quiet. They would need to find a safe haven before nightfall. Would he ever know the feeling of safety or normalcy again? Once he embarked on this course, there would be no turning back. His fate would be sealed. Any dreams he might have had about furthering his academic career would go up in smoke.

Jet lag had started to settle in, but he fought it. He had to get back to Bend Oaks. "I'll need a copy of the ritual," he said.

"I'll get you one from my study."

"I'll also need some instruction before I leave and, of course, your prayers."

The old priest nodded and headed back inside. "You'll have both. You also have another form of protection."

"What's that?" Rich asked.

Malachi set his goblet on a table and removed a silver ring from his finger. He handed it to Rich. "This."

Rich turned it over in his hand.

"That once belonged to St. Ignatius. Do you know anything about his ministry?"

Rich thought a moment. "I'm afraid I'm a little rusty on the lives of the saints."

"The namesake of your current parish, St. Francis Xavier, was a follower of his. St. Ignatius Loyola was one of the Church's most powerful exorcists."

Rich studied the ring closely. "What is the significance of the wreath?"

"That's not a wreath. It's the crown of thorns. It's the only true symbol that can contain evil and render it powerless. That's why we have one attached to our front gate."

"Front gate . . ." A lightbulb came on: Rich remembered something of importance. "There's a wreath like this on the rectory's gate and, now that I think of it, the stone walkway that surrounds the house is fashioned in the same design."

"It seems that Father Stephens did his homework," Malachi said. "Put it on. It will protect you."

As Rich slipped the ring on his finger, he had an epiphany. "So that's how he contained it. That's how Father Stephens was able to keep the evil at bay."

It was all coming together now.

"I noticed the other day that the pathway around the house had been disturbed. Vance Edwell told me that it happened when the hearse came to take away Father Stephens's body."

"Didn't you say that the disturbances began right after his death?" Malachi asked, following Rich's train of thought.

"Yes, and Marvin said—"

"Who's Marvin?"

"Sorry, he's the groundskeeper. He said Father Stephens instructed him to build a circular pathway around the rectory at the same time that he had the crown of thorns installed on the front gates. It must have been a security measure. Father Stephens wanted to make certain that if the evil ever broke loose from the house, it would be contained within the property. That's why he had Marvin promise to be diligent in keeping those gates closed after dusk."

"Then what freed it?" Malachi asked.

Rich sank into a chair, overwhelmed by what he had unknowingly unleashed.

"On the night of the Mass, I overrode the system so the gates would stay open. I didn't want to have to trek down there later and close them after the women had gone." He bent forward and placed his head in his hands. "What have I done?"

"Not all is lost, not yet," Malachi said, patting his shoulder.

"What do you mean?"

"Until the demon has total possession of the woman, it's dependent upon her as a host. It's not yet capable of maintaining both its life force and the portal. But you must bring her back to the rectory and perform the exorcism there. It's the only way to ensure that the entry point is sealed."

sixteen

Something was terribly wrong with this picture, Ralph thought, running the vacuum over the kitchen floor. A few days ago, his life had continued along on the course it had taken since he and Gail were married. She took care of the home, his two kids, and his mother whenever she flew into town, and never complained (as his ex-wife had) that he was never around or that, when he was, he didn't spend enough time with the family.

He and Chirley had been divorced for several years when he met Gail at a friend's Christmas party. She was a sweet, quiet, and moderately attractive woman—the antithesis of the sexually raw types he dated on the road. She was easy to be around and, every once in a while when he was in town, he'd give her a call and they'd watch a movie or she'd invite him over for a home-cooked meal. It was pleasant in a platonic kind of way, which was just fine with him, since he had no intention of ever getting married again. Every week another port of call, every port of call another woman. No strings attached.

This lifestyle worked for him until one day he realized that many of his co-workers had received promotions while he had been stuck in the same job, with the same pay, for the past five years. When he analyzed it, he found that the only difference between him and the other guys was that they were married. One day he shared this insight with his co-worker Larry Hanson, who was a mediocre salesman with a mediocre record but had just been made director of sales.

"Why sure, you dope," Larry said. "The company figures that if they're going to put time and money into training you for an executive position they want to make sure you stick around and, statistically, married men stick around longer."

So, after some heavy inner dialogue, Ralph figured that if he ever wanted to make vice president of the northeastern sales territory he had better find a wife, and at that point in his life Gail was the only good candidate. They were married within the month.

Little changed after their marriage, and as far as Ralph was concerned his decision had been a good one. He still got to travel twenty-four days out of each month, and he continued to bed other women. Only now, the company brass treated him differently. There was even talk of making him director of New England territories.

Then his dumb ex-wife showed up one day and dumped his kids off on their doorstep. She wanted to resume her singing career, she had told Gail. What career, he asked himself? He'd heard her singing in the shower. She sounded like a cat in heat. He could have wrung Gail's neck when he discovered that she had actually taken them in.

"What was I supposed to do?" she had said over the phone that night. "They're your sons. You're their father. Their mother doesn't want them. You have to take them in."

Of course, she was right, but that didn't make it any easier to swallow. His life was fine just the way it was. Kids only complicated things. But he needn't have worried. Nightmares about coaching Little League and building soapbox cars quickly vanished. Fortunately for him, the kids took after their mother. They weren't joiners.

And so his life remained basically unchanged until a few days ago. The discovery that Kay Sprage knew about the woman in Boston had been a seismic shock. He had been cheating on Gail for so long, it never occurred to him that one day he might actually get caught. The vacuum cord caught on the table legs. He gave it a snap, making the table shake. Pieces of fruit displayed in a bowl bounced off onto the floor. He chased after them.

He still couldn't believe that Kay had had the balls to hire a private detective to tail him. He had never liked her. She was a stuck-up broad, with her fancy clothes and her expensive sports car. He never could figure out what Gail saw in her. They were total opposites in every respect. And what business was it of hers, anyway, what he did on business trips? What was he supposed to do when he was away from home? Order room service, watch TV, and call it a night? That's what other guys might do, but not him. He was too young to rot on the vine.

He had spent the past few days thinking about Kay's ultimatum and had come to a decision. He wasn't going to let some skinny, designer-suit, uptight broad from New York City tell him what he could and couldn't do. No, sir. He planned on doing just what he had always done, only this time he'd be more careful now that he knew someone might be tailing him.

The vacuum sucked on a sock and was now making a strange sound. Cursing, he turned off the machine and heard the phone ringing in the background. He figured Gail would pick up, but she didn't. Pick up the phone! he thought. It went on ringing. Great! Did he have to do everything around here?

The last time he had checked, she was staring up at the bedroom ceiling. She had been acting weird ever since she came home from the hospital. Vera said it was just the side effects of the concussion. Well, she'd better snap out of it soon. He didn't plan on playing housewife much longer.

"For Christ's sake," he said, stomping back into the kitchen and snatching the receiver off the wall.

"Yeah?"

"Ralph? This is Rose. I have Jerry here with me."

His bad mood just went up another notch. Just what he needed, to be dragged down to the school.

"So what did he do this time?"

"Nothing," Rose said curtly. He was one of the few men on the planet that she'd rather cut off a leg than have anything to do with. "I'm concerned about Gail. Jerry says that she's not acting like herself and seldom comes out of her room. I thought some company might cheer her up, so I'd like to stop over after school."

"Well, don't expect coffee and crumpets," he said.

She ignored the sarcasm. "If it's all right with you, I'll give Jerry a lift home. We'll be there, say, around four o'clock?"

"Sure." Then a wild thought occurred to him. "You know, since you're coming over anyway, would you mind staying with Gail for a couple of hours? I have some errands to run. You know how it is. I don't feel comfortable leaving her alone in her condition," he added for effect.

"No, that would be fine. In fact, why don't I bring something along for dinner? I could stop over at Ming's. Gail likes their General Tsao's Chicken."

"That sounds great. See you in about an hour, then."

He felt his spirits begin to rise and made a quick call. "Joanna? This is Ralph. How would you like to meet for a drink, say around five? Where? How about at Saints and Sinners over in Harveyville. You can? Great. Oh, and Joanna. Wear the lacy red underwear."

Gail carefully replaced the receiver on the nightstand phone. She was seething. The rat! So what she had overhead Kay accuse him of that night was true. He was having multiple affairs, and all the while she was playing the dutiful wife—taking care of their home and caring for *his* children. She wanted to strangle him.

"You should make him pay," the voice said.

Yes . . . she should.

Images of the kind of retribution that Ralph richly deserved, which included dismembering vital parts of his anatomy, flooded her mind. Normally, she would have been horrified at such thoughts. But now, strangely, she found them comforting, almost titillating.

"*You should teach him a lesson,*" the voice said.

Yes, she should, but how?

The voice answered. She closed her eyes and listened carefully. An evil smile played across her lips. Yes, that's exactly what she would do. The plan made her tingle all over. Why, she hadn't felt this excited since she was a teenager and spray-painted her ex-boyfriend's car with yellow daisies after he ditched her at a school dance.

She ran a comb through her hair, pinched her checks, and went down to the kitchen to tell Ralph how much better she was feeling. When he mentioned that Rose was coming for a visit, she innocently suggested that he take the whole night off. Call some of his friends. After all, he had been such a good husband, taking care of her and the house. He certainly deserved a night out with the boys. She could almost read his thoughts as he smiled in gratitude. How stupid he must think she was. He figured she had no idea what he was up to. Wait until later. He would be so surprised.

When he left, she made herself a cup of tea using the china that was usually reserved for special occasions. After all, this *was* a special occasion. After tonight, Ralph Honeychurch would never cheat on her again.

She sipped from the delicately shaped teacup and carefully plotted the rest of her plan. When Rose arrived, she would pretend that she was exhausted and needed to go back to bed. She'd tell Rose that she was too tired to eat—maybe she'd have something later. But she would insist that Rose and Vera enjoy their dinner. Vera would be home shortly. She'd enjoy the company.

Then she would wait until they had drunk several glasses of wine before sneaking out. Ralph had been using the garage since he had been home. Her car was parked on the road, so they wouldn't hear her drive away. She glanced down at the piece of paper in her hands. She had written down the name of the bar where Ralph and his mistress would be meeting: Saints and Sinners, Harveyville. Wouldn't he and his lady friend be surprised when she showed up?

She washed out her teacup and placed it in the dish rack to dry. Making certain that everything was in order, she headed out of the room. Rose should be here shortly. It was important that she find her upstairs, weak from the trauma that she had sustained. She would insist on being left alone to sleep. She passed the rack of knives. Oh, yes . . . she mustn't forget to bring one of these along. She removed a butcher knife and paused briefly to study its razor-sharp edge.

It was almost dark. In the distance, streetlights flashed on. RJ looked at his watch. The guy had said he needed some grass and that RJ should meet him at the old warehouse on the corner of Ash Street and Collins in Harveyville. That was over an hour ago.

RJ took another drag on his cigarette, then stamped out the stub with the toe of his Timberlands. Where was this guy? He had to make the florist before it closed, and he needed the money. He'd ordered a dozen white roses. They were Gail's favorite. He hoped they would help to cheer her up. She hadn't been herself since she came home from the hospital. Not that his father cared. All he was worried about was his stupid job. "I'm due in Tulsa tomorrow," he had railed in the car on the ride home from the hospital. "Now I have to cancel my trip and play nursemaid." RJ had looked across the bucket seats of the Volvo S40 and thought, *It's always about you, isn't it? No sympathy, no concern for Gail's condition—only annoyance that the accident has somehow complicated your plans.*

The building he was leaning against had absorbed the cold. RJ stuffed his hands inside his jacket, wishing he had worn something warmer. He deeply cared for his stepmother, although he didn't like to show it. She was the first person who ever took any interest in him or his brother. Chirley (they had never called her Mom) had never cared a fig about either of them. She was just like their dad—interested only in *her* needs, *her* wants, always saying how much better her life would have been "if only" she hadn't had any kids. What did she expect them to do—apologize for being born?

The best thing Chirley had ever done was to drop them off with Gail. Oh, Gail could be a royal pain in the behind, always after them about homework or chores, but in a strange kind of way it was comforting to know that finally someone cared enough to nag. That's why he felt so bad when he was caught selling pot in the boys' room. Gail had gone ballistic. He didn't try to explain why he had done it. It was too embarrassing. It was the dumbest thing he had ever done in his entire life. At the time, however, it seemed like a cool way to make a few quick bucks—money he desperately needed to take Cathie Johnson out on a date. Cathie was the hottest girl in school. Once he had dated her, his status among his peers would be set.

He thought about going to his dad for the money, but he knew he'd only get a lecture. And he knew that Gail was tapped out. She had just learned that Jerry needed braces. He had already spent all of his birthday and Christmas money for front-row tickets to the Kanye West concert at the Hartford Civic Center. Cathie had a thing for Kanye. That was how he got her to say yes. Now all he needed was a little extra for food and drinks.

He told his best friend, Todd Meadows, about his financial problem and he said he knew of a way to make some quick cash. All RJ had to do was pick up some "merchandise" at a certain address and let his schoolmates know that if they were looking to score this weekend, he was the man. Todd handed him a piece of paper in chemistry class with a phone number.

He knew it was a dumb thing to do, but the thought of Cathie Johnson in the backseat of Gail's car and the look of envy in his friends' eyes the next day was too hard to resist. He had never done anything like this before, and didn't intend to do it again. It was just his luck to get busted. The worst part was seeing the look on Gail's face when she came to bail him out at the police precinct. There weren't many people whose opinion he valued, but Gail was one of them. Seeing her eyes fill with tears of disappointment had made him swear he'd never do it again.

So why was he out here tonight, dealing again? He wanted to buy her flowers, and he was dead broke. His father should have done it, but he hadn't. Not that it surprised RJ. But it made him sad, seeing all those flowers from other people and not one bouquet from her own family. It wasn't right.

He swore to himself that tonight was absolutely the last time he'd ever deal drugs. In fact, since Gail's accident he had been thinking a lot about his life or, at least, the life she kept telling him he was destined to live. "You have a wonderful, analytical mind," she said. "You could do anything you wanted to if you just applied yourself. You could be a scientist, an engineer, even a doctor. You have no limits other than the ones you place on yourself."

Car lights beamed up ahead, then turned into the dark parking lot. A van with tinted windows pulled up alongside. He couldn't make out the color. It seemed to be absorbed by the darkness. The window whined down.

"You RJ?" the guy asked, peering at him over a pair of sunglasses even though it was pitch-dark out.

"Yeah," RJ said. "About time you showed up."

"My girl here had to make a pit stop," he sneered. "You got the stuff?"

RJ pulled a small plastic envelope out of his pocket. The guy reached for it, but RJ pulled it away.

"Cash first."

"Sure, man. That's cool." He gave a nervous laugh. "Marilee, hand me my wallet. It's in my jacket."

"I can't see anything in the dark," a familiar voice answered.

The guy flicked on the overhead light, and RJ caught a glimpse of the girl. It was Marilee Edwell! What was she doing with this creep? He had heard rumors about this dude. His name was Tye. This was not the kind of guy a girl like Marilee wanted to be messing around with. But he kept his thoughts to himself as he watched Tye count out five twenties. "You said a hundred, right?"

"Thanks," RJ said, pocketing the cash and handing him the small plastic bag.

"Cool, man. Until next time," Tye said and took off, leaving the sound of peeling rubber in his wake.

RJ didn't tell him that there wasn't going to be a next time. After tonight, his cell-phone number was being changed. He glanced at his watch. He had about fifteen minutes before the store closed. If he hustled, he could make it.

The side streets were nearly deserted, and he made good time. He brought his bike to a stop and waited for the traffic light to turn green, glancing idly over at the Saints and Sinners Bar and Grill, which seemed to be doing a lively business for a Wednesday night. A group of construction workers piled out of a beat-up Chevy truck. By their unsteady gait, he knew they were already three sheets to the wind. They swayed and fumbled their way across the parking lot and into the bar.

A small motel composed of six units was at the rear of the small complex. From previous jaunts through this town, RJ knew that "ladies of the night" (as his grandmother Vera referred to them) frequented this area. He couldn't imagine having sex with a woman who had just done the wild thing with one of the gorillas inside the bar. He figured she'd pass along more than just a good time.

The light turned yellow, and he revved the bike's motor ready to make his turn when something caught his attention. He leaned closer. It couldn't be!

A woman who bore a striking resemblance to his stepmother was headed toward one of the rooms located a few doors down from the bar. She was wearing a bathrobe and bunny slippers.

"Holy crap!" He raced toward the parking lot.

It was Gail, all right, and in her hand was a butcher knife.

It was the persistent knocking that got him riled.

"Go away, you stupid redneck. Can't you see that this room is occupied! That does it," Ralph said, throwing the sheets to one side and marching to the door clad in only his birthday suit.

Joanna giggled and slithered down under the sheets.

"You want a knuckle sandwich," he threatened, yanking open the door. For a moment he stood there dazed. He had expected a tall, burly man, drunk as a skunk, who had mistaken this room for his. What he encountered, however, was his wife wielding a five-inch butcher knife. He jumped out of the way and nearly fell backward.

"Now, Gail. You don't want to do this," he began.

Joanna screamed and fled into the bathroom, locking the door.

"Oh, don't I?" she sneered, bringing down the knife with enough force to castrate a cow.

His reactions were slow, impeded by the half bottle of scotch he had consumed and the exhausting lovemaking. The blade sliced his right arm. Blood dripped to the floor and seeped onto the carpet.

He couldn't believe she had cut him. "Are you crazy?" he screamed, holding his arm and trying to stem the flow of blood. "What's the matter with you? Have you lost your mind?"

Gail threw back her head and laughed—an eerie, sinister sound devoid of all true mirth, reckless and evil. Then it stopped as abruptly as it had begun. Her eyes narrowed. "What's the matter with me? you ask. You're the one who's been caught committing adultery. You think that you can treat me like this and get away with it?" she asked, steadily advancing toward him.

Ralph flew behind the bed for safety. She was crazy. "Now, honey, you don't want to do this. I know this looks bad, but we can work it out," he said, hoping to buy some time. He surveyed the distance between his wife and the open door. If he could get her to move a little to the right, he could scale the mattress and make it through.

As though reading his thoughts, she took hold of the foot of the bed and, with superhuman strength, lifted the mattress and box spring. Ralph watched in amazement. It was as though they weighed no more than a feather.

He was truly scared now. Nothing separated them. He was dead meat, and he knew it. There was no place for him to run. He crouched down cowering, his hands covering his head, and pleaded. "Please, Gail. Don't! Don't kill me."

"Mom, put down the knife," RJ said quietly. He had never called her Mom before, but somehow it seemed appropriate.

"Thank God you're here," Ralph whined. "She's trying to kill me."

"Mom, you don't really want to do this," RJ said, advancing slowly into the room. "Believe me, he's not worth it."

A conflict of emotions played across Gail's face. She turned toward her stepson and, for just a moment, her eyes softened.

"RJ . . ." she whispered. She looked down at the knife still clutched in her hand as though she were seeing it for the first time.

"It's going to be okay, Mom. I promise." He removed his jacket and placed it around her shoulders.

Sensing that the immediate danger was over, Ralph stood and covered himself with a sheet. "She's gone nuts!"

In the distance, police sirens sounded. Someone must have passed the open door and seen what was happening. Gail began to rock back and forth on her heels, mumbling some gibberish that no one could understand.

"Please, Mom. Drop the knife. Do it for me. You're all Jerry and I have."

In Gail's mind, the boy's voice was growing distant. It was as if she were being sucked into a black vortex. She fought against it, as a drowning victim fights to stay afloat. But the current was too strong. Her hand shot out and pushed RJ. He flew across the room and landed in a heap by the front door. She faced Ralph with murder in her eyes and brought the knife up over her head.

Ralph screamed in terror. There was no place for him to run.

She lunged forward, just as an off-duty policeman who happened to be in the bar barged into the room and tackled her to the floor.

seventeen

Jane waylaid Marilee as she stepped through the front door. "Where were you? I thought you were studying with Jenna at the library?"

"We were," Marilee said, making a hasty retreat to her room.

Jane was quick on her tail. "I went to the library—"

"You were spying on me!" Marilee spun around and glared. "How could you?"

"I wasn't spying. Alex needed a book for his history report and, in case you don't know, there are other people in this house who use the library's facilities."

"We finished early and went for something to eat. All right?" Marilee threw her purse on the bed and switched on her CD player. Jane walked over and flicked it off.

"Hey, I was listening to that."

"Right now you're listening to me, young lady."

Marilee sighed. "Whatever."

"I want to know where you went."

"We went for a soda."

"Where?"

"I don't know. It wasn't my pick. A place in Torrington."

"I gave you permission to go to the library and that was all, to do research for a school project. You're grounded, remember? So how did you get there?"

"We drove."

"Who's *we*? Jenna's mother?" Jane could see her hesitate, weighing the risk of lying.

"No, it was a friend of Jenna's. A girl. I don't remember her name."

"So you got into the car of a perfect stranger, someone you just met?"

"She was an experienced driver. She's had her license for almost six months."

"That's comforting," Jane said, folding her arms across her chest. "Nevertheless, I don't want you taking rides with people I don't know, got it?"

Marilee rolled her eyes and turned away.

"I asked you a question, Marilee."

"Yes, I got it."

"Also . . . when you tell me that you're going to be someplace, that's where I expect to be able to find you. Any change of plans I want cleared with me first. That's why we gave you a cell phone."

"Anything else? I have homework to do," she snapped, collapsing onto the bed.

Jane exhaled a deep breath and tried to suppress the urge to wrap her hands tightly around her daughter's neck. Instead, she tried reasoning. "I know you think I'm trying to stop you from enjoying your teen years, and that's just not true. I want these years to be filled with wonderful memories. In some respects, this is the greatest time of your life. It's just that I'm trying to help you find a balance, to protect you from—"

Marilee never let her finish the sentence. She jumped off the bed and looked at Jane as though she were the enemy. "Protect me? From what, Mother? I'm not a child. I'm almost fifteen. In three years I'll be going away to college. What are you going to do then, rent a room on campus so you can protect me?" She emphasized the last two words by making quotation marks in the air. "Why can't you trust me instead of going behind my back and spying on me?"

A light rap on the bedroom door stopped Jane from possibly making an even bigger mistake by telling Marilee just how stupid that statement really was.

"Hon? Vera is on the phone," Vance said quietly. "You need to get down to the police station. Gail's been arrested for attempted murder."

The hookers were gathered around the large wooden work table at the back of the café. Vance had bravely offered to take care of things out front this morning while the group discussed the events of last night. Father Rich had arrived minutes ago, unshaved and slightly rumpled from his return flight from Rome.

"Where is she now?" Myla asked Vera.

"In Ridgecrest Hills under heavy restraints. Any more of that coffee?"

Jane had filled a large insulated thermos before the women arrived. She took Vera's cup and refilled it.

"Where's Ridgecrest Hills?" Kay asked. "I'll take a refill, too." Kay had arrived from the city only moments before Father Rich. The coffee and a half-eaten PowerBar in the car had been breakfast. What she really wanted was a plate of eggs.

"It's about twenty-five minutes from Bend Oaks and as close to hell as you can get here on earth," Rose informed her. "I can't believe Ralph allowed her to be taken there."

"I still don't understand how she managed to get out of the house without alerting either of us," Vera said.

"I've been trying to figure that out myself," Rose said, rubbing between her eyes. She felt like crap. She hadn't slept all night, her makeup had turned into a mud slide, and her clothes looked as though they had been slept in. She glanced over at the wall clock: 7:15. That gave her fifteen minutes to make it to school on time. If there hadn't been a huge assembly today, she would have called in sick.

"The only way she could have gotten out unnoticed was during that tea-kettle incident," Vera offered.

Rose explained to the others. "We put the kettle on for tea and all of a sudden it started making this horrible, high-pitched noise. Not a whistle, exactly, more like a kind of eerie moan." Rose's cheeks turned slightly red. "I know it sounds weird, but I can't explain it any better than that."

"Rose is right," Vera added. "And the noise wouldn't stop, not even when I took the kettle off the jet. It gave us both the willies."

"My guess is that while we were both dealing with that, Gail slipped out," Rose concluded. "I feel horrible about this. If we had kept a better watch on her none of this would have happened."

"I still can't believe she actually tried to kill Ralph," Myla said, wringing her hands, a new habit she had recently formed.

"Hell, if I were married to that man I might try to kill him my-self," Kay said. "He's been cheating on her all around the country."

"How do you know that?" Rose asked.

"I had him followed."

"You what?" the group cried in unison.

Kay told them what she had discovered in Boston, and her later confrontation with Ralph. "He didn't try to deny it. In fact, his only concern was whether I was going to tell Gail."

"And did you?" Rich asked.

"No," Kay said quietly. "I couldn't do that to her."

"When was this conversation with her husband?" Rich asked.

"The night of the Mass. Gail was running late. She and I were going to drive over to the rectory together, so we had made plans to meet at her house. She was late and Ralph and I were in the kitchen, so I let him know what I found out and what I planned to do if he ever cheated on her again."

"Is it possible that Gail slipped in somehow and overheard your conversation?"

"I suppose so . . . Why?"

"I was just trying to understand her state of mind when she arrived at the rectory that night."

"What bearing does that have on anything?" Vera asked.

"I think Gail may have become the host to whatever possessed the rectory."

"You mean like in demonic possession?" Myla asked.

Rich nodded, watching fear and disbelief flood the women's faces. He turned and glanced at Kay. "It's my guess that Gail overheard your conversation that night with Ralph and was filled with a complexity of emotions. Fear of losing her husband to another woman. Betrayal, anger, hurt. All entry points for demonic possession."

"But I get miffed at people all the time," Rose said. "As far as I know, I've never been possessed."

"Some people might debate that by the way you dress," Myla said, giving Rose's outfit—a low-cut spandex blouse exposing her ample cleavage, a skirt slit to her upper thigh, and four-inch stilettos—a quick once over.

Rich smiled. "No, Rose is right. Those emotions alone wouldn't trigger it. It might influence you to do something counterproductive, but that's not what happened here. That night, we were expelling a powerful demonic force from the house, an ancient entity that's been around for millennia. It's cunning and deadly. Sensing its demise, it did the only thing it could to survive. It looked for a host."

"And the host it took was Gail, using her anger over the discovery of her husband's infidelity as an entry point," Jane added.

"How can you be certain that Gail is possessed?" Vera asked. "She suffered a concussion. Maybe it clouded her thinking, made her act crazy."

Rich turned toward Jane. "Maybe it's time you shared what you've discovered?"

She hesitated.

"It's okay. We're all friends here," he told her.

"Please, Jane, tell us what you sensed," Rose said.

Jane cradled her coffee mug nervously. "As soon as you called, I rushed to the police station. The sheriff and Vance are buddies, so he sneaked me in to see Gail before she was taken away. It was horrible. They had her in a windowless cell, seated in a chair and bound in a straitjacket."

Vera's eyes filled with tears. "Poor Gail."

"I know, it hit me hard, too," Jane told her.

"Were you able to pick up anything?" Kay asked.

"Yes, in fact I had been sensing a dark force gathering around her for weeks, ever since our first hookers' meeting at the rectory."

"You think she might have picked up something in the basement? She did act kind of strange afterward," Vera said.

"And I'll never forget that scream," Myla added.

"It might have been tracking her from the beginning," Rich offered.

"Why Gail?" Rose asked.

"She was the easiest target, right?" Kay asked Rich.

"It looks that way."

"Poor Gail," Myla murmured, wringing her hands tighter.

"Go on, Jane," Vera said. "What else happened at the police station?"

The room had grown absolutely silent except for the sound of a fly trapped inside the back screen door.

Jane's face filled with a mix of terror and heartbreak. "She looked up at me, but it wasn't really Gail behind those eyes."

"Good God," Myla whispered.

"What are we going to do?" Vera asked.

"There's only one thing to do," Rich said. "I'll have to seek permission to perform an exorcism."

"You're kidding, right?" Kay said.

"No, I'm dead serious," Rich said. He went on to tell them about the parchment that he and Kay had discovered at the rectory, and its connection with the one in Rome. He also detailed Louisa's story, concluding with the exorcism.

"And is the child all right now?" Rose wanted to know.

"Sadly, she had to be committed to a mental institution. The trauma she underwent was just too much for her young mind to bear."

"How awful," Vera said.

"And you still want to go on with an exorcism for Gail?" Kay asked.

"We have no choice," he replied.

"Excuse me for being the only doubting non-Catholic in the room," Kay said. "But what makes you believe that Gail won't end up the same way?"

"You're right," he said. "There are no guarantees."

"I say let's do it," Vera said. "Without an exorcism, Gail's a goner for sure."

"But how?" Myla asked. "Ridgecrest won't let anyone in to see her. I know—I've already called, and they told me they have strict instructions not to allow her any visitors."

"It wouldn't work there anyway," Rich told them. "The exorcism has to be performed at the rectory. That's where the portal was opened."

"So how are we going to get her out?" Rose asked.

"Ralph sure isn't going to give his permission," Vera said.

"There's only one way," Kay said.

The group waited for her to continue.

"We're just going to have to kidnap her," Kay said, freshening up her coffee.

"You're kidding, right?" Rose asked.

"No. I'm not kidding."

Rose shrugged. "I'm up for it. Anyone else want to join in?"

The others thought a moment.

"I'm in," Vera said.

"Me, too," Myla added.

"How about you, Jane?" Rose asked.

"Sure."

"Then we're all agreed," Rose concluded. She turned toward Rich. "I think you'd better hang at the rectory and set things up. We women will take care of the kidnapping."

He nodded.

"Good. That settles it," Kay said, emptying a packet of Splenda into her coffee and stirring it around. "And I was afraid country living might be boring."

Ridgecrest Hills, a huge, imposing complex, was thought to be the most modern facility for psychiatric treatment in the nation when it was built in 1932. It was a self-contained facility with its own hydroelectric plant, greenhouses, laundry, bakery, upholstery shop, and, at one time, even a firehouse.

A row of maple trees lined the driveway that wound for more than a half mile before coming to the main compound—a group of Greek-columned buildings that rose like the Colossus from the sylvan setting (lots of meadows and woods). It was chosen to induce feelings of peace and tranquillity among the patients, who were never actually allowed to walk the grounds. This would have incited too much fear among the neighboring residents. The patients had to be content with looking out at the countryside from one of the screened rooms.

Eventually, time and modern psychology rendered Ridgecrest Hills obsolete. With each passing year, more buildings were closed and less of the grounds maintained until, presently, only one of the two large central buildings remained in use. The others were boarded up.

The lower floor housed patients who needed only minimal supervision. The second floor was designated for more serious illnesses. It contained sixteen cells that were filled with an assortment of psychotics and psychopaths, all of whom were considered a danger to themselves and to society. Gail was now listed among them.

RJ watched the old security guard head off to his car for his after-dinner nap. He leaned back against a tree and checked his watch. He'd give him about ten minutes before starting out. RJ was no stranger to Ridgecrest Hills. Almost everyone at school knew about this place. It had a cool network of tunnels that ran beneath the property and connected all the buildings. They had originally been designed as an unobtrusive way to transfer patients from treatment facilities to their dorms. The local kids now used them for drinking and drug parties.

RJ entered one of the smaller buildings and found the stairwell that led to the tunnels. Within minutes, he was winding his way along the dark passages, heading toward the main building. This place was the pits. His father was such a jerk for allowing Gail to be brought here, although he could understand why Ralph was so ticked off. She did try to kill him.

The whole incident had RJ deeply confused. Gail didn't have a murderous bone in her body. If she had, she would have killed him and his brother a dozen times over for all the grief they had caused her these past few years. But she wasn't that kind of person. It wasn't in her nature to be mean or cruel. She was the kindest, most forgiving person he had ever known, and he was sick to his gut just thinking about her being locked up in a place like this. His dad should have sent her to a place where she could get the help she needed. Hadn't he figured out that it was the concussion that had caused her strange behavior? She must have suffered some kind of brain damage when she hit her head. That would explain her actions, right? If he could just talk to her, get her side of the story. Maybe then he could persuade his dad to have her moved to a decent facility.

RJ threaded toward the main building, swinging the flashlight's beam back and forth and flooding the long, narrow tube with light. Every once in a while, he'd swear he heard someone coming up behind him. He'd swing around fast, but no one was there. The place creeped him out. Finally, he came to the wrought-iron staircase that led to the main building. It shook violently under his weight, his footsteps sounding hollow and metallic as they echoed in the darkness.

The landing was just up ahead. The red glow from the exit sign on the first level provided a modicum of light and a temporary sense that he had reemerged into the land of the living. The feeling, however, was fleeting. Almost immediately, he felt a deep unrest, as though the very walls were pressing in on him. He headed up one more flight and carefully opened the heavy metal door. The hinges creaked and groaned. The smell just about knocked him over. He covered his nose and slowly leaned into the corridor. It was empty. He stepped in and quietly closed the door.

It was a moonless night, and the three emergency lights (the only light source) did little to dispel the thickening shadows. Voices babbled away in imaginary conversations from behind closed doors. Occasionally, a piercing laugh broke forth. It gave him the shudders. Poor Gail. He had to get her out of here.

His sneakers squeaked as he made his way down the hall. At each door, he peered through the small openings that were used to dispense food trays.

"Gail?" he whispered.

"Who's there?" a spidery voice called from across the corridor. Unwashed fingers jabbed through the opening, trying to snag whatever passed by.

He finally found her. She was in the last room on the left.

"Gail?"

He could make out her outline. She was seated on a metal-framed bed, staring out into the starless night through a heavily grilled window.

"Pssst . . . Gail? Mom? It's me, RJ."

The figure slowly turned around and faced the door. It was hard to make out her features. He leaned in closer. The room was in shadow.

"I need to talk to you," he told her.

"Come closer," a female voice mimicked next door. "I need to talk to you." Shrill laughter rippled along the cold tiled floor.

"I can't stay. I just need to know that you're all right," RJ said.

The figure slid off the bed and made its way over.

"RJ?"

He exhaled. It was her.

He rushed on. "I came to make sure you're all right, and to tell you that I'm going to find a way to get you out of here. I really miss you, Mom." The sound of the word brought unexpected tears to his eyes.

"Give me your hand," she said. "Slip it through the opening. I just want to hold your hand."

He reached out, then hesitated.

"Slip your hand through, RJ."

For some strange reason, he couldn't do it. He couldn't put his hand through the slot.

"GIVE ME YOUR HAND," the voice on the other side of the door commanded.

That wasn't Gail's voice. He felt a shiver of fear. It took him several minutes to muster the courage to inch forward.

Without warning, something shot through the opening in the door, splintering the wood. He keeled backward onto the tile and scurried farther away. His heart was beating a mile a minute. He stared at the door. Was he having some kind of hallucination?

An arm, ancient and withered, had thrust itself through the opening. Only instead of a hand and fingers at the end, there was a cloven hoof.

eighteen

The Honeychurch house had grown quiet except for the ticking of the kitchen clock.

Rose had rushed over directly after school. Kay had been called back into the city to babysit a client but promised to return by nightfall. Ralph had left early this morning on one of his business trips, and the boys were supposedly visiting with friends. But it was Gail's absence that everyone felt most acutely.

Vera, Jane, and Myla sat staring into their coffee cups.

After what seemed an eternity of uncomfortable silence, Rose spoke. "I've been over Kay's idea a hundred times, and I still don't see how we're going to get Gail out of that place without being caught."

"It can't be that hard," Vera said. "There are only two men on duty at night—the security guard, who I hear is older than dirt, and a male attendant."

"What we need is a distraction to divert their attention," Myla said sagely.

"I suppose we could always start a fire," Vera offered. "There's a lot of old brush around some of those buildings."

"But then we'd risk the police and the fire department swooping down on the place," Jane said.

"Oh, yeah."

"To be honest, this whole thing seems really out there to me," Rose confessed. "I mean, we're talking about kidnapping a woman because we think she's possessed by the Devil. I don't mean to discredit your gift," she said to Jane, "but it does seem slightly over the edge."

"Slightly?" Myla piped up. "It seems completely loony, but . . ."

"But?" Rose waited for her to continue.

"Look, I'm just as confused and concerned as the rest of you for Gail's sake. The woman Jane described bears no resemblance whatsoever to the woman I know. I keep remembering what happened at the rectory. We can try to rationalize what we experienced up the wazoo, but let's face it, girls, it defies all sane explanations."

"I wish Father Rich were here," Myla said. "He could explain things to us—help us feel a little more settled about it. Where is he, anyway?"

"The bishop's secretary called. Archbishop Kerry has just been released from the hospital. I think Father Rich is hoping to finally get his hands on Father Stephens's diary," Jane offered.

"This discussion calls for something stronger than coffee," Vera conceded. "We've only got a few hours to devise a plan." She pulled two bottles from the liquor cabinet. "Scotch or vodka?"

"Scotch," the women said in unison.

"You know, if we don't settle this thing at the rectory soon we're all going to turn into blooming alcoholics," Myla predicted.

Vera grabbed Ralph's prize bottle of fifty-dollar Glenfiddich and poured liberal amounts into four tumblers that her daughter-in-law had found at a church tag sale. She grabbed two and felt an undertow of sadness begin to drag her down. Her lips quivered, and tears flowed copiously.

"You all right, Vera?" Myla asked. Vera never cried.

"No, I'm not," she said, setting the drinks on the coffee table. "I'm worried sick about Gail, and afraid for her. In fact, I'm afraid for all of us. I know what Father Rich is suggesting is strange and frightening. I mean, if we accept that this inhuman entity has attached itself to Gail the thought that follows next is what would stop something like this from happening to us. It's scary. So we sit here, trying to rationalize it away. We say it's a psychosis, a mental breakdown. God knows she's overdue, having to live with my son. But in my gut I know that it has nothing to do with the physical realm."

"All right, just for argument's sake, let's suppose what you and Jane are saying is true—that Gail is really possessed by something evil," Rose told Vera. "Do you really think that just by chanting some ancient ritual we can deliver her? I don't mean to play devil's advocate—no pun intended—but isn't it a little like swatting a Teratornis with a flyswatter and expecting it to roll over dead."

Myla frowned. "A Tera . . . what?"

"A giant prehistoric bird."

"I keep forgetting you're an educator. But for this discussion could you restrict metaphors to modern-day species?"

"Sorry . . . but my point is, what makes Father Rich think this will work?"

"Because it has a long history of working, going all the way back to Christ," Jane said, setting her glass on the coffee table. "I know it's hard to believe—"

"Damn impossible."

"Be that as it may, it's the only way that Gail's soul can be set free. The longer we wait, the more entrenched the demon becomes, making it harder and finally impossible to deliver her from its clutches, and the more of her life source it will use in order to survive."

"You mean that she might die?" Myla asked, wringing her hands. It was obvious that this hadn't occurred to her.

"Yes," Jane said simply.

"So that brings us back to the original question," Myla said. "How are we going to get Gail out of that place without getting caught?"

"I can tell you how," RJ said, dropping his schoolbooks on the counter.

Vera shot up out of her seat. "RJ, what are you doing here? I thought you were going over to Ron's house to watch videos."

He shrugged. "I didn't feel much like it."

"What do you mean you know how to get Gail out?" Rose asked as he walked into the room.

"I went there last night to see her," he confessed, leaning on the arm of the couch.

"You what?" Vera said.

"Grandma, something is really wrong with her, and I don't think it has anything to do with her mind."

"How is she?" Vera asked. "Is she all right?"

"She's . . ." He lowered his head.

Vera rushed over and put her arm around her grandson. "It's all right, RJ. We'll get her out of there."

"You said that you knew a way in?" Rose asked.

"There's a set of tunnels that weave underneath the hospital grounds. Gail's being held in the main building on the second floor. I know those tunnels. I can get you through without anyone seeing you coming or going."

"What about the security guards or the attendants?" Rose wanted to know.

"They won't be a problem," RJ said. "I think I know a way to keep them busy." He opened the liquor cabinet and removed two more bottles of his father's prize scotch.

"What if they were to get a surprise delivery?" he said with a devilish grin.

Hope was infused back into the room. The women smiled.

"And I know the perfect delivery person," Vera said, staring at Rose's red satin bustier with the black lace.

RJ turned red.

"Great. Now let's call Father Rich on his cell phone and tell him that tonight is a go," Jane said.

"Call Kay, too," Rose said. "She can meet us at the Big Y parking lot at about a quarter of seven. We'll carpool from there."

"I hate to leave without knowing she got home safe," Jane told Vance as he tossed three macaroni-and-cheese dinners into the microwave and hit the "frozen dinner" function. The unit began to hum.

"She's only a couple minutes late," he reminded her, taking out some glasses. "Hey, Alex. You want milk or orange juice?"

Alex looked up briefly from his PlayStation "Crash Team Racing" just as Coot was kidnapped by Emperor Velo.

"Chocolate milk."

"Good try, buddy," Vance said. "Plain milk it is."

"Maybe I should stay until she gets here," Jane said, setting her car keys back on the granite counter.

Vance picked them up and put them back into her hand. "Go. She'll be here in a few minutes. Meanwhile, if you don't leave now you'll be late, and you don't want to miss breaking your friend out of the clinker. Just know that I'm standing by, ready to bail you all out if you get caught."

"Funny," she said, smiling. He had doubled over with laughter earlier when she had told him of the hookers' plan.

Staring up into his soft brown eyes, she was overcome with love for this incredible, supportive man. How many men would take a wife's psychic powers in stride, and even be willing to bail her out of jail if she got caught while trying to rescue a demon-possessed friend? She grabbed him around the neck and planted a passionate kiss on his lips. God, she was lucky.

"Ummm . . . I think you should engage in kidnappings on a more regular basis if it makes you this passionate," he teased. He folded her into an embrace, his hand searching out the small of her back, melding her body with his.

"And if you keep this up I may not want to go at all," she said.

He released her with a sigh.

"All kidding aside, I'm scared," she whispered, so that Alex wouldn't overhear.

He moved away slightly, brushing a stray hair away from her eyes. "I'll tell you what I tell the boys' soccer team."

"What's that?"

"A little fear is a good thing—it keeps you on your toes." He looked down into her face and smiled gently. "Honey, I know that you've been running away from this thing ever since the night of your parents' accident. Isn't it time you faced it? Not that I'm exactly crazy about having a wife who can see demons and devils, but I figure you must have been given this gift for a reason. Maybe tonight you'll finally discover what it is."

She broke away. "I know you're right. I just wish that so much wasn't at stake. What if my powers fail and I can't help Father Rich? What if we can't save Gail from this thing?"

"Listen up, you," Vance said in his best coach's voice. "Father Stephens had great faith in your abilities, and so do I. Now go." He pushed her toward the back door.

"And Marilee?"

"I'll call you on your cell as soon as she gets home."

"I want to go home," Marilee said, pushing Tye back over to the driver's side of the van.

She was tired of his beer-soaked breath and his hot, clammy hands trying to snake their way up her blouse. God, he even stank like he hadn't bathed in days. He was a pig. She folded her arms across her chest and shot him a nasty glare. What had ever made her think that he was cool?

"Would you turn on the heat? It's getting cold," she said. She should have brought a sweater.

"Need a cuddle?" he said, all mushy-like. He reached out, grabbed her around the waist, and crushed her to his chest. "Come here—I'll relight your pilot."

She stiffened. "I said I want to go home. Now, Tye. I'm not kidding."

He tightened his hold. "Yeah, well, you can't always get what you want, now, can you? You'll go home when I say it's time to go home."

Suddenly she realized how vulnerable she was and felt a shiver of fear. They were parked along a back road, miles away from anywhere. If she screamed for help, who would hear?

Tye opened the window and tossed out the can of beer, then turned toward her, his eyes red-rimmed, his lips moist. "I thought you wanted to play with the grown-ups," he said. "You keep mouthing off about how your parents treat you like a kid instead of a grown-up. Welcome to adulthood, my sweet. First lesson: if you want to play grown-up, you have to learn to share your toys." He fondled the buttons on her blouse.

"Let me go, you creep," she said, slapping his face.

"Don't you ever hit me, you bitch." He yanked her hair, snapping her head back. "I think it's time I taught you some manners."

He covered her lips, forcing his tongue into her mouth while his hands searched for her breasts.

Rich checked his watch. He needed to reach Bend Oaks before nightfall, but he still had an hour or so. He cast around for someplace where he could be alone to study the package that was tucked under his arm. It had been given to him only moments ago by the bishop's secretary, Father Connors. His gaze fell on the small chapel annexed to the archbishop's residency. He hurried along. There wasn't much time, but it was imperative that he find out what secret the diary held.

He pushed against the paneled doors, which opened soundlessly, and slipped inside. Even though the building sat along a heavily traveled road in Hartford, the room was surprisingly quiet and, thankfully, empty. He needed to be alone.

Four sets of pews fronted a small altar draped in a white linen cloth. Behind the altar three stained-glass panels depicting the divinity of the Godhead—the Father, the Son, and the Holy Spirit—provided soft rays of filtered light tipped in reds, yellows, and blues. He turned toward the tabernacle, genuflected, and slid into a back pew. Whatever was inside the journal, the forces of evil had done their best to prevent him from reading it.

"I don't know what this package contains, but since the archbishop ordered it removed from the vault nothing but misfortune has plagued us," Connors had said, handing Rich the package. "I'll be glad to see it gone. First the bishop's heart attack. Then two unexplained house fires. And just this morning, moments after you called to make arrangements to collect it, one of our seminarians was injured."

"How?" Rich asked.

"I asked him to retrieve the diary from the bishop's office. While he was there, he was nearly blinded by a freak accident," Connors explained.

"Blinded! My God, what happened?" Rich asked.

"The gardener was mowing the lawn and a rock kicked up from underneath the blade of the mower and flew through the bishop's window." He turned, his face sober. "The glass flew out, slashing the young man's cheek. A few inches higher and he would have lost his sight."

Rich studied the package. These incidents were not accidents. He was sure of that. It all revolved around this diary. What could it contain that so threatened the powers of darkness?

Connors folded his arms across his chest, his face as dark as a stormy sky. "Archbishop Kerry told me in confidence what you were about to undertake. I admit I don't know much about demonology, but this much I do know. Whatever it is you're about to vanquish is a powerful source of evil. I admire your courage and wish you Godspeed."

Courage? The term had almost made him laugh. If only Connors knew how frightened he was. Any entity that had the kind of power over the physical world that had been displayed both here and at the rectory was a formidable enemy. He picked up the package and began to untie the string. His hand shook slightly. Satan had gone to great lengths to prevent him from obtaining this diary. Whatever it contained must be of major importance.

An envelope with the archbishop's seal was tucked inside the diary.

> *Dear Father Melos:*
>
> *I trust that the contents of this book will remain confidential. The public must never know what has taken place at St. Francis Xavier's rectory. Such knowledge would only place an unfavorable spotlight on our Church.*
>
> *I have read the diary's chilling account and must urge you to take every precaution to protect yourself and those you serve against the dark force that resides there. God bless you on your mission. I join the saints in their prayers for your protection.*
>
> *In Christ's service,*
> *Archbishop H. Kerry*

Rich tucked the letter back inside the envelope and set it aside. Taking a deep breath, he opened the diary and began to read.

> *Today I have set about to record the events of the past few weeks in hopes that it might help me clarify in my mind what is taking place here at the St. Francis Xavier rectory. I preface this account by stating that I have left no stone unturned in seeking*

*out a rational explanation for what I have encountered before
turning to the subject of the paranormal. Unfortunately, as of this
writing no physical cause has been uncovered that could account
for what I have experienced since my arrival.*

*I came to St. Francis Xavier's two months ago to assume the
role of pastor. Since my arrival, however, several strange and
troubling disturbances have led me to conclude that something evil
inhabits this place. This is not a statement that I make lightly.
Although I do not consider myself a mystic, I cannot shake the
feeling that I am being subjected to a malevolent force that seeks
to instill fear.*

*Most of these occurrences happen between the hours of 9 PM
and 3 AM. They begin with loud rapping noises that seem to come
from inside the walls. This is always followed by the sound of
footsteps marching up and down the hallway outside my bedroom
door. When I investigate, I find the hallway empty.*

*Most recently, I have seen a black mistlike substance forming
in the corners of my room. I instinctively sensed that it was
imperative that I not allow it to take shape. I blessed the room
with holy water and anointed the doorway and the windows with
holy oil. Since then, the substance has not reappeared.*

*I have questioned my sister Judith, who assists me as my
housekeeper, seeking to discern if she has experienced any of these
disturbances. She told me she has not. Apparently, whatever evil
resides here wishes to single me out. The question remains,
however, why?*

The next few entries echoed the same type of disturbances, the
same perplexity on Father Stephens's part in trying to understand
their significance. In one entry, he alluded to a visit with Archbishop
Jack Halpert, who held the office at the time. Rich remembered stories about him. He had not been greatly loved and had a reputation

for distancing himself from the parish priests. Somehow, however, Father Stephens had gained an audience.

> *I have grown increasingly concerned about the unexplained disturbances here at the rectory, which suddenly seem to be aimed at making me question my faith. As the shepherd of a large and growing flock, I felt it my duty to bring this matter to the attention of my bishop. Archbishop Halpert, however, made it perfectly clear that he did not believe in the paranormal and questioned the state of my mental health, insinuating that perhaps the pressures of overseeing such a robust and rapidly expanding parish was proving too difficult for me to handle. I assured him that was not the case and invited him to come visit and witness these disturbances himself. He, however, declined and gave me an ultimatum. I was either to desist from making what he labeled "wild and unbelievable claims" or I would be replaced. It is quite clear that I must handle this matter alone.*
>
> *Fortunately, another priest friend of mine, in whom I might confide without fear, has offered to lend me several books that deal with the subject of saints and the paranormal.*

Well, that explained Father Stephens's book collection, Rich mused.

He quickly scanned several more months of entries before coming upon Jane's addition to the household.

> *Jane awoke again with nightmares last night and shook the house with her screams. Judith tried to console her, but the child was consumed with fear.*
>
> *Is this due to the trauma she has endured, or is it something else? Has the evil that I feel is contained within these walls shifted its attention over to Jane? I pray not.*

Several other entries echoed the same concerns.

Jane complains about her room being as cold as ice during the night. I've had Marvin check out the heating system, but he assures me that nothing is amiss.

I've recently acquired a book written by St. Theresa of Avila. It speaks about this phenomenon in cases where demonic entities are present. If this is the cause, my worst fears have been realized.

Jane, however, insists that she is experiencing nothing out of the ordinary, yet I feel the child is not telling the truth. I perceive that she has a rare gift of discernment. On several occasions, I have caught her fleeing a part of the house where I, too, felt something evil was lurking.

This, however, leaves me in a quandary. Jane has no living relatives. If she is forced to leave here, she would become a ward of the state and be placed in the care of a foster home—an event that I fear would cause additional trauma. She's already been through enough with the death of her entire family.

I pray daily for wisdom.

The shadows were thickening outside. The chapel, too, had grown dim. Rich looked at his watch. It read 4:45. Bend Oaks was a good hour's ride from here, and that was only if there was no traffic.

He knew he'd better be going. He had left Marvin a detailed list of how the library must be set up; still, he needed to check everything out, make sure nothing had been left undone. He glanced at the diary and felt a wave of frustration. Whatever Father Stephens had discovered about the evil that had taken possession of Gail was in this diary, yet there were still hundreds of pages left to read. He'd never make it back in time if he stayed to finish it. He laid the book on the pew, then leaned forward and pleaded with God for help:

Dear God, What am I to do? The information I need is inside this book, but I don't have time to go through it all.

A strong current of wind crept into the room, curling around his feet, then fanning out across the room. The candles in front of the statue of the Madonna flickered and the linen altar cloth blew in the breeze. He turned. Had someone come into the chapel and forgotten to close the door? The chapel was empty. He glanced down at the diary. The wind had moved the pages. His eyes fell across the mention of St. Ignatius. His heartbeat quickened.

> *I've sent Jane to the Cape with her friend Gail. Judith is safe visiting with her aunt Violet in Maine. Their absence will allow Marvin and me to work at putting together the safeguards spoken of in the text I've just acquired on St. Ignatius.*
>
> *He refers to the power inherent in Christ's crown of thorns, a symbol that down through the years has become associated with his gift of exorcism.*

Rich unconsciously twisted the silver ring on his finger.

> *It is this symbol that I will use to contain the entity, for I lack the power to vanquish such a powerful force. According to St. Ignatius, only one order, a secret priesthood, possessed that kind of power. He was one of them.*
>
> *He refers to them simply as the "Ancient Order of the Magi," and states that they can be recognized by the mark of the crescent moon that they carry.*

RJ had hitched a ride with Jane. The plan was for him to show the women the way into the building and then act as a decoy if Gail put up a fuss. They made the turn off Main Street in Southbury, heading the back way along the river as the last rays of daylight began to fade. Jane switched on the headlights.

"Thanks for doing this for my mom," RJ said quietly as they crossed the small steel bridge that separated Southbury from Sandy Hook.

Jane glanced his way and smiled. "I think that's the first time I've ever heard you refer to her as Mom."

His face reddened slightly. He looked away. "Yeah, I guess I haven't been a very good stepson."

"She really loves you, you know."

"Yeah, I know."

"And when she finds out how you refused to leave her in that place she's going to be very proud of you."

Her cell phone rang.

"I hope that's my husband with news that our daughter has finally arrived home safe and sound," she said. "Hi, honey."

"Mom, you've got to come get me," Marilee said, her voice a hoarse whisper.

Jane could tell she was crying. Something was wrong. "Where are you?"

"I don't know, exactly. I'm somewhere in Waterbury."

"Waterbury? How did you get there?"

"I'm so sorry, Mom. I should have listened to what you said. It's Tye."

"Slow down, Marilee. What are you doing with Tye? Your father and I told you to stay away from him."

"Give me back the phone," Marilee screamed. "Tye, please . . . I just want to go home."

The connection went dead.

"What is it?" RJ asked.

"My daughter's in trouble. She's somewhere in Waterbury with a creep named Tye."

Jane clamped down on the brakes and made a U-turn, heading back toward I-84. She had no idea where to find Marilee. All she knew was that she had to try.

"If this is the same creep that was with her last week, I might be able to help you find them," RJ said.

"You saw her with him last week? If you knew this kid was trouble, why didn't you say something?" Jane asked incredulously.

"I didn't think it was any of my business." He opened his cell phone and scanned through the last week of received calls. Tye had called to arrange to pick up the pot. He recognized all the entries except one. He punched in the number and waited for Tye to pick up. He answered on the third ring.

"Hi, Tye? It's me, RJ. I just got a shipment of some great grass that I thought you might be interested in. No, I can't meet you later—it's now or never. In fact, I'm heading into Waterbury right now. Oh, you are? Tell me where you are and I'll meet you."

Jane handed him a pencil and a dry-cleaning receipt.

He cradled the phone and jotted down some street names. "Yeah, I know the place," he said. "Say in about twenty minutes. Oh, and Tye, if that sweet-faced girlfriend of yours is there, I hear this stuff drives them wild. She is . . . then I'll pack a little something extra."

RJ hung up, carefully avoiding Jane's laserlike stare. "He's got her, and she's all right. At least for the moment."

"I won't ask how you know this creep or why he thinks you're a drug dealer," she said. "Just tell me how to get there."

nineteen

The women leaned against Kay's roadster, which sat beneath a yellow pool of light in the Big Y's parking lot, and tried to decipher what was being said on the other end of her cell phone. It sounded as though Jane wasn't coming, which meant that neither was RJ. So how were they going to find their way inside Ridgecrest and rescue Gail?

"All right. I'll tell the others. Good luck," Kay said, flipping the phone closed and slipping it into the back pocket of her tailored jeans.

"She's going to be late, right?" Vera asked.

"Seems like Marilee got herself into some trouble," Kay told them. "Jane and RJ are heading over to Waterbury to bail her out."

"Now what?" Myla said. "Father Rich said that we had to be at the rectory before dusk. If we wait for Jane, we'll never make it there in time."

"Then we have to do this without them," Rose said, rolling back the door to her boss's minivan.

"I agree," Kay said, hitting the lock mechanism on her Beemer. Lights flashed and the horn beeped once, followed by the sound of locks slipping securely into place.

"But how will we find our way through the tunnels?" Myla asked as Rose pushed her into the backseat.

"RJ and I talked a little about his last trip. I have a general idea how to find our way through," Kay said, heading toward the passenger side. She saw them hesitate. "Come on, girls. Where's your sense of adventure?"

Rose adjusted her blouse, making certain to show just enough cleavage to incite interest, then pulled open the door to the main entrance and walked her best sassy, hip-swaying walk toward the two men seated at the front desk.

The old security guard was napping, his chin resting on his chest. The other, an attendant, came to life as soon as he saw Rose walk through the door. She checked him out. Not too bad—looked around forty. He stood about five feet ten. He was broad-shouldered, with tight abs. Must work out on a regular basis. She liked a man who cared about his body. As she drew closer, she slyly checked his ring finger. Empty—hot stuff! Under any other circumstances, she would have stuck around to see what she could drum up. Darn Gail! She'd better appreciate what she was giving up.

She pulled her stomach in, thrust out her 38D-cup chest and headed straight for him as he nudged the old gent awake. The four-inch heels she was wearing gave her hips just the right amount of sway.

"Hello, gentlemen," she said, giving them her brightest smile.

The old man tried to get up but was having trouble. The younger one leaned against the wall behind the desk and gave her an amused smile. She knew the look. He was playing it cool. She liked his style.

"What can we do for you?" the young fellow asked.

She set a shopping bag down on the desk. "I'm from the liquor store up the road and I have a delivery," she said. She removed a bottle of scotch, making sure they could read the label. "Seems like someone wants to thank you for services rendered." She set out three paper cups on the worn wooden desktop. "You don't mind if I join you for a drink, now, do you?"

Thirty minutes later, the men were well on their way to an alcohol-induced haze. Rose made her excuses and left. As soon as she hit the outside, she removed her heels and ran toward the row of small buildings at the south end of the compound. The others were waiting outside the van.

"Everything go okay?" Vera asked, handing Rose a pair of Nikes.

"Piece of cake."

"I found the door to the tunnels that RJ told me about," Kay said. "It's inside that building over there."

"You stay in the van," Rose told Myla. "Keep the motor running."

"Right, in case you need to make a fast getaway." Myla felt a rush of excitement, a sense of life returning to her predictable, uninteresting world. Suddenly she understood why Vera took all those risky trips. If the cops didn't get them for kidnapping or the legions of hell failed to overtake them, she just might join Vera on her next adventure.

Kay led the way through the tunnels.

"This reminds me of the caves I once explored in Yucatán," Vera said. "Only I hope this one doesn't have any bats. If there's one kind of rodent I hate, it's bats."

Kay shined the flashlight on a side corridor that veered off sharply from the rest. "This is where RJ said we were to make a left."

"A left it is, then," Vera said, stamping through a puddle of foul-smelling water as though she were having the time of her life.

"My God, this place is gross," Rose said. "The floor is coated in slime."

"I wonder what the kids do down here," Vera said as she marched full steam ahead.

Kay looked at Rose and shook her head. If Vera didn't know, they weren't about to enlighten her.

"Stop," Rose said. "Did you hear that?"

"Hear what?" Vera asked.

"I heard someone behind us."

"It's just your imagination," Vera said, shining her flashlight in the cavern of darkness behind them.

"Let's just hurry and get Gail out of here," Rose said. "This place gives me the creeps."

They came to a fork.

"Now what?" Rose asked Kay.

"RJ didn't say anything about this." She reached for her cell phone and hit redial. Nothing. "We're too far down to get service."

"The building that Gail is being held in is due east," Vera said, taking something out of her pocket.

"What's that?" Kay asked.

"A compass."

"You always carry one in your pocket?"

"If there's one thing I learned on all my adventures it was always to carry a compass and water."

"So where's the water?" Kay joked.

Vera pulled out a small canteen. "Thirsty?"

"So which way?" Rose asked, not amused. "The sooner we get out of this pit, the better."

Vera consulted the compass. "We stay to the right."

"RJ said that we should come to a staircase that leads to the main building. Do you see anything up ahead, Vera?" Kay asked, trudging through a small river. Fortunately, she had had the presence of mind to wear sneakers, but even those were now soaked through.

"Tell me you didn't hear that?" Rose said, grabbing Kay by the arm.

"Hear what?" Vera asked.

The three woman stood perfectly still. This time they all heard it. Footfalls sounded.

"Who's there?" Rose asked.

The air was turning bitterly cold. No one answered. The footsteps grew louder. Whispered voices could be heard in the distance.

"Let's get out of here," Rose said.

"I'll second that," Kay said.

Something flew past their heads, then another, then another. Vera shined the flashlight up toward the ceiling.

"Yikes!"

Bats! Suddenly the tunnel was flooded with them.

"Look!" Kay shouted, pointing behind them.

Amber orbs of light, like the eyes of a giant cat, had begun to glow. The women took off at a run.

"Let me drive in alone," RJ said, unbuckling his seat belt.

They were approaching the abandoned road that had once been used by the brass mills to transport metal from the freight yards.

"You've got to be kidding," Jane said, putting the car in park. "That's my daughter in there. I'm going to kill that creep for bringing her out here."

"Exactly," he said, opening the passenger door and slipping out. "And if Tye sees you there's no telling what he might do. But if I pull up alone he'll think it's just another buy."

Jane hesitated, watching RJ walk around to the driver's side.

"It's our only chance," he said through her open window.

"All right." She slipped out and let him slide in. "But if you're not back in ten minutes I'm calling the police."

"Deal," he said, heading out.

A quarter of a mile up the road, his headlights caught the front of Tye's van. He slowed to a crawl. He wanted Tye to think that he was playing it cautious, checking things out. He fought against the urge to rush in. He parked a few feet away, walked over, and rapped on the van's back door. He heard a scuffle inside. "Hey, man. I don't have all day. I've got other deliveries to make," he said.

The back door opened slowly. Tye tumbled out and nearly fell to the ground. "What took you so long?" he asked, steadying himself against the rear of the van. The guy was wasted and smelled like the inside of a blue-collar bar.

RJ got a quick look inside. Marilee was backed up against the driver's seat, her eyes wide with fear. She recognized him and started to stay something, but RJ threw her a warning glare.

"So where is it?" Tye asked, growing impatient.

Tye's eyes told RJ that he was already pumped up on something and could be dangerous. "You know the drill," he said. "I see the cash first, then you get to see the goods."

"I don't think so. First the pot, then the money." Tye took a menacing step forward and grabbed him around the throat. The sudden movement took RJ by surprise.

"Okay, man, settle down," RJ said, lifting his arms in surrender. "We'll do it your way. I've got it right here in my shirt pocket. You just gotta back off a little and let me get at it."

Tye pushed him away.

RJ made a big fuss about searching his coat pockets. "It's here somewhere. Oh, yeah. I got it." He turned away, forming a fist, then swung around in an explosion of power, cuffing Tye across the face. For just a second, his eyes registered disbelief before rolling back into their sockets. He crumpled to the ground.

RJ threw open the back doors to the van, and Marilee tumbled out.

"You all right?" he asked, helping to steady her.

She nodded.

He could tell that she was on the verge of a meltdown. "Your mom's right down the road," he told her. "Come on, I'll take you to her."

"Gail's room should be down here," Kay said, her heart still hammering wildly. Their encounter in the tunnel had been like something out of a classic B horror film: *Women Meet Beast from Hell*.

Fortunately, Vera had had the presence of mind to invoke St. Anthony's protection, and Kay had surprised them both by taking out a vial of holy water and sprinkling it into the air. The screams that followed were still reverberating in Kay's head, but at least whatever had blocked their path had been vaporized.

"Here it is," Vera said, peering through the door opening. "I see her. She's lying on the bed. Gail . . . it's me, Vera. Kay and Rose are here, too. We've come to get you out."

Gail didn't answer.

Kay tried the door. It was locked. "I don't suppose any of you have a key?" Her pick was in her purse, locked in her car.

"Give me a minute," Vera said. "I'll figure something out." She spied a stack of dinner trays. "I think I've got it." She picked up a fork and bent the tines. "This should do nicely." She inserted it into the lock, moving it back and forth until they heard it click. "Another little something you learned in the wild?" Kay asked, amazed.

"I once helped release a cargo of golden spider monkeys from a poacher in the rain forest," Vera said.

"Really?" Kay asked. "We really have to spend some time together when this is all over. I smell a television special in there somewhere."

The three of them rushed in. Gail lay staring out into space.

"Gail, you've got to get up," Rose told her. "We've come to break you out of here."

"She's not responding," Vera said. "What are we going to do?"

"See if you can get her to stand," Kay said.

"Then what?" Vera asked. "We'll never make it back through the tunnel with her in this condition."

"Then we'll have to go out the front door," Rose said.

"Oh, that's a good plan," Kay quipped. "You think the men downstairs won't notice us leaving with one of their patients?"

"My guess is the old guy's asleep," Rose said. "As for the other one"—she adjusted her neckline—"I think I can distract him long enough for you and Vera to slip her through."

Jane turned the car onto Route 8 and headed toward Bend Oaks. Marilee sat quietly in the backseat. She hadn't said a word since being rescued.

"Should we call?" RJ asked. "See how the others made out?"

"No, not yet," Jane said, easing over into the right lane. "They said they would call us when they had Gail safely en route. We just have to wait."

"But what if they need help. I mean . . . finding their way through those tunnels could be tough."

"I'm sure they'll make it. In case you haven't noticed, they're very resourceful women."

"Are you talking about Mrs. Honeychurch?" Marilee asked. "I thought she was at Ridgecrest Hills."

"She was, but your mom's friends are breaking her out."

"RJ and I should have been there to help, but we were both . . . detoured," Jane said, glancing into the rearview mirror. It was a nasty thing to say, but she was so mad at Marilee that she wanted to thrash her.

"I'm sorry, Mom," Marilee said, suddenly breaking down. "I thought I could handle it."

"A girl your age has no business dating a nineteen-year-old,"

Jane said. She didn't care how sorry Marilee might be. She wasn't letting her get off that easily. She could have been raped or murdered by that pervert. The mere thought chilled her to the bone.

"I know, and I promise from now on I'll listen to what you and Daddy say," Marilee said, feeling every bit a child of fourteen.

"If only I had a tape recorder," Jane mumbled under her breath.

twenty

Was it possible that he was somehow connected to the Magi? Rich wondered as he drove the back roads of the Litchfield hills. The idea seemed preposterous.

He fingered the scar on his neck, the one that Malachi had spied when they first met. It was just some strange co-incidence, right? Or was it? During the past few months a string of circumstances had continued to link him to an ongoing flow of events that seemed to be propelling him into the unfathomable realm of exorcisms.

First there was the meeting with Malachi a few months ago in Rome, and the entrance into a domain that he had no idea existed in this modern-day age, coupled with Malachi's prophecy that Rich was destined to follow in his footsteps.

Once he arrived in Connecticut, things got even queerer. The parish he was asked to temporarily oversee just happened to be ex-periencing some very strange, unexplainable events whose basis, he would later discover, was linked to an ancient parchment that was a sister to the one he had deciphered in Rome.

But the coincidences didn't end there. The parish was called St. Francis Xavier—teacher to St. Ignatius, the famed exorcist, whose ring he now wore. The wreath that encircled the ring (which turned out not to be a wreath at all but a rendering of Christ's crown of thorns) Father Stephens had discovered was a powerful symbol that could be used to contain evil.

Anddddd . . . as if that weren't enough, Rich thought, stopping for the traffic light at the intersection of Route 63, apparently the only person who could actually vanquish this evil was a descendant of the Magi, whose crescent-moon sign he had on his neck.

A car beeped behind him. He hadn't noticed that the light had turned green. He rubbed his neck along the birthmark. Malachi had hinted that it was the insignia of some ancient priesthood. He must have known more about it but had declined to delve into it further. Did he feel that Rich must come into both the knowledge and the acceptance of his destiny on his own? He remembered how he had balked at the priest's suggestion that he might have been preordained as an exorcist.

If he was part of this lineage (and that was a very big "if"), what did this order stand for? He tried to remember what he may have read about the Magi. He knew that they had lived in Persia, which was now Iran. They were Zoroastrians, noted astrologers and teachers who believed that the alignment of the stars was a portent of the future. In the Book of Matthew, they are mentioned as bringing gifts to the Christ child. Later, they are warned in a dream of Herod's plot to kill the child and told to travel home by another route.

Rich mulled this over. Why would God take such an interest in the welfare of three astrologers? Unless . . . What if they were a secret order of priests used to fend off evil's plan to destroy God's gift of salvation?

A few miles out of Bantam, he turned right and headed north. This section of the highway was deserted. He stepped on the accelerator, hoping to make it back to the rectory before the women arrived. He wanted to make certain that Marvin had set things up correctly.

A car appeared, seemingly out of nowhere. Rich shook himself.

He had to stop daydreaming behind the wheel. He had been so deep in thought since leaving Hartford that he barely remembered the ride up to this point.

The car seemed to be gaining speed rather rapidly. Rich was instantly alert to its erratic behavior, weaving back and forth across the center line. Just this past month, two people were killed in collisions with drunk drivers. He assumed that was the case here. Either that or it was a bunch of teenagers out joyriding.

Where was a cop when you needed one? Fifty feet ahead of him, the car switched over to his lane. This time it stayed there, heading straight into his path. Rich leaned down hard on the horn and flashed his lights, hoping that the driver would realize the danger he was putting them both in. To his disbelief, the car increased its speed. They were on a collision course.

He swung the wheel sharply to the right and into a recently harvested field of corn. He hit the ruts going forty.

That lousy son of a b . . . He jumped out of the car. He'd take down that idiot's license-plate number and get a good description of the vehicle, then he'd report this nutcase to the police. He was a menace and needed to be taken off the road.

He had a clear view of the entire road for nearly a mile. Even going as fast as it was, the car should still be in sight. Rich took a few steps forward. The road was empty.

Kay drove while Myla, seated in the passenger side of the van, helped her navigate the back roads. They had decided to avoid the major highways. Rose and Vera remained in the back. The seats had been removed and the van stripped bare. Gail lay on the floor between Rose and Vera.

As Father Rich had predicted, as soon as the sun began to set the demon's power increased. Kay had just eased the van onto the bridge that spanned the Housatonic River when she heard Vera gasp.

"Is everything all right back there?" She glanced in the rearview mirror.

"Something is happening to Gail," Vera said. "It's like her features are . . . changing."

It was hard to resist the urge to turn around and sneak a peek, but Kay wasn't familiar with these roads, which were filled with twists and turns. Still, she kept one eye on the rearview mirror.

"*Ohhhh myyyy Goddd!*" Rose said.

"What? What's happening?" Kay threw caution to the wind and turned around. What she saw nearly made her drive right off the road.

Myla turned, too, and screamed.

The contours of Gail's face were moving beneath the skin as though her skeletal structure were being completely refashioned. Her cheekbones were raised. Her nose was pushed in until the nostrils flared, and her mouth had stretched tightly across her face into an eerie kind of grimace.

"Make it stop!" Gail wailed in pain, gripping the sides of her head.

"What should we do?" Vera asked. Her voice had risen several octaves.

"I don't think there's anything we can do until we get to the rectory," Rose said. "But I'll tell you this . . . if I hadn't seen it with my own eyes, I would never have believed it."

"It's like watching a horror movie," Vera said, inching farther back into the van.

"*You think you're so clever,*" the creature raved. "*But you can't outsmart me, you whores.*"

"Did I hear that right?" Myla asked in disbelief. "Did it just call us whores?"

"Yep," Kay said, thinking how strange that the term should give Myla offense, since they called themselves the St. Francis Xavier Church Hookers.

Myla wagged a finger in Gail's face. "Someone should wash your mouth out with soap," she said.

"That priest of yours can't save this soul. It's already mine. And when I'm through with all of you tonight my master will cut out your hearts and feed them to the hounds of hell."

"Oh, *pleassseee*. Give me a break. 'My master will cut out your hearts and feed them to the hounds of hell,' " Vera taunted. "Can't you come up with something more original than that?"

"Now, Vera, don't tease the demon," Myla said.

The creature lunged forward and tore a section of Myla's seat off as easily as if it were a piece of paper.

"Now see what you've done," Myla said. "You've made him mad."

"It's not as mad as I am," Rose said, inspecting the damage. "Who's going to pay for this?"

"You will all pay with your souls," it cried, followed by shrieks of demonic laughter.

"Oh, yeah, that's what you think," Vera shouted. "I've just about had you up to here." She drew an imaginary line across her forehead. "You really burned my bums."

"I don't think you should . . ." Myla began.

"Just look what it's done to my daughter-in-law. Why, you big, ugly—"

"Vera, you're going to make him angrier," Myla cautioned.

"She's right. You might want to tone it down a little," Kay said. No one had thought to bring a rope, and from the looks of the back of Myla's seat this was one demon they didn't want to tick off.

But Vera was on a roll and would not be silenced. "It doesn't scare me. See if you can stand up against this!" She pulled out a rosary and brandished it like a weapon.

The creature screamed and lunged for her, tearing the rosary out of her hands and flinging it across the van. Then, with a wolfish grin, it clamped its hands around her neck. *"Call on your precious saints now, swine. See . . . they have no power against me."*

"You shouldn't call people swines," Myla corrected.

"Rose, I could use a little help here?" Vera said, gagging.

Kay didn't know which to be more amazed at—that there was a demon loose in the back of the van she was driving, or that Myla seemed hell-bent on giving it a lesson in etiquette.

Rose had ranked number one in women's wrestling in college, and she hadn't forgotten the moves. She grabbed a fistful of hair, yanked hard enough to pull it out by the roots, and tackled the creature to the floor. It screamed and released its hold, then rounded on Rose. With superhuman strength, it flung her across the cargo area. She landed against the back door with a loud bang.

"We'd better pull over," Myla cried. "I think it's killed Rose."

"It'll take more than that to kill me," Rose said, scrambling to her feet. "Kay, you keep driving. This is war."

If things weren't so desperate in the backseat, Kay might have laughed at the insanity of the scene. Rose and Myla were duking it out with a demon, while Myla solicited help from a litany of saints. Finally, Rose was able to pin the creature's arms behind its back.

"Quick," she told Vera. "Grab that bungee cord in the side compartment and wrap it around its hands."

Kay pulled up to a traffic light. "Maybe Myla's right. I probably should pull over," she said.

"No. Keep going," said Rose, who was sitting on top of what used to be Gail's body while Vera wound the cord around the creature's hands. It flung her off and scrambled in an effort to break free.

Kay hit the lock mechanism. All they needed was for this thing to escape and terrorize the countryside, although it might make for some interesting headline news.

A teenager in a small sports car pulled up alongside the van just as Gail let out a stream of obscenities that would have made a trucker blush.

"Oh, no . . ." Myla moaned, sliding down in her seat. "That's the grandson of one of my pinochle partners."

Kay threw on the radio and turned the volume up to the max. A rapper's voice sounded, screaming obscenities far worse than the ones that were coming from the back of the van.

"They'll never ask me back to play cards again," Myla moaned.

The kid glanced over at the van, smiled, and began to bob his head along with the beat. The light turned green. "Gray Panthers' rock," he shouted over the din, then gave the thumbs-up and sped away.

"Who's he calling a Gray Panther? Is that like the Black Panthers?" Myla wanted to know.

Kay passed a sign that read "Bend Oaks, Founded 1825, Population 2,455." She glanced in the mirror and cringed. A black mist, like the one Jane had described, was gathering directly behind Vera and Rose. She felt inside her jacket pocket for the holy water. "Ah . . . ladies. I think we have a visitor," she said. "Look behind you." She pitched the vial over her shoulder. "Vera, catch."

Rose swung around. "Oh, gross!"

Vera removed the cap and doused it with holy water. It vanished like a whiff of smoke. "If I knew how useful this stuff was going to be I would have bought a gallon's worth," she said.

"How much longer until we reach the rectory?" Kay asked Myla, switching on the high beams.

"About twenty minutes," Myla said, anxiously eyeing the nearly empty bottle of holy water in Vera's hand. "I sure hope our supply of holy water holds out."

"I hope my thighs hold out," Rose said. She had Gail's body in a leg lock.

Rich had managed to make it back to the rectory without further incident before nightfall and discovered that Marvin had done a good job in preparing the library. He was glad to have him on board for tonight's event. Marvin was to remain outside by the gates.

He sensed that Marvin's loyalty to both Father Stephens and the women would provide another weapon in the fight that was about to be waged. The more souls that were committed to vanquishing this evil, the more power Rich would have to draw upon during the exorcism.

Meanwhile, he had stripped the library bare except for a small table that held a crucifix, holy water, and a red leather book embossed in gold leaf titled *The Roman Ritual of Exorcism*. Extra copies for the women were stacked alongside.

Lighted candles glowed from several stands that Marvin had brought over from the church and screwed into the floor. Electricity could not be counted on this evening. A faulty transformer, or any one of a dozen other incidents, might plunge the house into darkness, giving the demons a decided advantage. Rich's aim was to provide as little assistance to that side as possible.

In fact, everything about the physical setup of the room was designed with an eye to how it might be used as a weapon against him. At the villa in Italy, Rich had witnessed firsthand a demon's extraordinary power to affect the physical world. The bookshelves had been emptied of every book. Every piece of furniture—chairs, ottomans, tables, sofa, lamps—had been removed. Even the windows had been boarded up for fear of flying debris and the fireplace sealed shut so that nothing could scurry down the chimney and gain entrance to the room.

Once the women arrived with Gail, he would lock the pocket doors and, for better or for worse, they would be sealed inside the room until the ritual had been completed. It was a bold plan. He had made all of this perfectly clear to the women, fully expecting that perhaps one of them would back out. He could hardly blame them. He told them what he had witnessed in Rome, realizing that words alone could not adequately prepare them for what was about to take place. Except for Jane, the women could not truly fathom the horrors they were about to experience—feelings of despair, hopelessness, and, ultimately, fear so terrifying that some, like the first men who had taken up residency in this house, had been literally scared to death.

But if he was to successfully combat the demon, he needed their support. The friendship they held for one another was a powerful spiritual force. That, coupled with their prayers during the ritual, would provide the kind of stronghold Rich needed to close the portal and send the demons fleeing back to hell.

Even so, it was a risky plan. There was no denying it. Their lives would all be in jeopardy. He had made certain they understood the gravity of the danger they were placing themselves in. But they were too concerned for Gail to worry about their own welfare. And, as Vera had so succinctly put it, "If Satan messes with one of us, he messes with all of us."

Rich walked outside and waited. The air held a sharp chill, and the shadows had begun to cloak the ground in darkness. He tucked his hands under his surplice. Where were they? He had told them repeatedly that they needed to arrive before sunset. Demons drew their power from the nightscape.

"You sure I can't come?" RJ asked Jane as they pulled into the Honeychurches' driveway.

She had tried to explain to RJ as simply as possible what had happened to Gail and the exorcism that was planned for tonight.

"That's creepy," Marilee said when she finished. "You sure you'll be all right?"

"I'm sure. I've read the last chapter in the Good Book. The good guys win," she teased.

"You'll call as soon as it's over?" RJ asked.

She nodded and put the car in gear. Then, seeing the worried look on his face, she added, "We'll get her back. I promise." She blew them both a kiss and headed out across town.

She arrived moments after the others had pulled through the

front entryway. Their taillights were just up ahead as she turned into the driveway.

Marvin stood beside his battered station wagon by the foot of the driveway. Jane waved as she rushed past. He waited until she was a safe distance inside the grounds before closing the heavy metal gates. Then, threading a heavy chain through the ironwork, he padlocked them shut, sealing both the good and the evil within.

"Are you ready?" Rich asked the women.

Gail's arms and legs had been lashed to a small metal cot that had been placed in the center of the room. Rose, Vera, Myla, and Kay surrounded her, holding copies of *The Roman Ritual of Exorcism*. Jane was stationed just behind Gail's head.

"About as ready as we're ever going to be," Vera said.

Formally robed, Rich positioned himself in front of the cot, made the sign of the cross, blessed the room with holy water, and began. As soon as he began to speak, a sharp, chilling wind coursed through the room.

"Gee, it's getting cold in here," Myla complained.

"*Deus, in nomine tuo salvum me fac et in virtúte tua:* Save me, O God, by thy name, and further my cause by thy power. O God, hear my prayer; give ear to the words of my mouth."

The creature lifted its head off the mattress and sneered at the priest. "*You have no power over me. I am many,*" it said.

"You mean there's more than one demon?" Myla whispered to Vera.

She shrugged. "I sure hope Father brought enough holy water."

"Let the enemy have no victory over her," Rich continued.

Gail's body arched, looking as though it were about to break in two. One by one the restraints snapped.

"And let the Son of Iniquity not succeed in injuring her. Send her help from the holy place, Lord, and give her heavenly protection."

Slowly, Gail's body began to rise. The women each grabbed for a limb, then simultaneously withdrew their hands and backed away. It was like holding the hand of a corpse. They watched in horror as the creature slowly began to spin—arms outstretched as it looked out over the group with sightless eyes.

"Take out your rosaries," Myla ordered, and dropped to her knees. The others followed. Soon their prayers overlaid those of Father Rich, and a strange kind of symphony of prayer was formed.

Rich looked across at Jane. "It's time," he said.

A thousand thoughts flew through Jane's mind, not the least of which was that she had never used her gift in this way before. Father Rich was counting on her to guide him, but what if she failed?

He saw her hesitate.

"Now!" he shouted. "Don't let the enemy instill fear or doubt."

Jane glanced up at the body that had once been her best friend. It was beyond recognition. Nothing of the sweet, kind, gentle Gail remained. The demon had overshadowed her soul. She thought how it had almost killed Ralph, and that if it had succeeded it would have destroyed Gail's life forever. If it was left unchallenged, Gail would be lost for eternity. She couldn't let that happen.

"I'm ready," she told Rich.

Taking a deep breath, she closed her eyes and gave herself up to the force that swept her into the black void. Through spiritual eyes, she saw that a dark tunnel was up ahead. She paused only slightly to utter a prayer before heading into its cavernous depths.

Clawlike hands reached out, snatching at her clothes, her hair. She wanted to run, but something stopped her. She paused. It was the prayers of her friends. Even in this dark place, she could hear their voices petitioning God for her protection. She let them wash over her, forming a barrier until she felt renewed. Only then did she dare to continue.

Voices cried out from the darkness, pleading for her intercession.

They hadn't known that hell was real, they cried. They had bought the lie from the father of all lies that hell was a myth and heaven pure fantasy. But there was nothing that she could do. They had forged their own destiny, link by link, knitting a chain that now anchored their souls to hell for eternity. Like prisoners consigned to death row, their voices grew more desperate as she passed by, and for a moment she feared she would go mad. "God, please help me," she prayed simply. She couldn't find her way. It had grown too dark.

Meanwhile, in the library a strong hum like that of electrical current forging through a transformer began to fill the room. The candles flickered.

"What's that noise?" Rose asked. Her eyes fell on Rich's hand. "It's coming from your ring, Father."

Rich lifted his hand. The crown of thorns was glowing, pulsating. He watched in sheer amazement as its holographic image lifted off the ring, expanding, widening farther and farther, until it encompassed all those present in the room. He watched in disbelief as three shadowy figures emerged on its perimeter. They were garbed in decorative robes and bejeweled turbans.

"Do you see them?" he asked, nodding toward the images.

Vera and Rose glanced around. "See who?"

"Don't tell me something else got loose?" Myla said in alarm, checking behind her. "Kay, move next to me just in case."

Suddenly Gail's body crashed back onto the cot as a scream of rage tore from her lips.

"What's happening?" Jane said from the other side.

"Power is being funneled through my ring, but apparently I'm the only one who can see it," Rich answered.

"Well, I can see it. A circle of light. It's encasing some kind of opening up ahead."

"That must be the portal," he said.

The three apparitions nodded in agreement.

"What else do you see?"

"Dozens of horrible creatures are trying to escape, but something seems to have stopped them."

"The ring must have temporarily severed the channel between their world and the one being held open by the demon here."

The creatures had spied Jane. She stepped back, uncertain. Two morphed into a funnel of black smoke and headed her way.

"Hurry, Father. I don't know how much longer I can hold the vision."

He turned his attention back to Gail. He had to know the name of the demon who held open this portal in order to seal it: "*We exorcise you, each unclean spirit, each power of Satan, each infestation of the enemy from hell, each legion, each congregation, each satanic sect, and command you to tell me your name!*"

The cot's metal frame began to pound against the floor like a jackhammer. Gail's body convulsed. Vera covered her face. She couldn't bear to watch.

"I COMMAND YOU IN JESUS' NAME."

Thunderous rappings sounded inside the walls, and the house began to shake. Outside, shingles were being torn off the house.

A sudden burst of red-hot pain seared the skin around his birthmark. He clutched his neck and sank down onto his knees, gritting his teeth. He lifted his head briefly to see the apparitions point their hands in his direction and move their lips in silent prayer. Each wore an identical ring. The pain slowly began to ease.

"Are you all right?" Kay asked, helping Rich back onto his feet.

He nodded. Meanwhile, Gail's body lifted off the bed, then flipped up into a standing position. Her feet dangled several feet off the mattress. She looked like a puppet suspended by invisible strings.

"GIVE ME YOUR NAME!" Rich demanded.

A fissure began to form across the ceiling, raining plaster down into the room. Gail's body floated toward him. Inky black eyes, like the caverns of hell, stared out. The demon's mouth opened. It began to gag. It was as if the words were being pulled from its throat. It fought to contain them.

Rich held up the cross. "GIVE ME YOUR NAME."

Gail's body began to vibrate as though it had made contact with a high-voltage wire.

Vera screamed. "It's killing her. Make it stop!"

"GIVE ME YOUR NAME."

"My name . . . my name is . . ." Its face contorted in pain. "My name is Baalzephon."

Jane felt a sudden release. The entities were being sucked back into the vortex. They screamed in agony.

Rich lifted his hands; the ring took on a high-pitched whine. The image of the wreath that encompassed them began to vibrate, then suddenly flipped over and spun like a top. One of the mystical figures nodded to his companion. Both stared briefly in his direction. He felt a strange kinship. And then they were gone.

He breathed in deeply and shouted one final command, his voice sounding like thunder. "In the name and by the power of our Lord Jesus Christ I command you, Baalzephon, to leave this body and to gather the others who followed your call from the underworld. I consign you and your legions to the hell from whence you came. The portal has now been sealed."

Gail's body went limp and fell back onto the cot.

The vision disappeared, and Jane opened her eyes.

Everyone stood absolutely still.

"Is it over?" Vera asked, looking around.

A piercing cry, the sound of which all those present would carry with them to their graves, shrieked from the bowels of the house. Windows exploded. Myla screamed. Everyone ducked.

The library doors blew off their tracks, and then there was silence. Jane looked over at Rich and nodded. It was finished.

twenty-one

The women gathered around the large piece of burlap in the rectory's library, studying the intricate design that had been penned by Myla. How many times down through the years had they taken the same posture, running their hands over the rough fabric, trying to imagine the completed design?

The room had grown silent—a comfortable emptying of sound that only close friends can share. The hall clock chimed twice, and outside the sun slipped out from underneath a low cloud cover, casting a sunbeam across the burlap and caressing it with a golden ray.

"With all the nonsense of the past few weeks, we're behind schedule," Myla complained, walking over to the window and adjusting the shade. "But I figure if we work straight through until this evening we'll catch up. So, no more dawdling. Everyone grab a chair and let's get going."

"Yes, drill sergeant," Rose teased. "So where's Gail?"

"She'll be here later," Vera said, moving her chair into place. "She had some things to take care of at the house."

"I heard she sold the old Demmings place," Jane said. "How long was it on the market?"

"About a year," Vera said. "She says the real-estate market is finally starting to move again. She picked up four new listings this past week alone."

"She's back to work already?" Kay asked, glancing around the room. In the light of day, it was hard to believe what they all had witnessed here. "I thought she'd need at least a month to recuperate."

"Fortunately, she doesn't remember a thing," Vera said, searching her tote bag for her metal hook.

"Thank God for that," Myla said. "I'm certainly never going to forget what I saw. I may never sleep with the light off again."

"I'm just glad it's over," Vera confessed.

Vera had worked hard the past few days—getting the rectory back in order, erasing all traces of the past few weeks. Under her ministrations, the library had been transformed to its former elegance. Paneling once again glowed soft and golden. The brocaded drapes, recently dry-cleaned, looked fresh and crisp against the spotless panes of glass. Books lined the shelves, and all the upholstery had been steam-cleaned. The only portion of the room that bore scars was the ceiling. But Vera had already called the plasterers. They were coming early next week to repair, paint, and hang a new chandelier.

As the others hooked, Vera glanced around the room and smiled in satisfaction. A fire glowed in the hearth, adding to the feeling of warmth and comfort. It had been carefully laid by Marvin earlier this morning. He had nodded shyly to Vera as he slipped through the kitchen door, his plaid wool jacket smelling of burning leaves, his arms laden with a bundle of logs. Vera had smiled and offered him a cup of freshly brewed coffee. He had whistled in a fashion that Vera now understood to mean "As soon as I'm done with this."

Although she would never admit it to a living soul, she was growing fond of this quiet, gentle man. He appeared odd to most people, but she had always been attracted to those who marched to the beat of their own drum, and Marvin certainly did that. Father Rich was right. Marvin's form of communication wasn't that hard to understand once you got the hang of it.

It was especially nice having Marvin around now that Father Rich was teaching part-time at the university. Even though the rectory had been exorcised of all demonic forces, there were moments when she still felt a chill snake along her spine, as when she passed the spot on the staircase where she had almost tumbled to her death. It also gave her the willies knowing that beneath this house was once a portal to a world filled with unspeakable horrors.

But none of this had stopped her from resuming her position as housekeeper. In fact, Father Rich had just upgraded it to a live-in position, and yesterday she had moved in lock, stock, and barrel, taking the room right off the kitchen, which caught the first rays of morning light.

Meanwhile, she had also placed a moratorium on her Elderhostel trips. With all that had taken place these past few weeks, she didn't need to march off to the wilds in search of adventure. There was enough excitement going on right here. And now that Father Rich had accepted the roles of both St. Francis Xavier's pastor and a teaching position at Yale, Vera figured that things were never going to be dull in Bend Oaks again. She also had a gut feeling that, once the smoke settled, Father Rich might be called on again to perform other exorcisms, and if he did, she and the women would be right there to lend him their support.

The women's hands moved steadily along with the conversation. Over the course of the next hour, they exhausted an array of subjects: the garden club's decision to plant a row of maple trees along Main Street to replace the ones that a recent ice storm had toppled; the new stop sign at the end of Benson Road, which townsfolk refused to obey; Emily Woodruff's announcement that after five years as Garden Club President she was finally retiring; Kay's first black-bear sighting—"At first I thought it was an exceptionally large dog. . . ."

Back and forth, a seamless thread of conversation wove in accompaniment with the thin woolen strips.

"You haven't told us much about your love life recently," Myla said to Rose.

"That's right, how is the online dating service going?" Kay asked, completing a row of evenly spaced loops. She smiled to herself with immense satisfaction. Maybe she'd get the hang of this yet.

"I haven't spent much time on the computer lately," Rose said.

"Does this have anything to do with a male attendant who works at Ridgecrest?" Vera teased.

"Vera . . ." Rose cautioned.

"You didn't!" Myla said, amazed.

"All right . . . I did. Thanks a lot, Vera. He was cute and unattached, so I went back and made him an offer he couldn't refuse."

"Dare I ask what that offer might have been?" Myla said, gazing over her granny glasses.

"He told me that they had a patient mysteriously disappear—a Gail Honeychurch, and I told him that if he took me to dinner I'd explain the mystery."

"And?"

"We went to a lovely little restaurant in Newtown, and I told him how we kidnapped Gail."

"Rose! You didn't," Myla moaned. "I hope you didn't give him our names. I'm too old to do time."

Kay smiled, trying to picture Myla in prison garb.

"It was the darndest thing, really," Rose answered, going back to her hooking. "He said he was glad to discover that her disappearance could be explained."

"What's that supposed to mean?" Myla asked.

"He said there had been other unexplained disappearances."

Vera shivered. "That gives me the chills."

"That *place* gives me the chills," Jane said.

"According to Gerald, there's a whole lot of things happening over there that are weird."

"What kind of things?" Vera wanted to know.

Rose pulled another strip of wool out of a plastic bag. "He said that I'd never believe it if he told me."

"Yeah, right," Kay said. After what she had seen, she'd believe anything.

"Anyway, he said that they're closing down the facility. Some developer has bought the place."

"What are they going to do with it?"

"Put up some high-end housing. They're calling it an Equestrian Community."

"What the heck is that?" Myla wanted to know.

"Homes built around riding trails and private stables and riding rings."

"That should cost a pretty penny," Myla said.

"Gerald said the homes are starting at around one and a half million."

"When I think that my grandfather bought this land for the rectory and the parcel that my house sits on in 1925 for twelve hundred dollars—why today's prices are just unbelievable."

"Gail says that you can't touch a piece of property for under a quarter of a million dollars. Can you imagine that?" Vera said, shaking her head. "I don't know how young couples today can afford to own a home."

Kay finished a seashell. "Speaking of Gail, she called me at the office yesterday. She said something about making a few changes."

"I don't know if I should be the one to tell you this, but . . ." Vera began. All hooking stopped as the women waited for her to continue. "She's given Ralph the boot."

"She has? Good for her!" Kay cheered, but, remembering that he was Vera's son, tempered her jubilation. "I mean, I think that might be best considering what he did to her."

"I couldn't agree more," Vera said. "Son or no son, the man's a pig."

Rose laughed. "Why don't you tell us how you really feel?"

"What about Jerry and RJ?" Jane asked. RJ and Marilee had become fast friends. Even Vance had taken a shine to the boy and had talked RJ into helping him coach Alex's soccer team.

"Ralph has signed over guardianship to me," Vera said.

"What about his ex-wife?" Myla wanted to know.

"Chirley? Other than Christmas cards, we haven't heard a peep from her since she dropped the boys off. Anyway, Gail has invited them to stay with her on a few conditions: RJ has to stop dealing drugs, and they both have to start making an effort with their schoolwork."

"I'm glad to hear that," Rose said.

"Are you women talking about me?" RJ asked, standing in the doorway with Gail at his side, a broad smile etched across his face.

Rose couldn't get over the transformation. It was the first time she had ever seen the boy smile. In fact, he looked genuinely happy.

"Sorry we're late," Gail said, dragging two large plastic bags behind her. "RJ, grab one of these, will you?"

As RJ lifted the bags on top of the table, each woman studied Gail's face, searching for any residue of the evil that had held her captive these past few horrifying weeks. But all were greatly relieved to see their dear friend returned, her eyes sparkling with a deep maternal love for the boy who had been her staunch supporter.

"I see you began hooking without me," Gail said, pretending offense.

"We have a deadline to meet and we're weeks behind," Myla said defensively. "The festival will be here before you know it."

Gail studied the design. "It's going to be the best one yet."

Everyone laughed. This was what she said every year.

"So what's in the bags?" Myla asked.

"I heard you were in need of some more wool," Gail said innocently.

Myla opened a bag and pulled out several pairs of men's woolen slacks. "Gail . . . ?"

Smiling like the cat that had just eaten the canary and enjoyed every morsel, Gail laughed. "You said you needed wool for the rug's background. Consider it a donation from Ralph."

Rich had taken Route 7 up to Vermont, winding through Arlington and Manchester, then into Rutland. All the leaves had fallen, but he could still imagine the beauty of this place set against the rolling blue mountains when spring returned.

He had driven straight through, stopping only briefly for a quick lunch at the Lion's Inn in Stockbridge, Massachusetts, before driving on. Hunger hadn't made him stop, but he felt the need for a glass of claret to help steady his resolve.

As he turned off Route 7 and headed west, the scenery changed. A sense of beauty and spaciousness was suddenly replaced by narrow roads, flanked by heavy pines that blocked the sun as if a huge curtain had been drawn across its warm rays. For the first time since starting out, he turned on the heater.

His thoughts leafed back through the annals of time until they came to rest on the page depicting a small, frightened young boy who had been abandoned on the front steps of the orphanage, too stunned to cry, and too hurt to call out. The pain and hurt had not been tempered by time.

A weathered road sign, barely discernible, read "St. Theresa's Cemetery." He turned right and headed down a narrow dirt road filled with potholes and oozing mud like an open sore. He bounced and swerved and swore his way along the three-mile road. Twice, his tires got mired in the mud and he wondered if he had gotten this far only to be turned back. The sun was already setting. In an hour, the sky would grow black. He'd never find his way back.

Just when he began to despair, he spied a metal arch with "St. Theresa" lettered across the top. The cemetery looked as forlorn as the untraveled road, and he parked the car and got out. He wore boot-cut jeans, a turtleneck sweater, and a parka—the one he had bought for a skiing trip to Switzerland a few years back. Even this seemed inadequate for the Vermont cold. Water seeped over the edges of his gumshoes. He sucked in his breath in dismay but refused to be turned away.

"Get behind me, Satan," he commanded. Nothing was going to steer him away from what he knew must be done.

The road leading into the cemetery was strewn with years of debris. The going was hard and exhausting; every footfall met with resistance. He stoically persevered, casting an eye across the rubble of fallen trees and a dense overgrowth that had obscured or toppled all but the most deeply rooted headstones. For just a moment, he felt a flash of despair so deep that tears came to his eyes. How was he ever going to find what he had come in search of amid these ruins?

The sun had already begun its slow descent. The air grew steadily colder. A damp, clammy chill snaked down his back. He lifted the hood of his parka and pulled on a pair of insulated gloves. They did little to protect his hands. The headstones felt like blocks of ice. Within fifteen minutes, he could no longer feel the tips of his fingers. Finally, he peeled off his gloves and tried to blow warm air onto his fingers. The warmth of his breath lasted only seconds, but it was enough to give him some relief.

"Where are you?" he called across the graves. From habit, he fingered the silver ring on his right hand, turning it around and around as one would a talisman. Hundreds of bodies had to have been buried here over the years. The chances of his finding the one he was looking for suddenly seemed impossible. In defeat, he turned away and glanced back at the car, its outline slowly disappearing in the thickening shadows.

"This was a fool's mission" an inner voice whispered. He should have waited until next summer or, at least, started out earlier in the day. But he had felt it was imperative that he settle this matter now and not wait. Besides his duties as pastor at St. Xavier's and his part-time teaching schedule at Yale, he had been asked to take on the role of head exorcist for the United States. He would oversee a secret network of priests, similarly called to this esoteric sector of the Church. No one, apart from him and a special Vatican council, would know who these men were. It would be his duty to see that they received spiritual and moral support, and to personally attend to the more difficult cases.

He could no longer deny his destiny. It was not a path that he would have chosen for himself, but the events of the past few weeks had convinced him that Malachi was right. As a priest, he must not question, only obey.

He did know, however, that this position would place him in constant danger. Satan's forces would stop at nothing to thwart him. Therefore it was imperative that he rid himself of any trace of sin, lest it be used as an entry point.

A crow landed on a nearby branch and began to caw, its sharp, staccato voice growing more insistent. Rich watched it carefully for several moments, then walked over to the area just below its perch. He bent down to clear away a fallen branch and felt the tears in his eyes.

Joseph Edward Melo
Born June 12, 1919
Died October 27, 1966

His father had been dead for more than forty years.

"Dad," he said, the words tasting bittersweet on his lips. "I've come to ask for forgiveness for my anger all these years. Please forgive me, as I have forgiven you."

It was after midnight by the time he let himself into the front door of the rectory. The women had long since gone home—not even Myla's stern reprimands could keep them working so late.

"We do have other lives besides this place," Rose had told her, and left a few minutes after nine. She had a hot date with Gerald.

Rich paused in the foyer. He could hear Vera's television coming from the back of the house. It was a comforting sound, and he smiled, feeling for the first time in his life that he had finally come home.

twenty-two

It was a perfect spring day for Bend Oaks's annual Strawberry Festival. After a long, hard winter, the seventy-degree temperatures felt almost balmy to the legions of New Englanders who came from as far away as the Connecticut shore to share in the first of the season's festivities for the state's northwest corner.

The fair was held on the town green among a cluster of dogwood trees, most of which had been planted twenty years ago in memory of the townsfolk who had lost their lives in wars protecting their native soil. Their pink and white blossoms added a cheery note to the widely anticipated celebration, competing with the rows of red and white tents that held an array of wares that warranted investigation.

There were dozens of craftspeople stationed both inside and outside the tents in front of the town hall, many of whom had garnered quite a following down through the years. Customers came early to get the best pick of hand-painted furniture, crocheted baby sweaters, beaded jewelry, pottery, and quilts. Vendor table space sold for thirty-five dollars, and the proceeds went to the volunteer fire department for new equipment.

Just as loyal were the people who arrived an hour early to pick over the Episcopal Church's tag sale. Eight-foot-long tables were lined end to end under a tent in the center of the green, where a set of eight dinner plates could be purchased for two dollars, or four folding chairs and a matching card table for ten. There were glassware, kitchen utensils, pots, pans, table lamps, furniture, children's games, and enough Christmas ornaments to decorate all of downtown.

The next tent held the strawberry-shortcake concession run by the Congregational Church. The day before the fair, the church ladies arrived at March Farms in Bethlehem to handpick a hundred quarts of strawberries, which would be served along with twenty-seven gallons of whipped cream and acres of shortcake, all made fresh by the church women.

Across the street at St. Francis Xavier, a set of double doors had been thrown wide open in invitation to come in and view some of the finest examples of hooked rugs in all New England. An entrance fee of two dollars was collected at the door by Marilee Edwell, who was dressed in a new outfit purchased at the mall with money she had earned by helping out at her mother's café. Since the incident with Tye, mother and daughter had grown much closer. Marilee found that she actually enjoyed working beside her mother. She had even taken on some of the baking.

Women were lined up halfway around the church, eager to get inside and view the kaleidoscope of rug designs that the hookers had carefully draped over all the wooden pews. Included among them was a whole busload of hookers from upstate New York who had come to "Ooh" and "Aah" their way up and down the church aisles and pick up a new trick or two. And if the St. Francis Xavier Church Hookers had anything to say about it, these women would find their two dollars well spent.

Just about every rug-hooking design was represented inside. There were the intricate floral patterns filled with an assortment of flowers, baskets, birds, and wreaths—all appearing as though they had been plucked from a fine painting. Most of these rugs had been hooked by mothers or grandmothers when life was simpler and there was more time to spend on crafts. Modern-day hookers all agreed that these incredibly beautiful designs took the patience of Job to complete. They were made with scant, one-eighth-inch-thick strips of wool that had been hand-dyed in myriad rainbow shades later woven into shadows and lights.

Showcased alongside these classical beauties were the whimsical rugs that contained landscapes of the surrounding countryside or depictions of fish, cats, dogs, and barnyards, as well as dozens of bold geometric designs.

Toward the front of the sanctuary, the raffle rugs were displayed. These were the creations that had been hooked by the St. Francis Xavier Church Hookers since its inception, creating a sort of time line.

Down through the years, it had become something of an unspoken promise that each year's winner would allow the hookers to display her winnings. Fortunately, most winners were proud to take part and lived within a twenty-mile radius. However, that might change this year, Myla was thinking as she sold another round of chances (five for ten dollars). Kay had sold more than two hundred chances herself to her Hamptons friends. Myla couldn't imagine that any of them would be interested in driving up each year to have their rug displayed.

Meanwhile, business was so good this year that neither she nor Vera had taken a breath since the fair began—mainly because this year's rug (hung over a makeshift close line to their right) was attracting scores of people.

Myla smiled whenever she glanced that way. Gail was right: it was the best one they had ever made. The women had really outdone themselves this year, adding new elements as they went along in keeping with the nautical design. Dozens of tiny seashells and schools of bright-colored fish had joined the original design.

As one woman said, handing Myla a ten-dollar bill, "It's too pretty to be stepped on. It should be hung on a wall." It was a nice sentiment, and certainly a wonderful tribute to the women's skills. But Myla believed that these rugs were meant to be used. She liked the feel of a hooked rug underfoot, and the knowledge that it had been made by loving hands.

Kay and Gail were making their way through the crowd. Myla waved them over. It took forever for Gail to reach their table. Her arms were laden with shopping bags filled with tag-sale items. Her stepson Jerry lagged behind, scooping whipped cream and strawberries into his mouth. RJ was talking on his cell phone.

"I just sold a few more books," Kay said, reaching inside the pocket of her linen slacks and withdrawing a wad of crisp ten-dollar bills along with several orange ticket stubs.

"My Lord! There must be over a hundred dollars here," Vera said, counting out the cash. "Who did you sell them to?"

"The news crew from Channel 8," Kay said, smiling. "I kind of hinted that I might be able to get them an interview with Faith Hill."

"And I've bought out the tag sale's complete supply of used coffee mugs," Gail said proudly, letting the shopping bags slide out of her hands and onto the ground.

"Why?" Rose asked.

"Didn't you hear?" Vera asked. "Gail has landed the listing on that fancy new equestrian development. She's hiring a slew of new people."

"The Ridgecrest property?" Rose asked incredulously. "So you think that's wise?"

Jane and Myla grew very quiet.

"I know what you're all thinking, but really . . . it's all right," Gail assured them. "I don't remember anything about that place. Besides, it's being completely redesigned. The builder is a brilliant guy with an incredible vision. The houses are going to be something to die for."

"I do hope you mean that in the metaphorical sense," Rose said.

Gail rolled her eyes. "Oh, stop. It's just a piece of property—a very expensive piece of property that I have an exclusive listing on."

"As long as you're truly all right with it," Rose said.

"You know what they say. You have to face your *demons*—pardon my pun," Gail said, smiling.

"*Aughhhh . . .*" the women said in unison.

"Anyone see Father Rich?" Jane asked, dumping several bottles of water onto their stand. "He's supposed to draw the winning ticket in about twenty minutes."

"I saw him with Marvin a little while ago," RJ said, closing his cell phone. "They went off to help the fire chief at the barbecue pit. There was a fire over in Warren. Some of the volunteers got called away."

"I'll go get them," Kay said, grabbing a bottle of water. "Father Rich manning a barbecue pit. Now, there's something I've got to see." She left the others debating whether they should donate some of this year's proceeds to the high-school scholarship fund. Kay smiled with deep satisfaction. It seemed that the hookers had exceeded their goal by some two thousand dollars. Bless her friends at the East Hampton Yacht Club.

She followed the path that led toward the back of the firehouse, wishing she had brought along a camera. Somehow she couldn't image Father Rich flipping hamburgers. He seemed too cosmopolitan for that. But then the man was full of surprises.

Funny, she would never have thought him capable of something as archaic as an exorcism. He had the suave, debonair air of a world traveler, a learned man—and he was. Kay had recently mentioned his name at a party of Columbia alumni. Several guests were quite familiar with his work in the field of ancient texts.

If they only knew what else he was an expert at, she had mused over her glass of champagne. She had gone into this whole thing a skeptic and come out a believer. As much as she hated to admit it, the experience had opened up an entirely new world. Suddenly the terms *good* and *evil* had taken on a whole new meaning.

The crowds had thickened around the food booths. She was forced to elbow her way through before circling around toward the back of the firehouse. She came upon a small knoll and nearly gasped with delight. Stretching before her was a sweeping view of the valley and the lake below. Row upon row of yellow daffodils lined the banks, their sunshine glow reflecting off the water in a happy medley. Soft tufts of grass, lime green—the color of spring—grew here in clumps. She spied a blue heron poised among the reeds, its eyes fastened on the water gently lapping at its feet. Tears formed unexpectedly at the corners of her eyes. The scene was absolutely breathtaking in its simplicity.

Suddenly it came to her in a flash: Bend Oaks had become home. It was filled with the people she deeply cared about. She thought about the hookers. She had never known the true meaning of friendship until she met them. They were more than just friends—they were women she had grown to trust, and she had become a part of them. She smiled as she thought about Gail. After all, how many people would take on a demon for you?

The smell of charcoal and barbecued meat brought her around. A cluster of men were gathered around a huge grill. She headed that way, suddenly overcome with a craving for a hamburger smothered in onions and gobs of ketchup. As a rule, she didn't eat red meat, but what the heck. This was a special occasion. It was a celebration of spring. New beginnings.

The hookers' meetings would officially end now for the summer. As Vera pointed out, "It's hot enough during the summer as it is. Who wants a heavy piece of wool lying on your lap?" They would still meet for coffee at the Sit and Sip Café on Saturday mornings. They'd plan their next rug and talk gardens and the latest tabloid stories. Kay's approval rating among the women continued to climb. Whenever they wanted the truth about a celebrity rumor, she simply made a phone call. They were thrilled to hear that she planned to spend the entire summer here, luxuriating in her lake house.

She could almost point it out from here: its green tin roof was tucked behind a cluster of elms at the south end of the lake. She had grown to love her little cottage. Funny. She had paid well over ten million for her New York apartment, and that didn't include the decorator's fee or the monthly maintenance charge. Yet this twelve-hundred-square-foot cottage, with its leaky roof and floorboards that warped in the summer, making it impossible to sit at a table that didn't rock and roll, held more charm.

She had decorated every square inch of it herself, filling it with "shabby chic": chipped and peeling painted tables, overstuffed chairs she had slipcovered in chintz and linen; odd accoutrements (like a brass horn she had found in a dusty antiques shop in Torrington) she had wired for lamps. It was the antithesis of her stylized Manhattan apartment, which had twice graced the cover of *Architectural Digest*, yet she loved it more.

Was it really this sweet cottage that had captured her heart, or was it the town? Life was lived at a much slower pace out here in the country. People were seldom in a hurry. They took time for small things, like gardening and chatting over their picket fences with neighbors. Recently, even she had found a way to unwind. Marvin had strung a hammock between the two maple trees that looked out over the lake. She planned to spend several uninterrupted hours beneath a leafy canopy, devouring dozens of romance novels—Barbara Delinsky, Nora Roberts, Dorothea Benton Frank—reading material that would have been frowned on by her high-society friends. Heck, she might even toy with the idea of writing one herself. And why not? It was time she slowed down, took time for herself. Had a little fun. Her whole life had been nothing but hard work. She was due some serious R & R.

She fingered the strange crescent-shaped mark that had suddenly appeared on the nape of her neck. It worried her. What if it was some type of skin cancer? She had always taken precautions when she was out in the sun. Still, these things sometimes cropped up.

Well, there was no point in worrying now. She had an appointment with one of the top dermatologists in the country next week. Julia Roberts had given her his name. She searched the men flipping over beef patties and chicken wings. Father Rich was in the center, dressed in jeans and a loose-fitting plaid work shirt with a white T-shirt underneath. Jane's husband, Vance, was beside him. Vance said something that sent the priest howling with laughter. Obviously she wasn't the only one who was becoming accustomed to country life.

It suddenly occurred to her that she might have spent her life working for the wrong things. What was money or fame really? Had she accomplished anything of real worth? One thing was for certain. She didn't wish to spend the next twenty years putting out fires for the rich and famous, or spinning copy that turned obscure individuals into megastars? There had to be something more worthwhile that she could do with her life, but what?

She pulled up her collar and walked on. She could almost taste that hamburger. Maybe she'd order a side of French fries. And maybe she'd find the answers she sought here in Bend Oaks among her new circle of friends.

READING GROUP
COMPANION

1. The women of the St. Francis Xavier Church Hookers share a special bond. How do their personalities complement each other? What role does their friendship play in overcoming evil?

2. Jane has kept her psychic powers hidden from everyone, including her husband. Why? Would you share your talents if they were considered outside the norm? How would one come to grips with paranormal powers while maintaining a sense of normalcy?

3. Father Rich was abandoned as a child. How does this affect his role as a priest/pastor and his new role as an exorcist?

4. Why is it necessary for Rich to join with the women in order to realize his full potential as an exorcist?

5. Besides the anger Gail felt at her husband's infidelity, what are other reasons she might have been vulnerable to demonic possession?

6. Kay seems an odd member of the rug-hooking group, considering

her jet-setting lifestyle. Why is Kay drawn to the group? What do they have that she desires?

7. Compare the exorcism in Rome and the one at the rectory. What are the similarities? What are the differences, and why do they matter?

8. Marilee deliberately disregards her mother's warnings and puts herself at risk. Jane will disregard her inner warnings and put herself at risk as well. How are these two cases parallel? How are they different?

9. There are many reported instances of haunted houses. Do you believe in them? Why are certain places prone to these disturbances while others are not? If you moved into a home that you later felt was haunted, would you stay and try to exorcise the evil, or would you flee? What role would the Church and your faith play in your decision?

10. *The Haunted Rectory* highlights the subject of evil. Does evil have its origins in the organic mind and social conscience, or is evil an external force?

ABOUT THE AUTHOR

KATHERINE VALENTINE is the author of *Grace Will Lead Me Home*, *On a Wing and a Prayer*, *A Miracle for St. Cecilia's*, and *A Gathering of Angels*. She lives in New England.